HIDDEN *Target*

Book 4

O'Connor Girls

RHONDA BREWER

Dedication

This book is dedicated to all our military heroes and their families, especially David and Tammy Forristall, my brother-in-law and sister-in-law. They can never erase the memories of his time overseas but he has all the love and support of his entire family.

Acknowledgments

With so many people in my life to thank for making publishing this book possible, I could almost write another book on that alone. However, a simple thank you never seems like enough to convey my gratitude, but I will try to do that the best I can with this acknowledgment.

First, thank you belongs to the many authors who have become both friends and mentors to me. Then there are the amazing ladies who help with editing and errors. A special thank you goes to Michelle Eriksen, Abbie Zanders, and Amabel Daniels for their constant support and keen eye. To my dedicated betas and dear friends, Jackie Dawe Ford, Nancy Arnold-Holloway, and Karie Deegan thank you so much for the support and constant encouragement. To my readers, you are the reason that I can continue to do this.

To my husband who supports me everyday and To my two children Laura and Colin, both of you show me every day how proud you are and how much you love me. To my beautiful granddaughter, Emma. You may not be old enough to read yet, but your smile gives me the inspiration to keep going. I love all of you.

Chapter 1

"Mom, you have to stop asking him to come to dinner." Pam Nightingale groaned as she glanced out the window of her parents' living room.

"Pam, the sooner you realize he's your future, the sooner you can stop with this nonsense," her mother repeated for the hundredth time as she checked whatever she had put in the oven.

Pam pressed her lips together to keep from making a sarcastic comment. When Cora O'Connor-Nightingale had her mind set on something, there was no changing it, especially when it came to her Cupid powers.

Pam's mother was known as Cora the Cupid by practically everyone who knew her. Probably because she'd predicted every marriage in their family for years, not to mention the number of couples she brought together outside the family. The fact her mother was zoned in on her made Pam uncomfortable. It meant Pam made a colossal mistake all those years ago when she left him.

Pam left Damon Blackwood in Ontario more than five years earlier, expecting never to see him again. Then he showed up in her hometown of Hopedale, Newfoundland a few months earlier to help save a couple of teenagers who had been kidnapped.

She'd met him almost ten years ago when he'd first returned from deployment in the Middle East. Damon was an Elite Special Forces Sniper for the Canadian Army before he was medically retired. His hearing had been compromised when he ended up too close to an explosion. He'd been lucky, because there were only two other soldiers who had survived.

Damon would never talk about any of the things he saw while he was deployed. In the almost three years, they were together, he would never talk about it. Once she'd asked him what it was like to be over there, he'd replied with a statement that gave her chills.

"It's a hell nobody should have to live through," he told her.

There were nights Damon would wake her shouting in his sleep. Other times he would wake up soaked in sweat and trembling. She worried about him and was relieved when he started to see the therapist the military had suggested. The truth was, she loved him back then and would have done anything for him. Anything except be honest about who she really was.

To Damon, she was Trixie Knight, the full-time bartender, part-time dancer, and costume designer for the other exotic dancers at *The Glitter Pole Gentlemen's Club*. Most people would call the place a strip club, but the dancers didn't strip down to their birthday suits. They danced erotically for the patrons with skimpy costumes, that was it.

Nobody in Pam's family knew where she worked while she lived in Ontario. Somehow, they got the impression she was employed by a lingerie designer. Maybe because she kind of steered them in that direction when they asked about her job.

Since Pam was close friends with a couple of girls who did work for a designer, she was able to keep her secret when anyone in her family visited her. It killed her to lie to them, but they wouldn't understand why she wasted her business degree and her talent to design clothes on creating costumes for dancers.

When she first started at the club, she'd made a suggestion to one of the dancers about her costume. The girl asked Pam if she could help. That night, Pam designed a beautiful sexy bra, and thong with sequins. The girl was over the moon about the outfit and paid Pam a considerable amount of money. From that moment on, all the dancers asked her advice on what they should wear and paid her well for her designs.

Pam turned it into a part-time income, and the money she made helped her finance her shop. She still designed unique costumes for the few dancers she was close to and she would ship them to Ontario.

Now, she was co-owner of *Cupid's Closet* with Elaine Bradshaw. Their store sold accessories, lingerie, underwear, casual and formal wear for women. All designed and made by Pam or Elaine. Pam took care of the actual store, and Elaine handled everything online. They worked well together, and since Elaine's sister was married to Pam's cousin, they were practically family.

"Pam, answer the door, please." Her mother motioned toward the front door.

Pam knew it was pointless to argue with her mom. She didn't want to face him; in fact, she would rather stick hot pokers in her eyes. It was the third time Damon had been invited to her parents' place for supper in a week.

Pam was living with her parents until the apartment over her store was renovated. Pam would have lived in her store, if she had known her mother would use the time to shove Damon in front of her every chance she had. Pam made the decision as she walked to the door to call her cousin Jess and see if she could stay with her for a few days.

Pam opened the door and looked up into Damon's dark hazel eyes. The same eyes she used to get lost in every night. He gave her a soft smile, and Pam stepped back so he could come into the house.

"Nice to see you again, Trixie," Damon whispered low enough so only she could hear it.

"Don't use that name around my parents, please," Pam snapped and turned away from him to make her way to the kitchen.

She heard him mumble something behind her, but she didn't bother to ask what he'd said. The truth was, Damon didn't do anything to make her angry with him. Pam was the one who snuck out in the middle of the night, and it was the hardest thing she'd ever done.

5 years ago,

Pam giggled when Damon rolled off her and blew out an exhausted breath. She'd been teasing him all night at the bar, and he swore when they got home, she was going to make good on all her promises.

"You had me stiff as one of those fucking dance poles all fucking night." Damon sighed. "But you did everything you promised you would."

"Don't I always?" Pam wiggled her eyebrows up and down and snuggled into his side.

"Trixie, you always keep your promises." Damon turned onto his side and gazed into her eyes.

"What?" She smiled as he ran a finger down her cheek.

"I must have done something damn good in a previous life to have you walk into my life." He kissed the tip of her nose.

"You must have, because I'm pretty damn special." Pam smirked.

"You are special. You're the best thing that's ever happened to me, Trixie. I've never been this happy in my life, and the best thing about being with you is you don't have a stupid controlling family interfering in your life. Family sucks the life out of relationships. It's just you and me." Damon closed his eyes and pulled her into his embrace.

"Yeah." Pam swallowed hard because she hated that he didn't know the real her.

"Trixie, I love you," Damon whispered, and for a moment his body stiffened.

"What?" Pam lifted her head to look down at him.

"Shit. Thought I'd get away with that." Damon smirked.

"Damon." Pam looked down into his eyes. *"I thought you said love wasn't real."*

"I never believed it until I met you. It took me three years to realize that, because you make it real. Trixie, I grew up with a family where my father only spoke to us when he needed to show us off, my mother popped tranquilizers as if they were candy, mostly because she couldn't stand to be married to a heartless bastard, but she didn't have a choice, and my brother was brainwashed to think I was

6

a traitor to the family. I became a disappointment when I defied him and joined the Army." Damon's voice seemed to have no emotion when he talked about his family, but she could see the pain in his eyes.

"That's awful; you're a hero." Pam cupped his cheek.

"To my mother, I was a reason for her to pop more pills. To my brother, I didn't exist. To my father, I was a waste of his hard-earned money, because I didn't do anything with my life." Damon rolled his eyes.

"Baby, you don't believe that, do you?" Pam hated to see him like this.

"No, my father is a prick, but I'll give him credit for one thing. He taught me how to close off my heart, and it made me a damn good sniper. Until the day I walked into the club, my heart was closed off." Damon tucked a piece of her hair behind her ear. "Then I saw your beautiful blue eyes. I didn't know it then, but I know now, I fell head over heels."

"You only saw my boobs that night." Pam poked him in the chest.

"They are beautiful. Especially when that mysterious tattoo is peeking out." Damon glanced down to where her naked chest was pressed against him.

He'd asked her about the tattoo several times. Pam told him she'd gotten in memory of her grandfather. The truth was it was the

O'Connor family crest and everyone in her family had the same ink. Pam had gotten hers when she was eighteen.

Pam rolled her eyes, but she had a knot in her stomach the size of a bowling ball. She couldn't live like this anymore. There was no way she could have a future with Damon when she couldn't be honest with him.

"I grew up with a family who would lie their asses off so nobody would know how miserable they really were. You're real, and you don't care what people think about you. I want you to be with me forever. I know I can be an asshole at times, but I'd do anything to make you…" he whispered but she interrupted his words when she pressed her lips against his.

She couldn't let him go on. There was no future for them, even after all the sweet words. Once he knew the truth, he'd hate her for hiding who she really was. It was time for her to leave Ontario and go back to where she belonged. It was time to bury Trixie Knight.

After they made love again, Damon fell into a deep sleep, and Pam rolled out of bed, desperately holding back the tears as she made her way to the other room. Damon set up the second bedroom in his condo as a huge walk-in closet. It worked out great because it made it easy for her to pack the clothes she had at Damon's place and get out before he woke.

Pam knew she was a coward and he'd be devastated when he saw she was gone, but Damon would be better off with someone who could be honest about her life.

At four in the morning, Pam walked out of his life. On her way back to her apartment she booked a flight back to Newfoundland, and her wonderful, nosey family.

Pam absently pushed her food around the plate as she listened to her father talk with Damon about what teams were going to make it to the World Series. It was almost September, which meant baseball playoffs were the main topic of discussions. At least until hockey season started.

"The Blue Jays really got to pull their socks up, that's for sure," her father said as he cut a piece of roast on his plate.

"I can't remember the last time I saw them in the playoffs." Damon chuckled.

"Me either." Her father snorted.

"Brian, can we talk about something else besides sports?" her mother complained.

"I apologize, Mrs. Nightingale. You know how us guys are when we get together. Sports, sports, and more sports." Damon smiled, and Pam fisted her hand under the table to keep the sigh from escaping.

"Please, call us Cora and Brian. You're family." Her mother grinned, and Pam almost choked on her sip of water.

"Thank you, Cora. You do have a wonderful family." Damon's tone sounded sad, and Pam raised her eyes to meet his.

"Tell us about your family," her father interjected.

"Not much to tell, Brian. I'm afraid we aren't close. I haven't seen them in a long time." Damon shifted in the chair, looking slightly uncomfortable.

"I'm so sorry, Damon." Her mother reached across the table and covered Damon's hand with hers. "You will always have us."

Pam shot to her feet and snatched her plate from the table. She quickly vacated the dining room and stomped into the kitchen. After scraping the contents of her plate into the garbage, she put her dish in the dishwasher.

"That was so rude, Pam." Her mother entered the kitchen behind her.

"Mom, I can't do this anymore. I'm not comfortable with him here, but you don't seem to care." Pam kept her voice low.

She didn't want to make a scene, even if her mother deserved it. Pam just wanted to run to her uncle's house next door. Well, at least his garage. Jess lived in the little apartment over it, and she would definitely not make Pam live with this torture another day.

"Pam, don't be ridiculous. You heard him. He has no family in his life. Don't you feel bad for him?" Her mother was genuinely concerned about Damon.

"Yes, Mom, but that's not why you invited him here." Pam raised an eyebrow.

"Why are you fighting this so much?" her mother asked.

"Because it will never work, and I don't want this." Pam sighed.

She wasn't about to give her mother a chance to say anything else. Pam stomped out of the house without another word to her parents or Damon.

After a quick text to Jess, she headed around the garage to the bottom of the steps leading to her cousin's loft. Pam was halfway up the stairs when her phone rang. She was going to ignore it because she figured it was her mother, but when she looked at the screen, she didn't recognize the number.

"Pam Nightingale," she answered the phone.

"Hello, I got this number from your website," a man with a foreign accent replied.

"Yes, how can I help you?" Pam eased down and sat on the step.

"I would like a meeting with you," the man said.

"You understand we only sell ladies clothing and apparel?" Pam replied.

"Yes, yes. I buy clothes for my wife," he answered with what sounded like a fake accent.

"I understand. I can set up an appointment with you at my store." Pam didn't want to deal with anything at that moment.

"Yes, yes. I call tomorrow for a meeting," the man replied, but before Pam could say anything else, he hung up.

"Okay, I guess I'll talk to you tomorrow," Pam mumbled to herself.

Pam stood and proceeded up the steps to talk to her cousin about the impossible situation. Jess would probably say yes, but Pam was ready to beg if she needed to. Anything to avoid another uncomfortable dinner with Damon.

When her phone rang the second time, Pam breathed a sigh of relief when she saw Jess' number pop up on her phone.

"I'm out by your door. Come let me in," Pam answered her phone.

Chapter 2

Damon stared out the window of his Toronto apartment. He returned after he had his fill of everything. For several months, he'd hung around Hopedale, hoping Pam would give in and admit they were meant to be together.

It was time for him to go back where he belonged. Newfoundland ceased to be Damon's home the day his father bellowed at him for giving up what was important and choosing to join the Army.

To his father, his choice of career was too blue-collar for the Blackwoods. Just because his family was one of the wealthiest in the province didn't mean they were above everyone else. Hell, Damon had met his boss' in-laws, and even though they were well off, they seemed to treat everyone the same.

Keith O'Connor was not only Damon's boss, but he was also Pam's cousin. Keith had hired him when Damon helped the O'Connor brothers save two teenagers who had been kidnapped.

Damon shot the asshole who'd abducted the teens from less than four-hundred feet, a shot he could have made with his eyes closed. After that, Keith offered him a job with Newfoundland Security Services. NSS was a high-end security and investigations firm who dealt with a lot of politicians and other bigwigs. They were hired mostly by people who thought themselves important.

Damon was looking for a change and a reason to move out of the condo. It reminded him so much of the love he lost, and he quickly jumped at the job. Little did he know, that his reason for running away would be right there under his nose.

One year ago,

Damon stood in the small house, surrounded by his new boss' family. They were such a great bunch of people, and they felt like old friends from the moment he was introduced to them. His friend Elijah Grant seemed close with the youngest of the O'Connor brothers, but probably because Aaron O'Connor was seeing Elijah's cousin, Bethany.

She was the reason Damon now stood with a beer in his hand after knocking down the prick who'd abducted Bethany's nephew and his friend. One shot to the forehead, and he went down like a stone.

"Jesus, this is like a party." Adrian chuckled as he popped the top off the beer bottle in his hand.

Adrian 'Rock' Hudson was not only Damon's best friend, but he was, like Damon, medically retired from the Army. Adrian had taken a piece of shrapnel to his left eye and lost the vision in that eye.

"Not a party really, just family." Keith winked.

Damon turned around and glanced toward the small kitchenette. Aaron leaned against the counter, surrounded by a few women, including Bethany.

"I'm gonna go say hi to A.J.," Damon told Keith.

Damon figured out pretty quickly that the only one who called Aaron by his first name, was his girlfriend. Everyone else called him A.J., so Damon followed suit.

"Did you get the job?" Aaron chuckled.

"We're going to meet next week with all the details." Damon grinned.

"Since you're going to be staying, let me introduce you to some of my cousins and my beautiful lady." Aaron pulled Bethany closer to him.

"Beautiful she is." Damon winked.

"Bethany, this is…" Before Aaron could continue, Damon heard a small gasp

He turned, and for a moment, thought he imagined things. He blinked and shook his head, but she was still there in front of him. Her face was just as beautiful as ever, and her eyes widened with recognition.

"Trixie?" Damon practically choked on the name.

"Trixie?" one of the other female cousins said in confusion.

Damon didn't care who was there, because he couldn't pull his eyes away from her. If possible, Trixie was even more beautiful than he remembered. Her hair was a little longer, but those blue eyes still pulled him in.

"What ... what... are you doing..." she stammered.

"What am I doing here? I could ask you the same thing." Damon winced as the pain he felt when she ran out on him returned and hit him like a punch to the chest.

"Pam? Do you know Damon?" Aaron asked.

Damon was confused at the unfamiliar name. In all the time he knew her, not once had he ever heard her called anything but Trixie Knight.

"Pam?" Damon turned to Aaron.

Trixie, or Pam, took that moment to squeeze by them and escape from the house. Damon took a step to follow her, but Aaron grabbed his arm.

"What did you do to her?" Aaron narrowed his eyes, and his words came out like a growl.

"I didn't do anything, but I need to find out why she lied about who she was, and why she took off without a word after I told *her I loved her." Damon yanked his arm from Aaron's grasp and ran out the door after her.*

Damon ran down the steps and caught her as she was about to jump in her car. There was no way she was getting away from him until she explained why the hell she left, or why she lied to him about who she was.

"Not so fast, Trixie." Damon grabbed her arm and pulled her to a stop.

"Let me go." Pam pulled her arm from his grasp.

"At least you gave me a choice to let you go this time," Damon snapped as he dropped her arm.

"What the hell are you doing in Newfoundland?" Pam narrowed her eyes and glared as if he was the devil.

"Elijah told me there might be a job here with a security company." Damon crossed his arms over his chest.

"That's fucking great." Pam tipped her head back and looked up at the sky as she let out an exasperated sigh.

"Imagine my surprise when I see a woman who looks just like the girl who took off like a bat out of hell. Ran out after I told her I loved her and had the most intense night of love making I've ever experienced. Took off after I fell asleep." Damon hated it, but the thought of that night made him hard every time he let his mind go there.

"I left and came home to my family. I didn't run like a bat out of hell." Pam wouldn't look at him, but the flush in her cheeks told him she was affected by the memory as well.

"No, sweetheart, you ran away and left me in bed without a clue to where you were going." Damon grasped her chin between his fingers. "It was rather shocking to find out the next day you'd packed all your shit, gave your roommate two months' rent for leaving without notice, and disappeared without a forwarding address."

"Jesus, you make it sound like I left in the cover of the night like a spy." Pam pulled her head back to get away from his grasp.

"You did. Lola said she'd never seen anyone pack so fast," Damon continued.

When he had gone to Pam's apartment the next morning, he was heartbroken. Pam shared an apartment with one of the dancers from the club, and when she told Damon Pam was gone, he felt as if she punched him in the gut.

"I was tired of...living that life." Pam leaned against the car.

"You mean tired of the exotic dance club or tired of me?" Damon knew he should keep his voice down, but he was pissed.

"Keep your voice down. My family doesn't know where I worked when I was away." Pam grabbed his arm and dragged him further from the house where her family was celebrating.

"You've been back for what? Almost three years and they don't have a clue what you did in Ontario?" Damon was in shock.

"No. They don't know, and you're going to keep your mouth shut. That gentlemen's club helped me." Pam shoved him.

"Helped you how? You were dancing, bartending, and designing sexy costumes for the dancers." Damon smirked.

"Shut up." Pam tried to step around him, but he stopped her.

"Why?" Damon couldn't keep his voice from cracking.

"They wouldn't understand." She sighed.

"I don't care why you're hiding it from your family. Why did you leave me?" Damon swallowed the lump in his throat.

"Damon," she whispered.

"Why, Trixie? Or should I call you Pam now?" Damon took a step toward her, but she held up her hand.

"I just left," Pam whispered.

"You told me you loved me too." Damon stared into her eyes.

"Please, just forget about it." A tear rolled down her cheek.

"I know you loved me. What I don't know is how you could walk away from what we had." Damon cupped her cheek and wiped the tear away with his thumb.

For a moment, she looked at him the way she used to. The same gaze that used to drive him wild with need for her. She was adventurous and passionate. Funny and stubborn, but it was her compassion for the dancers at the club that first made him fall for her.

The first time he saw her, he'd been attracted to her instantly. He'd been glued to her performance on stage and couldn't believe his luck, when ten minutes later she was behind the bar handing him a drink.

He'd gone there for three weeks straight until he caught Pam on a night off sitting at the bar. She was giving a dancer some much needed advice. The dancer was ready to quit medical school because someone told her she wasn't smart enough to be a doctor.

"Yes, I loved you, but you didn't love me. You loved Trixie Knight, but that's not who I am. Not really. It was the name I used for my anonymity. My family thought I worked for a clothing designer." Pam dropped her head.

"But you weren't," Damon pushed.

"I was for a while, but the company closed down. I saw a position for a bartender in a Toronto hotel and got the job. I was there for a year when I met Drake at the hotel. He offered me a bartender job at his club. The dancing was just fun, and the money was even more fun." Pam lifted her head and glanced over his shoulder at the house.

"You were an exotic dancer, Pam. You didn't undress completely. You were good at it. Awesome, in fact. Why would you think your family would not support you in anything you do?" Damon was confused.

From the short time he'd gotten to know the O'Connor family, they seemed very supportive of everyone. Besides teasing each other now and then, they all seemed to care deeply for one another.

"Sure, they'd be overjoyed to know I was dancing for men to make money. Damon, my family is full of doctors, cops, a nurse, a chef, and lawyers. They wouldn't understand. Especially since I lied to them for so long." Pam leaned against her car and wiped away the tears.

"That doesn't explain why you ran away from me." Damon leaned on the car next to her and glanced at the house where Pam's cousin Keith now stood glaring at him.

"Do you remember what you said to me that night?" Pam must have noticed Keith and waved to him.

"I loved you." Damon shrugged.

"No, you said you loved me, and the best part was I didn't have any family who would interfere in our relationship. Family sucked the life out of relationships." Pam turned to face him.

"Pam, I told you what happened with my family and why I don't see them." Damon tried to reach for her, but she stepped back.

21

"I know. My family didn't know about my life in Ontario, but I talked to at least one of them every day. As big, loud and nosey as they are, I love each and every one of them. They're incredible, and they love me." Tears streamed down her cheeks, and she didn't seem to notice. *"I couldn't deal with not having contact with them. Being with you would mean I couldn't have my family in my life."*

"Jesus, Pam, I didn't know you had a family. You never told me. You never told me anything about you, as a matter of fact; I don't even know if I really did know you. Was any of it real?" Damon couldn't help the anger bubbling inside him.

"I don't think it was. You were in love with Trixie, not Pam. I can't be her. Here, I'm just Pam Nightingale, daughter of Cora the Cupid." Pam hopped inside before he could say another word and she quickly drove off.

"I don't know if I want to hire you if you upset Pam so much." Keith's voice rumbled behind him.

"You don't have to worry about it. I don't think she and I will be speaking again." Damon watched her taillights disappear.

"Maybe we should talk about how you two met and why she doesn't want to talk about her life in Ontario." Keith stepped next to him.

"We met at a club, we had a few dates, and you'd have to ask her about her life. If you want to withdraw the job offer, I understand, but whatever the situation is with Trix... Pam, it's not

going to affect how much I want to work for Newfoundland Security Services. The ball's in your court." Damon started to walk back to the bunkhouse, where he and Adrian had stayed since they arrived in Hopedale.

"As long as you do your job and don't hurt my cousin, you're hired, Bullet." Keith smirked.

"Bullet?" Damon furrowed his brow.

"All my guys have nicknames. You're a sniper and took that asshole out with one shot. I'm calling you Bullet. Unless there's another we can call you." Keith grinned.

"No, it's just funny because they called me Bulletproof overseas because I managed to avoid getting my head blown off four times." Damon tried to force a smile.

"I know, Sandy did a background check on you." Keith raised an eyebrow.

"I should have known." Damon sighed and glanced toward where Pam had driven off.

"If it's meant to be, it'll work out." Keith slapped his hand on Damon's shoulder. "Let me get you a beer and introduce you to the rest of the guys."

Damon nodded as he walked silently next to Keith, wishing he could go back three years and keep his feelings to himself. At least then, Pam may not have run off, leaving him broken and lost.

Damon had been back in Ontario about a week when he ran into Drake. His old friend owned the club where he first met Pam. He was a good guy and offered Damon a job as a bouncer. The truth was Damon didn't need to work, but if he sat home and did nothing, he'd go crazy and probably drink himself to death.

He took the job and for the most part, only had to throw out a few over-excited assholes when they got a little grabby with a couple of the dancers. The rest of his duties consisted of standing on the sidelines of the club and protecting the girls.

Now nearly two months later, he cringed as he locked eyes with the one man he'd never expect to see walking into *The Glitter Pole*. The one man who made him feel like his life was a waste and all the years he put into fighting for his country was below him.

Damon stiffened as his father stalked toward him, with nothing but rage in his eyes. It wasn't going to be pretty, but the last thing Damon would allow was for his father to cause a scene in the club, especially since Damon didn't give a damn what the man thought.

"This is what a so-called hero does after his service to the country?" Damon's father snapped.

"What do you want?" Damon replied with just as much disdain.

"Such a wonderful way to greet your father." Alastair Blackwood sneered in his usual snobby tone.

"I thought when I defied you and turned down your deal so I could join the Army, I was no longer your son?" Damon repeated the last words his father had said to him.

"You need to return home." His father didn't even acknowledge Damon's question.

"I am home, old man." Damon turned as his father grabbed Damon's wrist.

"Your mother is sick and asking for you." His father's voice didn't change the tone, but Damon was almost sure he saw a flicker of sadness in his dad's eyes.

"What's wrong with her?" Damon pulled from his father's grasp.

"Years of abusing drugs and alcohol have taken their toll. Her liver is failing, and she needs a transplant." His father stood up straight and shoved his hands into the pockets of his trousers.

"Is she on the transplant list?" Damon asked.

"Yes, but Doctor Burton said all the family should be tested as well." His father shuddered when a man staggered into him.

"You just want me to go home to be tested." Damon nodded.

"She's your mother," his father snapped.

"She hasn't been a mother to my brother or me for a long time." Damon tried not to raise his voice.

"Malcolm at least had the decency to be tested. He's there next to your mother." His father's voice got louder.

"Probably because you bribed him. What did you offer him this time? A house? Car? No, wait, did you offer him a line of mistresses he can screw while his wife slowly kills herself with vodka and tranquilizers?" Damon replied through gritted teeth.

"Keep your voice down." His father took a step toward Damon.

"You can't bribe me, Father. I'll get tested because no matter what she has done or didn't do, she did give birth to me. I'm doing this for her, not you. It's not her fault she married a cold-hearted bastard." As Damon finished, his dad lifted his hand and slapped Damon across the face.

"Watch your mouth," his father said with a growl.

"That's the last time you'll ever get away with that. I'm not a little boy anymore. If you raise your hand again, be prepared to be on the receiving end of a fist." Damon turned and walked away from his father.

Damon was about two seconds from losing his composure and punching his father right in the face. He wasn't about to stoop to his father's level, but Damon would be tested to see if he could help his mother. He'd been right about one thing; it wasn't her fault. She'd been driven to the abusive life by the one and only Alastair Blackwood.

"I'll leave Doctor Burton's information at the bar. Do something good for your family, for once in your life." His father's voice blared from behind him.

Damon slapped his hand on the bar. A signal to the bartender he needed a drink and a strong one. It probably wasn't a good idea to drink the same stuff that had his mother on the verge of death, but it was a necessity after his father's visit.

Chapter 3

Pam walked down the spiral staircase from her apartment above her shop and flicked on the light at the bottom of the steps. With a frying pan she took from the kitchen in her hand, she slowly made her way to the front of the shop.

"Hello?" Pam called as she took a step into the main area.

The shop was illuminated by the lights from the window display and the streetlights outside. She held the pan over her head as she moved around the store. She searched the shop for what could've possibly made the loud crash that woke her out of her sleep.

"If someone is there, you better come out. I've called the police, and they're on the way," Pam warned.

Nothing.

She walked to the large glass entrance of her store and tried to look up and down the street. It was quiet, and since it was almost three in the morning, all the other shops around were closed.

"Hmm, did I dream it?" Pam muttered to herself as she turned and dropped the frying pan down to her side.

28

As she took a step, something sharp stuck into the bottom of her barefoot, and she grunted in pain as she lifted her foot to see blood seeping from her heel. Probably because of the large piece of glass sticking out of it.

Pam glanced down to see broken glass shattered on the tile floor. None of her windows were damaged and she double checked to make sure. When she took a closer look, it appeared to be one of the water glasses they kept in the shop for customers. She didn't know why it would be next to the entrance.

As she limped back to one of the chairs next to the changing area, Pam saw something that caused a chill to skitter up her spine. The security alarm was off, and the rear entrance of her shop was opened.

Pam hopped on one foot to the bottom of the steps and clumsily made her way back upstairs to her apartment. Her hands trembled as she slammed her apartment door and locked it. She snatched her phone off the table and immediately called the police.

Pam hobbled to the bathroom to find her first aid kit. Her foot wasn't cut too deep, but it was enough to have a steady flow of blood seep from the wound on her foot.

She sat in her bathroom, to wrap the gauze around her foot. She'd just gotten to her feet when someone pounded on the main door to her apartment. Pam didn't need to see anyone to know who was on the other side of the door.

"A.J., you do realize it's the ass crack of dawn, and other people are sleeping. You could have knocked like a normal police officer," Pam said after she opened the door to let her cousin into her place.

"I was a little panicked when the dispatcher called to tell me my cousin called for help. What the hell happened?" Aaron asked.

"I stepped on glass in my shop. Are you here in an official capacity, or just as the closest relative to my place?" Pam asked as she closed her door.

"Both. What's going on?" Aaron asked.

Before she could answer, Jess arrived. It was apparent to Pam the dispatcher probably called a number of her family members to make sure Pam was okay. It was a perk, and a curse of being an O'Connor family member.

"Should I wait for the rest of the family before I explain why I called the police?" Pam sat on her couch and propped her injured foot up on the coffee table.

"Lois, you better start talking." Her cousin Keith's gruff voice echoed in the room.

He always referred to her as Lois Lane, and she would call him Superman. It started when they were kids, and she wanted to go out as Lois Lane for Halloween, but everyone tried to tell her nobody would know what her costume was. Keith, in his protective way, showed up at her door dressed as Superman and took her door to door.

"Fine." Pam huffed.

As she told them about the noise she heard and how her alarm had been turned off, her cousins listened intently. Pam might be acting like she wasn't a nervous wreck, but inside, she was scared to death.

Someone had been lurking around her shop while she slept upstairs. They were able to turn off her alarm, and that terrified her the most.

"Are you sure you set the alarm?" Keith walked to the alarm touchpad and seemed to inspect it.

"Yes, I'm positive." It was the last thing she did before she went to bed for the night.

"Could Elaine have come by?" Aaron asked.

"At three in the morning?" Pam scoffed. "Besides, she doesn't get back from Montreal until next week."

Elaine had flown up to meet with a few small clothing shops to talk about carrying some of *Cupid's Closet* products. Pam knew there was no way Elaine would get back to Newfoundland and not tell her about the meetings.

"How about Sabrina? Doesn't she work here part-time?" Jess asked.

Sabrina Burke worked for Pam and Elaine part-time two evenings a week. She also worked at Jess' parents' diner as well as *Snippy Gals*, the beauty salon owned by Keith's wife, Emily.

"I seriously doubt Sabrina would come into the shop so late. She certainly wouldn't leave the back door open and a broken glass on the floor." Pam sighed as her door opened and two uniformed police officers walked in.

"It looks like the alarm was cut outside. The door was pried open." The female officer handed the camera to Aaron.

"I don't understand why someone would break in here knowing I live upstairs." Pam pulled her knees up to her chest and tried to act as if she wasn't uneasy.

"Well, you're not staying here tonight," Keith said as he sat next to Pam and pulled out his phone.

"I'm not leaving my apartment." Pam shook her head.

"I'm afraid you will be, young lady." Kurt's gruff caused her head to snap up.

Pam knew it would be pointless to argue with her mother's brother. Not only was he the former chief of police and the current mayor of Hopedale, but he was also a pig-headed O'Connor.

"She can stay with Emily and me." Keith stood up and put his phone to his ear.

"I can't leave my shop unattended. Especially with the back door broken and my alarm out of commission. I've got a lot of valuable inventory here." Pam tried to argue, but with the way Keith, Kurt, and Aaron narrowed their eyes and glared at her, she knew she was beating her head against a brick wall.

"I'll post someone outside your shop, and we'll secure the door," Aaron told her as he left her apartment.

"You know it's pointless to argue, right?" Jess sat next to Pam and gave her a comforting hug.

"Don't I know it." Pam sighed.

For the next six days, Pam stayed with Keith and Emily. It wasn't convenient when she was restless. At least at her apartment, she could work when sleep evaded her. The only thing she could do at four in the morning at her cousin's was watch television or get lost in memories of Damon. Thinking of the first day she met Damon had her drifting into the past.

Seven years ago…

Pam was glad to be getting more time behind the bar than on the stage. She enjoyed the money from dancing, but it wasn't her favorite thing to do. Luckily, she only filled in a couple of days a week.

Behind the bar or the sewing machine was where she felt more comfortable. When she served drinks, she could talk to the customers and be tipped for a smile. Of course, her low-cut tank tops increased the generosity of the patrons.

After she had a chat with one of the regular dancers, Pam finished her break and hopped behind the bar. As she glanced down at the end, she saw her boss' handsome friend. He'd been coming by a lot over the last few weeks and always planted himself with his back to the wall on the end barstool.

"Hey, handsome. You want the usual?" Pam asked after she worked her way down to where he sat.

"Yeah," he said with a raspy voice.

Pam nodded, grabbed the whiskey bottle, and poured the gorgeous man his usual double, with ginger ale, no ice in a large glass. It wasn't anything unusual for her to remember drinks of the club's regular customers.

"Here you go?" Pam smiled as she placed the drink in front of him, and he sipped it immediately.

"Nobody makes the drinks like you, Trixie." He winked.

She wasn't confused at the strange name because it was what everyone called her. The only one who knew her real name was the woman in payroll and her boss, Drake. Pam didn't want anyone from home to find out where she was working and what she did.

"Of course not." Pam winked back as she took the money he handed to her.

Before she could pull back, he took her hand and smiled. Pam held her breath because, for the first time in ages, she got butterflies in her stomach at the touch of someone's hand.

"Have supper with me on your next day off?" he asked.

"Do you ask out all the bartenders who make you a drink?" Pam chuckled as she tried to pull back her hand.

"I haven't asked anyone out since before I was deployed." His face turned serious.

"You're in the military?" Pam asked.

"Sergeant Damon Blackwood, medically retired. Seems it's not good for my hearing to be close to an exploding bomb." His lips quirked up into what she knew was a fake smile.

"I'm sorry, but thanks for your service." Pam laid her hand over his on the bar.

"You can thank me by having supper with me." He raised an eyebrow.

"You're tricky." Pam narrowed her eyes and poked him in the arm.

She had to bite back the gasp as she felt nothing but sexy muscle. It was difficult to see his body with the jacket he wore. She stepped back and turned when someone called out to her.

"I'm not off again until Tuesday," Pam said as she turned back to him.

"That's too long. I can take you for a bite after you get off." He held out his phone to her. *"Put in your number, and I'll text you so you can have mine."*

"I don't get out of here until one in the morning." Pam chuckled as she tapped her number into his phone.

"I don't care." He winked. *"I'll be back."*

Later that evening, he stepped inside the bar with a white rose. Pam sighed as she saw him stroll toward her. At that moment, she knew Damon wasn't going to be just another guy in her life.

Chapter 4

Damon jolted up in his bed and gasped for air. Another nightmare, but it wasn't unusual. For the last week, all his nightmares consisted of him on an overlook, aiming at a terrorist who had Pam at gunpoint.

It always ended the same way. Pam lying on the ground and the terrorist with a bullet hole in the middle of his head. The problem was he'd always wake up before he knew if she was alive.

It played havoc with his already fucked-up brain. He'd talked to the therapist about it, but he knew why it was Pam who showed up in his dreams. He was worried about her.

Damon had stayed in touch with Keith and Aaron when he left Newfoundland. Mostly because besides Adrian and Elijah, they were the only friends he had left.

Keith told him someone had broken into her shop, and she'd been there alone. Damon had been tempted to head back to guard her himself. He knew it would never go well because she didn't want him around.

"Fuck it." Damon flopped back on the bed and snatched his phone from the bedside table.

It was almost five in the morning, and he was surprised he'd slept for nearly three hours. He tossed the phone on the bed and closed his eyes.

Damon was miserable. He was working, drinking, and going home to fall into bed. He had no purpose in his life anymore, and the fact he wasn't a match to help his mother only made him feel worse.

Since it was his day off, he planned to do a few errands and probably stop by the club to keep himself from going stir crazy. He knew Jess O'Connor was getting married that day. She'd made a point of calling him a few months earlier to invite him to her wedding.

Damon had declined but didn't get off the phone without promising to visit the family soon. It seemed like all of Pam's family wanted him to go back to Newfoundland. Everyone wanted him to return except the one person he cared about the most.

He was about to leave for the grocery store when his phone buzzed in his pocket. Damon pulled it out and glanced at the unfamiliar number. Without answering, he sent it to voicemail and continued out of the apartment.

A few seconds later, his phone buzzed again with the same number. Curiosity got the better of him, and he tapped the screen.

"Hello," he said as he hopped into the taxi he'd managed to flag down.

"Damon, it's Malcolm." His brother's voice echoed through the phone.

"Someone must be dead," Damon replied but immediately cringed as he remembered his mother's situation.

"No, but our mother is on borrowed time." For the first time, his brother's voice cracked.

"I see." Damon swallowed the lump that formed in his throat.

"Is that all you can say? She's your mother for Christ's sake," Malcolm shouted.

Damon didn't know what else to say. He did love his mother because she was his mom, but they hadn't spoken in more than six years. He'd tried several times after he returned from his last deployment but was always told she was unable to take his calls. He'd given up after six months of trying.

"What else am I supposed to say?" Damon sighed.

"You could say you're coming to make it look like you at least give a damn about the family," Malcolm snapped.

"Like the family gave a damn about me. Don't give me that shit, Mal. I ceased to be part of the family when I refused to marry Gail. You know, the woman you eventually married?" Damon said through clenched teeth.

According to his father, marrying Gail would help the family business win the merger with Gail's father. Carl Small ran a large finance firm, and Damon's father wanted to merge both companies. It would make him co-owner of the biggest investment and finance firms in the Atlantic provinces. It seemed owning a ton of commercial property didn't make enough money for the Blackwoods.

According to his father, in order to make it happen, Damon needed to marry Carl's daughter to ensure the merger wouldn't fall through. Alastair Blackwood didn't care if Damon wasn't in love with Gail, or Damon had a different career choice. It was why his father was so furious when Damon enlisted without discussing it with anyone in his family.

Damon felt a little guilty when three months later his brother called to say he would be getting married to Gail Small. It seemed since Damon had screwed up his father's plans, he'd bribed Malcolm to go along with the idea.

"You know very well why I married Gail. Drop it. I just want to know if you're going to grace us with your presence before mom dies." The venom in his brother's voice told Damon that Malcolm didn't want to talk about his marital situation.

Damon knew he'd probably regret it in years to come but considering how fucked-up his head was, it wouldn't be a good idea to put himself within ten feet of his father. He was probably a selfish bastard, but there was nothing he could do for his mother.

"No," Damon said adamantly.

"Fine, don't say you weren't informed." With that statement, Malcolm was gone.

Damon spent the rest of the day digging himself into a bottomless pit of guilt. His mother was dying, and he wasn't considering going to see her. How could he not go to say a final goodbye to the woman who raised him. His mother didn't deserve any of it. She'd been driven to her addiction by the unfeeling bastard she married. He hung his head over his lap and linked his hands behind his head.

"She didn't really have a life with the old man. He probably married her because it helped his business," Damon whispered as a tear slipped out and dropped to the floor.

He did remember when he was a kid, and she would take him and Malcolm to the lake behind their estate. They'd swim in the cool water during the summer and skip rocks. His mother was beautiful and loved them.

The year Damon turned twelve, something changed. He'd hear his parents argue all the time and they started to sleep in different rooms. That was when she began to sleep more, and as he got older, Damon realized why. She'd started popping pills and drinking. He'd asked her what was wrong once and she told him she was tired of being a wife in name only. She was tired of mistresses.

The truth made him ill, and he swore to never become anything like his father. Damon wanted to go his own way, and when he found the one he wanted to marry, she would know he would be faithful to her and only her.

That was what he'd hoped for with Pam.

Chapter 5

Things were finally back to normal at her shop, and Pam was happy to be back in her apartment. Of course, Keith upgraded the security in both her apartment and her shop. Cameras were placed outside along with motion sensors to make sure nobody could get near her place without being noticed.

Elaine was back and had gotten two huge contracts in Montreal for delivery of some of their clothing and lingerie. Their production warehouse was working hard to get the orders done and sent off by the end of the month.

Now Pam stood at the head of the church and watched her cousin marry the man of her dreams. Wade Rivers looked at Jess with such love that Pam couldn't help but feel a little jealous.

Then there was Jess' sister Isabelle, who was grinning ear to ear as she rested her hand on her pregnant belly. She and her fiancé Roman were waiting until their baby was born to marry. The youngest of the three sisters, Kristy, had gotten married a few years earlier and recently had their second child.

As Pam glanced around the church, her chest ached as she watched all her family smiling and happy with their spouses. Even Aaron and his six older brothers were happily married with families.

Pam was thirty-six, an only child, and the only one not in a long-term relationship. It sucked, but she hoped the date she brought would get everyone off her back. Especially her mother and grandmother.

Elizabeth O'Connor, or Nanny Betty as everyone called her, had her sights set on Pam. She was continually telling Pam to call the nice man she'd allowed to run away. Of course, she was referring to Damon because Pam's mom made it clear to the entire family that Damon was the one.

"Pam, ya know dat lad is not gonna wait fer ya," Nanny Betty said with an Irish lilt.

Nanny Betty was born on the Southern Shore of Newfoundland in a small community called Cape Broyle. The accent of the people, *up the shore*, as people would say, sounded Irish. She was in her mid-eighties, but it was hard to believe because she didn't act it and she certainly didn't look it. Especially when she was with Tom Roberts, her boyfriend, for lack of a better word, they'd been sweethearts when Nanny Betty was seventeen, but circumstances separated them, which was how she fell in love with Jack O'Connor, Pam's grandfather.

Tom came back into Nanny Betty's life a few years back, and they'd been dating ever since, or courting, as Nanny Betty called it. No matter what it was called, they obviously loved each other and were adorable when they were together.

"Nan, he obviously didn't. He left Newfoundland a while ago, and I'm pretty sure Mom is wrong this time." Pam wrapped her arm around Nanny Betty and kissed her cheek.

"My Cora is never wrong." Nanny Betty pointed her arthritic finger at Pam.

"You have such faith in Mom's cupid powers." Pam chuckled and turned as her date walked toward them.

"I do and dat lad comin' over here acts like a bedlamer." Nanny Betty huffed and scurried away.

Pam laughed at the term her grandmother used to describe Kyle. Newfoundlanders used the term for teenagers, mainly when they acted immaturely. Kyle O'Leary wasn't a teenager, but Nanny Betty wasn't exactly wrong with calling him immature. He was five years younger than Pam, but he acted as if he was still in his late teens.

Kyle partied every weekend and drank excessively. Pam wasn't really dating him, but she had gone out on a couple of awful dates with him. The only reason she asked him to the wedding was, so she didn't have to be the only loser without a date. She hoped if her mother saw her with Kyle then she would stop urging Pam to contact Damon.

He'd left town over a year earlier and hadn't looked back, but who could blame him? She didn't exactly make him feel welcome, but it was the hardest thing she ever did. Pam had to keep her life in Hopedale and the life she had in Ontario separate.

Pam needed an excuse to leave the wedding. Kyle started to give her hints that he wanted her to go home with him. It wasn't happening because after the wedding, she didn't want to see the guy again.

"We could really have a wild time tonight, baby," he whispered into her ear as he slobbered down to her neck.

Pam practically threw up in her mouth when he stuck his tongue in her ear. Pam politely pushed him back and forced a smile. The last thing she wanted to do was cause trouble at a family wedding.

She was about to make up an excuse when her phone vibrated in her purse. Pam held up her finger and put her phone to her ear as she made her way to the ladies' room.

"Pam Nightingale," she answered as she smiled at Sandy, her cousin Ian's wife.

"It's Vladimir Yugov." The man's voice echoed through the phone.

Pam rolled her eyes because this was the guy who had been buying an enormous number of items from her store for a year. He said it was for his wife, but Pam had never seen the woman. She didn't say anything because the truth was, he was tossing a lot of money her way.

"Hi, Mr. Yugov. What can I do for you?" Pam checked out her makeup in the bathroom mirror.

"I need my order first thing in the morning," he demanded.

"I'm sorry, Mr. Yugov, I was under the impression you didn't need it until Monday." Pam tried not to sound annoyed.

"Wife needs clothes tomorrow," he snapped.

"I'm at a family function right now, but I can put it all together in the morning." Pam leaned against the counter.

"Need at eight in the morning," he continued.

Pam realized this would be the perfect excuse for her to leave. Her family wouldn't want her to lose a considerable sale. It was also a way to get away from Kyle.

"Okay, I'll go to the shop and get it together. I'll see you first thing in the morning," Pam said.

"Good." The called ended.

Pam wasn't surprised by the abrupt end of the call because he wasn't exactly the politest person in the world. Pam didn't really blame him for being so cranky. He was in a wheelchair and from what she could see, needed to be pushed around by a large wall of muscle who came into the shop with Vladimir.

The only thing Pam knew about the man was he was huge, and the left side of his face was scarred terribly. He never spoke and he made Pam feel uneasy with the way he watched her. Vladimir called him Al.

Pam glanced around the beautifully decorated club, but it was as if the walls were closing in on her. She desperately wanted some fresh air, and to get far away from Kyle. Pam needed to get back to her shop and put together the order for the impatient Mr. Yugov.

"Hey, I need to run to the shop and box up an order. It should only take me an hour or so." Pam found her mother and father at the table with her grandmother, aunts, and uncles.

"Can't you do it tomorrow?" Pam's mother complained.

"Sorry, Mom. It's a last-minute order, and the guy is picking it up in the morning." Pam kissed her mother's cheek and hurried out of the hall to her car.

She felt like a coward leaving her date at the wedding with her family, but she didn't care. Pam needed to get away.

She was almost to her car when she heard her name being called out. Pam turned around and groaned as Kyle staggered down the steps. The wedding reception was held at the club owned by Isabelle's fiancée, Roman Young and his best friend, Ethan Norris.

There was a total of two steps to maneuver, but Kyle made it look like it was an obstacle course. She rolled her eyes as he missed the last step and slammed into a man who was stood next to a vehicle.

Pam was about to head over to apologize for Kyle, but someone placed something cold against the back of her neck. Pam stiffened as she was pulled back behind a truck and something was placed over her eyes.

"Don't make a sound or your friend over there will need a pine box in the morning, instead of a couple of aspirin." The voice in her ear wasn't familiar.

The next thing she knew, Pam was tossed into what seemed like the trunk of a car. Something was wrapped around her hands; then a trunk slammed above her.

"God, help me." Pam choked out the words as tears slipped down the side of her face.

She was jostled when the vehicle shot forward, and Pam closed her eyes. She prayed Kyle was sober enough to notice she suddenly disappeared.

Chapter 6

"You want another, handsome?" The pretty barmaid with the enormous tits leaned over the bar.

"Yep." Damon could have her on her back and be slamming into her in less time than it would take him to pull the trigger of a sniper rifle.

He just wasn't interested. Whenever he thought about taking another woman home, he felt guilty. Like he was unfaithful to his heart. It was stupid, but it was a feeling he couldn't shake. It was why he spent his evenings drinking himself into a stupor and heading home to pass out in his empty apartment.

"I'm off at two, if you're interested." The barmaid slid the drink in front of Damon and ran her long fingernail down his bicep.

"Thanks, maybe another night. Long day." Damon smiled and slammed back the drink.

He tossed a couple of twenties on the bar and headed out into the night air. He lived about a block from the club and made his way there while he fumbled in his jeans' pocket for his keys.

Damon was almost at his building and thankful because the humid July night in Toronto was stifling. As he unlocked the main door in the building, his phone buzzed in his pocket.

He thought about ignoring it, but the only people who called him were Drake, Keith, Adrian, or Elijah. They were the only ones that called him. If they were calling him at midnight, then there was a problem. Damon glanced at the screen to see a blocked number.

"Hello." Damon put the phone to his ear as he stepped on the elevator.

"Damon, it's Keith O'Connor," the deep gruff voice rumbled in his ear.

"Hey, Keith." Damon stepped off the elevator and headed down the hall toward his condo.

"Pam's missing," Keith choked out.

"I'll be on the next plane," Damon answered and ended the call.

He didn't ask Keith for details, nor did he care. Those two words Keith uttered were enough to stop Damon's heart and have him running back to Newfoundland.

Damon quickly tossed some clothes into his duffle bag and grabbed a few other essentials. He took a quick look at his gun locker and then shook his head. He refused to believe he needed any of his weapons.

It would also be too much of a hassle to get it on board the plane in such a short period of time. No, if he needed to take someone out, he was sure Keith would supply him with what he needed. The man had access to more weapons than anyone knew.

Damon was almost through security when his phone buzzed. He looked at the screen and cringed. This was the last thing he needed to deal with. Drake would be pissed that Damon left without giving him enough notice to cover his shift.

"Hey Drake," Damon answered.

"Jesus, thank fuck." Drake huffed.

"What's wrong?" Damon stepped aside so the people behind him could move on, and he wouldn't hold up the line.

"I got a call saying your family needs you at home right away," Drake said.

"What the fuck?" Damon didn't even try to control the volume of his voice.

"I thought you didn't have anything to do with your family," Drake said.

"I don't. I'm needed back in Newfoundland for another reason. I'm at the airport now," Damon said through gritted teeth.

"What's going on, buddy?" Drake asked.

"It's Trixie; she's missing." Damon wasn't sure if he should be telling Drake anything, but he knew his friend would understand.

"Fuck, let me know if you need anything, Damon. I mean anything." Drake's reply was expected.

"I will, thanks." Damon ended the call.

His phone buzzed with an email. He hoped it was from Keith saying they'd found Pam. His hopes were dashed when he swiped the screen. The picture he viewed made him feel as if his heart stopped. His hand trembled as he held the phone closer.

Pam was blindfolded and tied to a chair. It looked as if there was duct tape across her mouth, and she was dressed in what looked like a formal dress. It was the message attached to the photo that made his blood run cold

Unknown: You want your girlfriend back safe? Give us what we want, and I'll return this hot little piece of ass safely and untouched.

Damon stared at the picture as he tried to understand exactly what he was seeing. Did someone take Pam because of him? He and Pam hadn't been together in a long time, and when they were, everyone knew her as Trixie. He couldn't even reply to the email because it was blocked.

"Sir, are you coming through security?" The man on the other side of the body scanner appeared annoyed.

"Uh, yeah." Damon shoved his things into the tray and made his way through the security check.

When he got through, he waited for his belongings to make their way through the conveyor. It seemed to take forever as he watched the tray come closer. When it moved in front of him, he grabbed his things and immediately opened the picture again, but before he could get a better look, his phone rang again, and he answered it.

"Why did you hang up on me?" Drake asked.

"Sorry, going through security at the airport," Damon said as he made his way to the gate.

"Are you okay?" Drake's voice was filled with concern.

"I've got to go find Trixie." Damon didn't give Drake a chance to say another word and ended the call.

Damon forwarded the message to Keith with a note with his flight information. He didn't know what this person wanted, but at least if he sent it to Keith, he could get a jump on it before Damon landed. He didn't wait for a response and turned off his phone as he buckled himself into the seat.

For the next three hours, all he could do was sit on the plane and pray to God that Pam was found before the plane touched down in St. John's. It was hard to block out the images of what could happen to her. He'd seen too many victims of abductions to count, and most of them were never the same.

Damon studied the photo on his phone and shook with anger. Pam had to be scared, but she was tough. She was also stubborn.

Hopefully, she wouldn't tick off the assholes who took her because they could wound her. If the kidnapper hurt one hair on her head, Damon would rip them apart.

The flight seemed to take forever and to top it off; the plane had to circle a couple of times before it could land due to the fog. Typical Newfoundland weather and any other time, it wouldn't bother him, but he needed boots on the ground.

He turned off the airplane mode on his phone as he exited the aircraft. He wasn't surprised when seconds later his phone vibrated over and over. He looked at the screen to see several text messages from Keith, Adrian, and Drake.

Before he could call Keith, he looked up to see the large man stood next to the exit. It was apparent Keith hadn't slept. His clothes were rumpled, and his hair looked a tousled mess, but the dark circles under his eyes showed his exhaustion.

"What do they want?" Keith asked as soon as Damon was close.

"I don't have a fucking clue," Damon replied and walked with Keith out of the airport.

"Come on, Bullet. Think," Keith begged.

"What the fuck do you think I've been doing for the last four hours?" Damon snapped.

"She's been gone for more than twenty-four hours." Keith's voice cracked.

Damon knew Keith cared deeply for his family. Pam may be his cousin, but Damon realized early on, Keith and his brothers watched over her and the other girls in the family as if they were their sisters.

"What I don't get is why would someone take Pam to get to you?" The voice from the back seat of the vehicle startled him for a moment.

Damon turned to see Brent 'Crash' Adams in the back seat with another of the guys who worked for Keith. Lane 'Shadow' West was not only an employee of Newfoundland Security Services, but he was also the brother of Keith's sister-in-law, Sandy.

"Plus, I didn't know you two were dating." Shadow said.

"We haven't dated in a long time." Damon's leg shook up and down.

It was a habit he had when he was anxious, and he couldn't control it. He also wanted a drink more than he wanted to breathe, but his brain needed to be completely clear. Keith hadn't told him what happened, and he didn't want to miss anything.

"Tell me exactly what happened," Damon ordered as Keith pulled onto the highway and headed to Hopedale.

"We were at Jess and Wade's reception. Pam's date was a little drunk," Keith began.

"A little drunk, Rusty?" Crash scoffed using the nick name they guys used for Keith. "That fucking plug was more than a little drunk."

"He's a fucking dick." Shadow snorted.

"Aunt Cora said Pam had to leave to go finish an order for early the next morning," Keith continued.

"Who was the order for?" Damon interjected.

"Don't know. I've got Sandy and Smash looking into her customer records and checking her phone log," Keith explained.

Gage 'Smash' Hodder was one of the two computer analysts who worked for Keith, and Sandy was the other. She might be Keith's sister-in-law, but she was also one of the best in the country. Keith was lucky to have her and Smash.

"So, what happened after she left?" Damon asked.

"Kyle followed her, but when he got outside, he stumbled into a guy. We saw that on the CCTV cameras set up outside the club and Isabelle's restaurant," Keith went on.

"The last time Pam showed up in the video, she was crossing the street. She didn't make it to her shop," Shadow finished.

Damon swallowed hard. His heart felt as if it would pop out of his chest, and at one point, he felt as if he was about to have a heart attack. He was never so terrified in his life, and considering he spent time in a war zone, that was saying something. He refused to think about what could be happening to her because it made his stomach knot.

"How did you find out she was missing?" Damon managed to choke out.

"Her car was still next to the club, and her phone was shattered on the ground. When we searched further, we found her purse behind some of the trees," Keith explained.

"Her date or the other guy in front of the club didn't see anything?" Damon almost choked on the word date.

"Kyle O'Leary couldn't describe the guy right in front of him, let alone see across the street. The guy is like an overgrown adolescent." Crash obviously didn't like Kyle.

"I don't know if he's sobered up yet." Shadow sneered in disgust.

Damon didn't like the guy either but mostly because he'd been Pam's date at the wedding. He wondered how close Kyle and Pam really were. He hadn't been with Pam in a long time, but the thought of her with another man made him want to vomit. It was probably because he never stopped loving her. Pam somehow knocked down the walls he'd built up over the years, and he opened his heart to her.

Pam was the first woman to make him believe love really existed. When she left, he tried to find her, but Trixie Knight disappeared without a word. He begged Drake to give him all the information on her, but Drake couldn't or wouldn't tell him anything. Friend or not, Drake wouldn't break the law by giving Damon Pam's information.

He had to find her, and when he did, he wasn't letting her walk out of his life ever again.

Chapter 7

Pam crawled on to the large bed in the room she'd been locked in for what seemed like weeks, but in reality, it had been five long days. The only people she saw were the men who delivered her meals. She tried to speak with them, but they would drop the tray, leer at her, and then leave.

The room was comfortable, for a prison, and she had a full bathroom. There were several large windows, but they didn't open, and the only view she had was what looked like woods behind the house.

She'd also been given clothes, and surprisingly, a lot of it was from her shop. It made her wonder if the person who took her had been watching her, but she wouldn't know who it could be since a lot of her merchandise was sold online as well.

There was no television, computer, or anything in the room to kill time while she figured out how to get the hell away from her abductors.

She asked several of the men for books or cards, but they still hadn't brought her anything. Pam was going stir crazy locked up in the room and tried to find a way to escape.

The first night there, she tried breaking the window with a chair, but she stopped when the window didn't even crack. She tried to pick the lock, and only had her bobby pins taken from her by one of the large goons. She'd also tried fighting one of the guys, but he'd twisted her arm so hard she thought it would snap.

She did manage to find a pen and notepad in one of the dresser drawers and started to write letters to her family. She kept it under her pillow, and whenever she felt anxious or like she'd never see them again, she'd pull out the notepad and write to one of them. She even wrote one to Damon and cried the whole time she wrote. Pam always found it easier to write down her feelings, and maybe it was what she should have done when she left him.

"I've got to get out of here." Pam sighed and curled up on her side with her arm tucked under her head.

As night fell on her fifth night of captivity, she silently thanked God for the hundredth time that she was still alive. The night she'd been taken, Pam wasn't sure she'd be alive the next day. They knocked her out, and by the time she came to, the man who had snatched her had tied her to a chair, blindfolded her, and covered her mouth with tape.

Pam didn't know what they were doing, but all they did was take pictures. It was creepy, mainly because nobody talked to her. The only time she heard voices was when people were outside her room. The problem was they all seemed to be speaking a different language, and it terrified her.

Pam rolled over and hated to open her eyes. She was still in the room and had no idea why. A click of the door caused her to jolt upright, and she tensed as it opened slowly. A woman dressed in a maid's uniform walked into the room. She was followed by one of the goons, and he stood inside the door while the maid scurried into the bathroom.

Pam took in the man who stood like a soldier next to her door. He was big, but he wasn't in shape like her cousins and the guys who worked for Keith. This goon had a slight beer belly and a double chin. He also had large hands and wore a wedding ring.

It was the first time Pam had anyone besides the men come into her room. She slipped off the bed to make her way toward the bathroom, but the goon shook his head.

"I have to go," Pam lied.

The goon just shook his head and knocked on the bathroom door. The maid appeared again, looking confused, but she stepped out of the ensuite when the goon whispered something to her. He motioned to let Pam know it was free, and she hurried by the young woman. One look at the girl told Pam the woman didn't want to be there any more than Pam did.

While she was inside, she pressed her ear against the door to see if she could hear them speak, but all she could hear was silence. After what she figured was an appropriate amount of time for her to use the bathroom, she flushed the toilet and washed her hands.

When she walked back into her room, they were gone. The bed had been stripped and remade with fresh towels placed on the foot of the bed. Pam sighed as she eased down on her bed and blinked back the tears threatening to spill over.

She didn't know what to do and wondered if she was being held by some sex trafficker who wanted to sell her off to the highest bidder. It didn't make sense. What little she did know about the sex trade world she'd found out a few years ago when her cousin Mike almost lost the woman he loved to one of them.

"But Billie is younger than me. Who the hell would buy a woman in her late thirties?" Pam mumbled to herself.

It was tough to know what to do. The guards didn't tell her anything, and she was lonely. She missed her family and friends terribly. She would give anything to see them burst through the door to rescue her.

Damon.

If she hadn't been so stupid, she would've invited him to the wedding. Pam would never leave him the way she left Kyle. He certainly wouldn't have let her go back to her shop alone. Pam knew Damon would have gladly gone with her to help because he was that type of guy. How could she be stupid enough to let him go? He left Newfoundland because she pushed him away.

"If I get out of here, I'm going to find him and tell him exactly how I feel about him," Pam whispered as she curled up on the bed and allowed the burning tears to fall.

She hadn't let any of the goons see her cry since they took her, but Pam was exhausted. They had to be watching her; she saw the red blinking lights inside the air vent in the corner of the room. She prayed they would tell her soon why she was a prisoner, or let her go.

Pam woke suddenly when someone touched her arm. It was barely daylight, and she looked up into the eyes of one of the goons. For a moment, she could have sworn she saw compassion, but he pointed to the table.

"I don't want to eat at this hour," Pam griped as she lay back down.

He dragged her to the small table where the food sat and pointed to the chair. Pam was too tired to argue with him; it was why she plopped down on the chair.

"Could you at least say a word? At least I'll find out if you actually have the capability." Pam snapped as she pushed the tray of food back.

"Eat," the goon growled and stomped out of the room.

Pam stared at the door for several minutes after the goon left. He was the first one to utter a word to her since she'd gotten there. Even though he only said one word, she didn't hear any kind of an accent. So why did they talk in a foreign language?

Pam saw red when she glanced outside to see the sun just coming up from behind the trees. She grabbed the end of the table and flipped it over. The food flew to the floor, and the dishes shattered.

"Why. Am. I. Here?" Pam screamed as she glared up at the blinking red light.

Nothing.

Pam roared as loud as she could and then flopped down on the bed. Her heart pounded in her chest, and she was ready to explode with rage. If these people wanted to drive her to the brink of insanity, they were pretty close to achieving that goal.

"What would Damon do?" Pam murmured.

As if he whispered in her ear, Pam sat up straight and scanned the room. All she needed was something hard enough to knock out one of those goons but small enough she could hide it when they came into the room.

She searched the room, but after an hour, Pam felt defeated. She made her way into the bathroom and switched on the light. As if someone guided her to it, her eyes locked on the towel rack. Pam ran her hand along the rod and smiled. As all the hardware in the bathroom, it was cast iron.

Pam tugged on it, but it was secured to the wall. She couldn't give up. There had to be something in the room to help her pry it off the wall or remove the screws on one end. As she entered the bedroom, she spotted the spoon from her tray under the edge of her bed.

Pam glanced up at the red light. She wasn't sure if they really did watch her, but she decided it was better for her to remain casual. There was a mess on the floor, and she crouched down to pick up the broken dishes. As she did, she slipped the spoon into the waistband of her yoga pants.

She placed the tray back on the table with the broken dishes and the food. She made her way to the bathroom and closed the door. Pam had to hold in her squeal of excitement when the handle of the spoon fit perfectly in the screw. It took a little elbow grease to get the first screw loosened. When she had the one screw removed, she pulled the bracket at the end aside and removed the rod.

The bathroom was large enough for her to test the weight of the rod in her hands. She raised it above her head and swung it down with all her strength. Pam did it several times, each time becoming easier. The rod was like a spiral and thick enough for her to get a comfortable grip on it. Pam swung it a couple more times, and when she was satisfied she could give one of the goons a good smack with it, she put it back into the brackets but didn't replace the screw.

"I need a plan," Pam whispered as she stared at herself in the mirror.

For two days, she worked on a plan to get one of the goons into her trap. Since they usually didn't go any further than the entrance to the bedroom, Pam wasn't sure how to get them into the bathroom so she could whack them.

When she'd all but given up, an idea hit her. At lunchtime when they came into the room, she stood up and pretended to be lightheaded. The guy simply raised his eyebrow but didn't even move from the doorway.

"Sorry, I don't feel well. I'm not sure why I'm dizzy, and my tummy hurts too." Pam eased into the chair next to the table where the tray was placed.

The guy didn't say a word when he pulled out his phone and tapped in something. He looked up at Pam then back down to his phone. When he stalked toward her, Pam pulled back. He lifted his hand slowly and gently pressed the back of his hand against her head.

He immediately tapped something into his phone again and went back to his post at the door. Pam started to eat the sandwich, but before she'd taken a second bite, there was a soft knock on the door.

The goon opened the door, and someone handed him a small cup. He brought it to Pam and placed it on the table next to her tray. She looked down to see two pills in a blister pack.

"Tylenol?" Pam asked, and the goon nodded.

This was the time. Pam took the two pills and made her way to the bathroom. She removed the pills and hid them in her bra as she turned on the tap. After a few seconds, she turned it off and stepped behind the bathroom door, held her breath, and prayed.

For what seemed like several minutes, Pam stood with her back against the wall and waited. The goon didn't come in, but she wasn't losing the chance to make her escape. A few more minutes passed, and she heard the unmistakable click of the bedroom door.

"Damn," Pam whispered as she put the rod back and shuffled out of the bathroom.

As she stepped into the bedroom, she slammed right into another goon. It wasn't the same one, but it was the one who had spoken a few words to her.

"Okay?" It was only a word, but he did speak.

"Oh. Yeah. I'm just gonna lie down." Pam walked around him and crawled onto the bed as she silently cursed her luck.

"Eat." The goon pointed to her tray.

"I will. I have to wait for my tummy to settle." Pam curled up and wrapped her arms around herself.

"Fine," the goon grumbled and nodded to the other one.

They exited the room, leaving Pam to feel defeated and hopeless. She wondered if she would ever see her family or Damon again.

Chapter 8

Damon leaned against the doorframe of Keith's house and slowly sipped coffee out of the large cup he held in his hand. He probably shouldn't drink it so late at night, but it was better than doing what he wanted to do. Drink a bottle of whiskey until he passed out.

He'd been back in Newfoundland for five days, and they were no closer to finding Pam. He hadn't received any more messages, and they'd talked to the man who had called Pam the night she disappeared. He was in a wheelchair and seemed genuinely concerned about Pam's safety. He'd been more than a little miffed when Pam didn't show up for the meeting, but he swore he had nothing to do with her disappearance.

Damon did feel a little uneasy with the man's reaction. Vladimir constantly checked his watch and something about the accent was all too familiar, and it caused his heart to pound in his chest. Accents were probably a trigger for him, but Vladimir's accent was different from the ones he heard during his time in the Middle East. It did remind him to make a call to his therapist. Maybe she could recommend someone for him to see in Newfoundland.

It was hard for him to admit he had some form of Post Traumatic Stress Disorder, or PTSD. It was one of the issues he had with his therapist because he would never admit he had it. The therapist told him until he could face it, he'd never be able to work through it. Damon had nodded but never said the words.

When things got too hard for him, Damon would find his solace in the bottom of a whiskey bottle. Now his mother was dying because of her tendency to deal with her issues in the same manner. It was ironic how he'd sworn to never end up like that, but realistically, he was headed in the very same direction.

"You look sad, Uncle Damon." Keith's oldest son said from behind Damon.

Damon knew Noah was five because the little boy constantly reminded people he was a big boy. His mother said because he was going to Kindergarten, he was all grown up, or so the little boy declared.

All the kids in the O'Connor family referred to him as Uncle Damon because their parents didn't like them calling him by his first name. Since Damon refused to be called Mr. Blackwood, that was the choice. He didn't mind. It was probably the only time he would be given the title.

"I'm a little tired, Noah." Damon crouched so he was eye level with the little red-headed boy.

"It's okay to be sad." Noah put his little hand on Damon's shoulder.

"You're right. It is." Damon couldn't help but smile at the kid.

"If you need to cry, it's okay too. Daddy says even big boys like him need to cry sometimes," Noah continued.

"Yep, that's true." Damon nodded.

"If you need to cry, I'll get you a tissue." Noah turned, but Damon stopped him.

"Thanks, buddy, but I'm good." Damon ruffled the little boy's wavy hair.

"Noah, I thought you were coming down to get your teddy?" Emily stood behind them with her hands on her hips.

"I did, but Uncle Damon looked like he needed a friend," Noah explained to his mother.

"How can I get annoyed when he says something so sweet?" Emily sighed and shook her head.

"You can't." Damon laughed.

"Goodnight," Noah called as he ran down the hall and up the stairs.

"He's a good kid," Damon told Emily before she walked away.

"Yes, he is." Emily smiled as she followed her son.

"Keith's a lucky son of a bitch," Damon murmured.

"You won't hear an argument from me." The voice startled Damon.

"As long as you know it." Damon chuckled.

"I do." Keith plopped down in the old rocking chair on the front porch.

"I know I ask this way too much, but any news?" Damon asked.

"Sandy is still checking in to Vladimir Yugov. He might have seemed concerned, but it's a little coincidental how Pam disappears the same night he calls her. She also checked into the license plate on the car in front of the club. She tracked down the address, but we went there, and it looked like nobody had been there in a long while." Keith sighed.

"Where the fuck is she?" Damon huffed mostly to himself.

"I wish I knew, but they've got to make contact again soon. Have you figured out what they want?" Keith asked.

"Jesus, Keith, I got nothing. I live in an apartment with enough furniture to make it look like someone lives there. I have my sniper rifle and my medals. If they want that shit, I'll gladly give it to them to get her back if they'd just make contact." Damon tossed the remainder of his coffee into the bushes.

"Aunt Cora's a mess." Keith plowed his fingers through his hair.

"I know. I saw her this morning." Damon swallowed the lump in his throat.

Pam's mother was not the same cheerful woman he'd first met. She walked around like she was in a daze, and Pam's father wasn't much better. Brian told Damon that if they didn't find Pam soon, he didn't know what they would do.

"Have you talked to your family?" Keith asked.

"No," Damon answered abruptly.

"You're not going to let them know you're here?" Keith asked.

Damon explained everything about his family to Keith and Emily and how his mother was in the hospital. They were a little surprised he hadn't gone to see her, but they didn't push it.

"You can tell me to mind my own fucking business, but I think you should at least go see your mom before it's too late, Bullet." Keith stood up and dropped his hand on Damon's shoulder. "You don't want to have any more regrets in your life."

With those words, Keith walked into the house, leaving Damon alone. It was obvious Keith knew Damon regretted leaving Hopedale and giving up on Pam. So many of the family tried to talk him out of it, but it hurt too much to see her and not be with her.

Damon wasn't a religious man, but he was at a point in his life where he needed to try something to find Pam. He hated to think of what she was going through, and it made him sick when some of the possibilities entered his head.

Damon dropped his head into his hands as he flopped into the chair, and he did something, he hadn't done in way too long. He prayed.

"God, I know you don't hear from me often, and I guess I should be ashamed to say it. I need you to keep Trixie safe until I find her. Give her the strength to get through this. God, give me a sign that you're up there. I swear, I won't take another drink as long as I live if you bring her back to us." Damon lifted his head. "I hope you hear me up there."

As usual, Damon hardly slept. He managed to catch a couple of hours before sunrise, but he was up and had a pot of coffee made when Emily appeared in the kitchen with the youngest of the three kids.

"I swear this little doll has an internal clock that wakes her exactly at five in the morning," Emily grumbled.

"Do you want me to hold her while you get her bottle ready?" Damon asked.

"Damon, I carry her bottle on my chest. I only came down because I was afraid her screaming would wake the boys." Emily chuckled.

"Shit, right. I'll wait outside while you do…" Damon pointed in the direction of Emily's breasts. "That."

"I'm not feeding her here in the kitchen. I just wanted to get a cup of tea." Emily laughed.

"Oh." Damon picked up his cup of coffee and moved out of Emily's way.

"I should pump enough off for you to feed her in the morning. Then I won't have to get up. You seem to have the same alarm clock that Scarlett does." Emily poked Damon in the shoulder.

"Yeah, I don't think she wants to see this face in the morning. I'm pretty sure she'd rather see her beautiful mama." Damon smiled.

"Stop hitting on my wife," Keith grumbled as he walked into the kitchen.

"I… Fuck off. Did you piss in the bed?" Damon asked as Keith poured a cup of coffee for himself.

"No, the women in this house don't let me sleep." Keith smirked as Emily slapped his arm and walked out of the kitchen.

"For a little girl, she's got quite a set of lungs." Damon laughed.

"Scarlett is just like her mother," Keith replied.

"I heard that, Keith," Emily shouted from the living room.

"I love you," Keith called out.

Damon laughed when Emily grumbled something he couldn't hear, but he was sure it wasn't anything nice. Keith motioned to the front door, and Damon followed him outside.

"I'm up because I got a call from your friend Drake," Keith said as he closed the front door.

"Why would Drake call you?" Damon's body tensed.

"He said there was an older man looking for you last night." Keith pulled out his phone and tapped the screen. "He managed to get a photo of the guy, but it's a little fuzzy."

Damon took the phone and looked at it. He didn't have to see the clear image to know who it was. It was his father, which meant his family wasn't aware he was back in Newfoundland. Maybe Keith was right.

"That's my father." Damon handed Keith back his phone.

"Do you think he could be involved?" Keith narrowed his eyes.

The hair on Damon's neck stood up on end. His father? Damon wouldn't be surprised to find out his dad was involved in illegal activity, but what would his dad want from him? It didn't make sense.

His father didn't know about Pam. How could he? The communication between him and his family during the time he and Pam were together was a phone call a year to his mother to wish her a happy birthday. There was no way his dad would have even known about who he dated.

"I doubt it. Before he showed up to tell me about Mom, I hadn't seen or spoken to him in years," Damon finally replied.

"I'll still have Sandy look into him." Keith turned and glanced out to the road.

The idea that his father could be involved never entered Damon's mind until Keith mentioned it. Now he was compelled to check it out. If he was honest, he really needed to see his mother before it was too late. The problem was he wasn't sure if he wanted to see the rest of the family.

"I should go see Mom. If the old man is involved, I'll find out." Damon lifted the cup to his lips and held in the rest of what was on his mind.

If Dad did this, he'll be sorry.

Chapter 9

Pam woke up that morning soaked in sweat. The power had gone out during the night, which meant the air conditioning wasn't working. It wasn't a good thing since it was early August and the temperature outside was unusually hot, or at least she thought it was. Since she hadn't been out of the room for more than a week, she wasn't really sure what it was like outside.

Pam discovered the red light she'd seen in the vent was no longer lit up. She quickly tucked her pillows under the blankets, so when one of the goons came in with her breakfast, they'd think she was still asleep. Pam crouched behind the door of the room and waited. She had no idea what time it was or how long it would be before one of the goons would show up.

Pam had lost track of how long she'd been stood behind the door, but she didn't care if she was there all day. It would probably be the only chance she had to catch the goons off guard. Pam was going to escape the place, or she'd die trying.

"God, help me get out of here. Please," Pam whispered.

A few minutes later, loud footsteps echoed from the hallway. Pam shot to her feet and pressed her back flat against the wall as she waited for the door to open. The footfalls stopped, and the click of the lock had her heart thudding in her chest.

Pam held her breath as the door slowly opened and concealed her behind it. As usual, the goon placed the tray on the table. Pam peered around the door to see the back of the goon.

He cleared his throat as he moved toward the bed. She didn't hesitate because it would be her only chance. Pam quietly stepped from behind the door, lifted the iron rod, and brought it down on top of his head with every bit of strength she could muster. The goon grunted, and for a long second, he stood stock-still. Pam backed up as she waited for him to turn around. He didn't. The goon dropped to the floor on his knees and then fell flat on his face.

When he didn't move, Pam closed the bedroom door and slowly moved toward the motionless goon on the floor. She poked him a few times with the rod, but he didn't move. Her heart pounded in her chest as she kicked his foot.

"God, I hope I didn't kill him," Pam whispered as she walked closer and pressed her fingers against the side of his neck.

She blew out a sigh of relief when she felt a steady pulse. It also meant he could probably jump up at any minute and ruin her escape. Pam scanned the room to see if she could find the keys. She wanted to squeal with happiness when she saw them next to the goon's lifeless hand. As she made her way around the goon, she noticed a cell phone in his back pocket.

"I'll need this more than you do, buddy," Pam whispered and slipped it out of the goon's pocket.

Without a looking back, Pam tugged the door slowly to see if anyone was outside waiting to stop her before she could escape. The hallway was deserted and didn't look as clean as her room. Without a second thought, she closed the door behind her and locked it.

The last thing she needed was the goon waking up and coming after her. As she made her way down the hallway, Pam glanced down at the phone. If luck was on her side, she wouldn't need a passcode to use it. She tapped the home button, and the screen lit up.

"Thank you, God." Pam blew out a breath.

Pam found a stairway at the end of the hallway and whimpered when she saw the front door at the bottom of the stairs. The exit would lead to her freedom. Since she was smart enough to take the iron rod with her, she had protection in case someone tried to stop her. Pam wasn't about to let any of the other goons ruin her escape and keep her from going home.

She was halfway down the steps when the phone vibrated in her hand. It startled her for a moment, and Pam almost dropped it over the steps. She stopped at the bottom of the stairs and opened the screen. To her surprise, the message was in English, and it was from someone the goon had listed as Boss.

Boss: You'll have to stay there for a bit. I've got the other guys on something. I'm sure you can handle her for a few hours.

The good news was it meant nobody else was in the house. The bad news was the boss was probably expecting a response. Pam quickly typed in a reply. She prayed the boss guy didn't suspect anything, but Pam typed back the word okay and waited. A few seconds passed before another message popped up.

Boss: The power should be up and running in a couple of hours. According to the power company, a transformer blew.

Pam typed back another okay and hustled to the front door. She wrenched the door open and stepped outside. The area didn't look familiar, and she didn't know if it was miles away from Hopedale or not. All she knew was she needed to get as far away from this house as possible and contact her family.

Twenty minutes later, Pam braced her hands on her knees as she bent over to catch her breath. She'd run as fast as she could down the only road from the house where she was a prisoner. When she straightened, she scanned the area as her breathing returned to normal. The intersection at the end of the dirt road had a small house on her left and a dilapidated old barn on her right. There were no cars in sight, but she was anxious and wondered if anyone was in the house. If they were, they might be involved in her abduction.

She decided to continue down the road a little further. After what seemed like an hour, she spotted a small shack that appeared to be abandoned. The windows were broken, and the front door was gone. It was hot outside, and the sun was beating down on her. Not only that, Pam was exhausted. She had to get off the road before someone showed up looking for her. She scanned the area as she hurried up the gravel walkway.

Pam stepped inside the ragged house. It was bare inside the small structure except for an old wooden stool stood propped against the wall to her right. The floors creaked as she walked into the shack

Pam slowly spun in a circle, taking in her shelter for a moment. The wallpaper was faded and peeling from the walls. It smelled musty, and she could see water damage on the ceiling. She made her way to the stool and prayed it wouldn't break under her weight.

Pam pulled out the phone and brought up the phone app. It took her a moment to remember any phone numbers since all her family's numbers were saved in her phone. Did anyone really remember telephone numbers anymore? The only one she could remember was the one person she knew could find her faster than anyone else.

"Hello?" The voice had Pam's eyes filling with tears.

"Sandy," Pam choked.

"Pam?" Sandy shouted.

"Yes. It's me. I don't know where I am. I escaped and ran. Can you trace this phone and find me?" Pam hiccupped as the emotions she'd been hiding for the last week overwhelmed her.

"You're damn right I can. Hold on, honey." Sandy sounded as if she was about to burst into tears herself.

Pam smiled at the sound of the rapid clicking of computer keys. Sandy would find her, and she'd be back with her family before nightfall. Hopefully before any of the other goons returned and discovered she'd escaped. Pam licked her dry lips as she glanced around the little shack. There was a small kitchen counter on the other side of the ample open space with a sink.

"Got you." Sandy squealed.

"I stole the phone from one of the goons who took me. Should I leave it on?" Pam realized if Sandy could track the phone, so could the goons.

"I got your location. You're about an hour from Hopedale. Here's what I want you to do. Turn off the phone, but if you have to move somewhere else, turn it on and call me back. Got it?" Sandy explained.

"Got it. Please get here quick." Pam ended the call and did exactly what Sandy told her.

Pam turned off the phone and shoved it in her back pocket as she walked toward the sink. When she turned the tap, her heart sank when nothing came out of the tap but air. She was so damn thirsty because she never thought to grab the bottle of water off her tray. The only thing she had on her mind was getting out of the damn room and as far away from the goons as she could get on her own two feet.

She sat back on the stool and leaned her head against the dilapidated wall where she could still see out through the front window, but nobody would be able to see her. The heat in the house was stifling, but a slight breeze blew through the broken windows and gave her a reprieve from the heat for a few seconds. Pam pulled up her shirt and sighed at the cool air on her sweaty skin.

Sandy said she was about an hour from home and given where Hopedale was located, she could be in a dozen different towns. Pam didn't recognize the area, and she wasn't sure she cared. The only thing she cared about was someone getting there before the goons.

Pam turned her head and stared out through the window at the back of the room. The excitement of her escape started to wear off, and she began to tremble. She wasn't out of the woods yet and wouldn't feel safe until she was with her family back home.

Pam didn't know how long it had been since she'd talked to Sandy, but she started to count off the seconds in her head. She'd gotten to almost forty minutes when an engine roared in the distance.

Pam moved slowly toward the front of the house and peeked through the window. A large white truck bounced slowly up the unpaved road toward the house she'd escaped from. It felt as if her heart would jump out of her chest as she pressed her back against the wall.

"Shit," Pam whispered. "They're back."

She debated with herself whether she should turn on the phone and call to see if her recovery crew were close. Pam peeped out through the window again as she held her breath. The truck turned around and came back down the road toward her.

"Fuck it," Pam muttered as she turned the phone back on.

Before she had a chance to make a call, the phone started to vibrate in her hand. Pam whimpered when she saw Sandy's number on the screen because it meant they were close, or at least she hoped they were.

"Hello," Pam whispered but continued to watch the truck.

"Pam, thank God. They're close by, but they can't seem to find you," Sandy said.

"Who's here?" Pam asked.

"Keith and Damon, they're in a white truck Damon rented. They left before the police. Damon said they are in the area, but they can't see you." Sandy sounded panicked.

"I see the truck," Pam shouted and ran out of the shack to meet the vehicle.

"I'll see you soon, honey." Sandy hung up before Pam could say another word.

"Wait, did she say…" Her words stopped when Damon jumped out of the driver's side of the truck and sprinted straight to her.

"Trixie," he croaked as he wrapped his arms around her.

Pam didn't understand why he was there, holding her and making her feel safe. She clung to him as the heavy, uncontrollable sobs started. When he pulled back and gazed down at her, she saw tears in his eyes as well.

"Why…" Pam didn't get a chance to finish her question because he scooped her up in his arms and carried her trembling body to the truck.

"We can talk about who, what, where, when, and why as soon as we get home." Damon pressed his lips to her temple as he placed her in the back seat of the truck.

"Lois, you're a sight for sore eyes." Keith wrapped her in his massive arms.

"So are you." Pam sniffed. "What do I do with this?"

Before she had a chance to say another word, Keith took the phone and immediately turned it off. He dropped it into a plastic bag and tossed it on the front passenger side seat. Damon handed the keys to Keith as he hopped into the truck next to Pam.

"Let's get the fuck out of here." Keith pulled the truck into drive, and the tires spun on the rocks as they drove away.

"Don't you need to see where I was held?" Pam asked as Damon buckled her seatbelt.

"Don't worry about it. Your uncle and cousins have more than enough coming here. We're just here on a retrieval mission." Damon took her hand.

"I'm just a mission?" Pam narrowed her eyes.

"Not by any stretch of the imagination. The only thing I'm here to do is to bring you home and make sure you're safe." Damon ran a finger down the side of her face.

"They'll find an unconscious goon in a locked room on the second floor." Pam swallowed hard mostly because she was thirsty, but a little because of his gentle touch.

Who was she kidding? His touch felt like heaven, even if it was just the light caress of his finger against her skin. It wasn't because it was the first human touch she had since she was taken; it was because it was Damon.

"That's my girl." Damon smiled as he gazed into her eyes.

His hazel eyes always mesmerized her. They were a light brown with flecks of green and gold in them. She used to tease him about the stars in his eyes because of the way they sparkled in certain lighting. They were beautiful, just like him.

"Why are you here?" Pam whispered.

"Because Keith called to tell me you were missing, and I took the next plane back." Damon lifted her hand and pressed his lips against her palm. "I'm not leaving you. Not ever again."

"Damon," Pam sighed.

There was no way they could make a go of it. Not with all the secrets she'd kept from her family. Then she lifted her head and met his eyes again, it took her breath away and she could almost believe they could make it work.

Damon had such a hatred for his family and Pam knew she could never shut out hers the way he did his. Would he be okay with her large family? Was she ready to tell them about her life in Ontario? After her ordeal, maybe she was.

Chapter 10

Pam didn't know who cried more, her mother, her grandmother, or her. She'd been whisked off to the hospital to make sure she was physically healthy. Since Keith didn't give her an option, she didn't even bother to argue. There was no point because Keith and Damon were stubborn.

The first question they asked was if she'd been sexually assaulted. Pam shivered at the thought but assured them she wasn't raped. Pam realized how lucky she was. Her captors may have locked her up and restrained her a couple of times, but she wasn't abused.

"Pam, I was so worried. I don't know what I would have done if…" Her mother sobbed as she hugged Pam for the tenth time.

"I'm sorry, Mom. I'm safe now." Pam looked up at her father.

Pam's dad was a quiet man and the perfect match for her extrovert mother. He always treated both his girls, like they were queens. Pam wasn't spoiled, her father just made sure that on birthdays, Christmas, or any other special occasions, Pam and her mother knew how much they were loved and appreciated.

Her parents owned *Nightingale's Private Care and Therapy*. It was a private business for people who wanted or needed home care. Her parents employed nurses, physical therapists, and home-care workers all over the province. Her mother had given up her career as a nurse after Pam was born and decided a place like *Nightingale's* was desperately needed. With the help of both sets of grandparents and the bank, her dad simply took his knowledge as an accountant and opened their business right after Pam started school.

Her parents worked well together and seemed to enjoy what they did. Pam's dad insisted working with his wife was the best decision of his life, next to marrying her.

"We're so relieved to have you home safe." Her dad cupped the back of her head and kissed her temple.

"I'm not exactly home," Pam grumbled as she shifted in the uncomfortable hospital bed.

The whole time her parents fussed over her, Damon stood in the corner of the room his back to the wall. He always did it wherever he went. She asked him about it once, and he said he hated to have anyone behind him, and it was easier for him to survey the room.

This time, his eyes were entirely focused on her, and he didn't flinch even when the nurse ran over his foot with the food tray. Usually, someone staring would make Pam uncomfortable, but not with Damon. He was obviously concerned, but there was something else she recognized. Fear.

"I hate to interrupt, but I've got to talk to Pam." Nick walked into the room.

Pam expected the police interview and couldn't be more relieved to see her cousin was the one to question her. With four cousins in the Hopedale division of the Newfoundland Police Department, her odds were good one of her family would be there.

"Nicky, can't we do this later," her mother asked.

Pam smirked when Nick rolled his eyes at the childish name her mother used. It seemed her mom and grandmother refused to drop the childish names they used for all her male cousins.

John was Johnny, James was Jimmy, Keith was Keithy, Nick was Nicky, and Aaron was A.J., which wasn't so bad, but Ian had it the worst. His nickname was Inky, and he hated it.

"Aunt Cora, we want to do the interview while it's still fresh in Pam's mind." Nick wrapped his arm around her mom's shoulder.

"Mom, it's okay," Pam assured her mother.

"I'll be staying, Cora," Damon spoke for the first time since her parents arrived.

"Good," her mom said as she walked out of the room.

Nick sat on the chair next to her bed, and after some small talk, he pulled a notebook and pen from his shirt pocket. After a quick glance at Damon, Nick turned his attention back to Pam.

Nick headed the department for special victims with the Newfoundland Police Department. Although Pam wasn't assaulted, abductions were handled by his division. He probably could have sent someone under him, but she was relieved he didn't.

"Okay, cuz. Let's start with the night of Jess' wedding. What happened?" Nick began.

Pam closed her eyes and let the memories of the last week flood her thoughts. The truth was she could tell him in detail everything up until she was grabbed and shoved into the trunk of a car. Then she was secured to a chair, and after the light flashes, she was pushed into that room.

"I was ready to go out of my mind. They didn't speak to me, but they brought food and clothes. There was one guy who I managed to get a couple of words out of." Pam remembered the goon she hit with the iron rod.

"How many guys did you see?" Nick asked.

"There were three different ones and a woman who came in to clean the room once," Pam replied. "The funny thing is, I heard them talk outside the door. They never spoke English but the text sent to the goon was."

"Do you know what language they spoke?" Damon interrupted.

"I know it wasn't French. Maybe Russian or German. It was one of those languages where they sound like they were angry with each other." Pam shrugged.

"Is there a reason you call these guys goons?" Nick smirked.

"They were about the size of Dean or Keith, but they were not in good physical shape. They just looked like goons." Pam didn't know their names either.

"Makes sense." Damon smiled.

"All the texts on the phone were in English." Nick went back into professional mode.

"Could be they didn't want Trix… Pam to know what they were talking about?" Damon walked closer to the bed.

"Maybe, but we still have to figure out what all this has to do with you." Nick raised an eyebrow.

Pam saw Damon shake his head. It was as if he wanted Nick to keep quiet. Pam watched his Adam's apple bob up and down as he met her eyes. He wasn't hiding this from her. She was tired of secrets, and as soon as she got home, she needed to talk to her parents about her past.

"What do you mean, Nick?" Pam turned back to her cousin.

"It's nothing you need to be concerned with," Damon answered for her cousin.

"I wasn't talking to you, Damon," Pam spat. "Nick, what does my abduction have to do with him?"

"We honestly don't know. Damon got a text with a picture of you tied to a chair and a message." Nick told her.

"Which said?" Pam waved her arm in front of her to tell him to continue.

"You know what we want," Nick told her.

Damon cursed and started to pace the small hospital room. It was something else she recognized with him. He tended to pace and hum to himself when he felt anxious. Pam had seen it several times after he'd woken from a nightmare.

"Damon, why would someone take me to get to you?" Pam asked.

There was something they weren't telling her, and from the look on her cousin's face, he wasn't going to be the one to enlighten her. She turned her focus back to Damon. He still had his back to her, but she could see the tension in his shoulders.

"Damon?" Pam swallowed hard when he finally turned around.

"My father is a suspect in your abduction," Damon spoke with a tone so cold it caused her to shiver.

"Your… your father?" Pam whispered the words.

"He's been trying to get me to come back to Newfoundland for a few months. He even went as far as coming to Toronto." Damon wouldn't meet her eyes.

"What aren't you telling me?" Pam slapped her hands down on the bed.

"My mother needs a liver transplant. She destroyed hers with all the drugs and drinking she's done over the years." Damon pressed his lips together.

"Why would he abduct me to get you to return? I mean, this makes no sense. You can't live without your liver so he can't expect you to give her yours." Pam was completely confused.

"If a person is a match, they can donate a part of their liver to the recipient." A strange voice echoed in the room.

Pam turned to the direction of the unfamiliar voice. She didn't recognize him, but from Damon's reaction, he definitely knew the man in the doorway of her hospital room.

"What the hell are you doing here?" Damon growled at the man who entered the room.

"I came to tell you he didn't do what you suspect him of." The man was cool and calm with his hands in his front pants' pockets.

"I see the police have talked to him. Did he send you to tell me that?" Damon snapped.

"No. I came to tell you she's fading fast. If you want to see her before it's too late, I suggest you make it soon." The man started to leave.

"Wait." Pam sat up in the bed.

The man turned slowly, and his eyes went to Pam. She looked back at Damon then to the other man. He was impeccably dressed and appeared to be in his thirties. He was quite handsome, or at least he would be if he smiled. It was apparent he had money by the clothes he wore, but there was something familiar about him.

"Who are you?" Pam asked when Damon didn't speak.

"My name is Malcolm. Malcolm Blackwood." He held out his hand to Pam.

"Blackwood?" Pam glanced back to Damon as she shook Malcolm's hand.

"Yes, Damon is my big, brave brother. A Canadian hero who fights for his country but won't try to help his dying mother." Malcolm jeered.

"I wasn't a match," Damon snapped.

"So you say." Malcolm scoffed.

"What the hell is your problem? Your brother risked his life overseas and almost lost it. He's suffered more than you will ever know. If he says he's not a match, then he's not, but I'm sure if you need it, he'll be tested again so he can shove it in your face." Pam's anger rose so fast it scared her a little.

How could a brother be so unpleasant to his own sibling after the man almost died? Pam found it hard to believe Damon's father would stoop so low as to kidnap her to get to him but then again, Damon told her his father was a cold-hearted man.

Pam flicked her gaze to Damon. His face was red, and although he stood steady as a rock, he was ready to explode. He'd fisted his hands by his sides, and his eye twitched the way it always did when he was angry. She'd seen it several times when a few of the patrons at the club got nasty or too rough with the girls.

"Pam? Is it?" Malcolm looked at her.

"Yes," she returned.

"I don't know what fairy tale my brother has fed you, but Damon isn't who you think he is. He may be a military hero, but he deserted his family when he was needed most." With his statement, Malcolm turned and sauntered out of the room.

"What a fucking ass." Nick stood up.

"He's actually the nice one of the family." Damon scoffed.

"Why don't they believe you were tested?" Pam asked.

"I have no idea; the papers were sent to a Doctor Dylan Burton weeks ago." Damon shrugged.

Before Pam could say anything else, a familiar face entered her room with a huge smile. Dr. Adam Cramer was a friend of her family and always seemed to be at the hospital when one of them had an emergency. He was a jovial guy, and Pam had never seen the handsome doctor without his friendly smile.

"I swear I should just open a private practice for the O'Connor family and their friends." Adam grinned as he pulled his stethoscope from around his neck.

"Do you ever go home?" Nick laughed.

"This place is home." Adam winked and proceeded to check Pam's heart and lungs.

"Can I go home?" Pam asked when he shoved his stethoscope into the pocket of his lab coat.

"All your blood work came back clear. You're a little dehydrated, so you need to drink plenty of fluids for the next few days and get some rest," he told her.

"I will, and thanks," Pam replied.

"I'm glad you're safe. My family prayed for your safe return." Adam placed his hand on her shoulder.

"Thanks, Adam." Pam smiled up at the handsome doctor.

"Anytime. I love to see you guys, but if you want to see me, you could just drop by and say hi. Bring me a cup of coffee or just invite me to supper. There's no need for all this." Adam chuckled as he headed out of the room.

"So, I can go home?" Pam was out of the bed before she finished her sentence.

"Whenever you're ready." Adam pulled the door open. "Stay safe, you guys."

Pam didn't need to hear another word as she grabbed the bag her mom brought and practically ran to the bathroom to change. She had to figure out what her abduction had to do with Damon. Were his family really involved? The first thing she was going to do was convince Damon to go see his mother, and she was going with him.

Chapter 11

Damon stared at Pam as if she'd lost her mind. As cute as she looked standing in the middle of the hospital lobby with her hands on her hips, he wasn't about to give in to what she just said. There was no way she was serious, but with the way her eyes were narrowed, he had a feeling she was.

"Are you out of your fucking mind?" Damon asked.

"No," Pam returned.

"I know my hearing isn't the best even with this hearing aid, but let me make sure I heard you right. You want me to go upstairs to see my mother and take you with me?" Damon repeated the words she'd said as they stepped off the elevator.

He suddenly wished he was in one of the larger provinces. At least then the chances of Pam and his family being in the same hospital would be cut down considerably. The east coast of the province only had two hospitals and the majority of people were brought to the bigger one.

"Yes," Pam replied.

"You did hear us when we told you my father could be involved in your abduction, right?" Damon asked.

"Yes, and it's why I want to confront him or at least see his reaction when he sees me." Pam crossed her arms over her chest.

"That's not happening, Trixie." Damon wrapped his arm around her shoulders and tried to guide her toward the exit.

He should have known it wouldn't be easy. Pam was stubborn as a mule. She ducked under his arm and stood defiantly in the middle of the lobby.

Damon glanced at Nick for some form of support, but all her cousin did was shrug. The man wasn't going to be any help. The last thing Damon wanted was to put Pam within arm's reach of his father, especially if he was responsible for kidnapping her.

"You're just going to stand there?" Damon snapped at Nick.

"I've been around the O'Connor women all my life. I know better than to argue when they look like that. Nan taught them the devil's glare when they were still in diapers, I'm sure." Nick chuckled.

"This is not a good idea," Damon grumbled.

"Either you come with me, or I'll go find your father alone." Pam headed back to the elevator.

"You're no fucking help." Damon shoved Nick aside and followed Pam.

"I'm going with you, aren't I?" Nick smirked as they stepped on the elevator.

The ride on the elevator went way too fast, and for the first time in his life, he wished it had gotten stuck. As luck should have it, the doors opened, and the three of them stepped off. Damon made his way down the corridor to the Palliative Care Unit with Pam by his side and Nick behind them. Pam had gotten the information at some point during her short couple of hours in the hospital without Damon knowing.

The rhythmic beeps of machines, the smell of antiseptic, and the din of people talking surrounded them as they got closer to the unit. Damon didn't want to be anxious, but the closer he got, the more his heart thudded in his chest. Pam walked next to him as they got closer to where his mother was dying.

"I'm here to see my mother," Damon managed to say to the nurse at the entrance of the room.

"Who's your mother?" The nurse glanced up at him.

"Tabitha Blackwood." Damon's mouth felt like a desert.

The nurse tilted her head and stared at him for a moment. It was almost as if she didn't believe him. Before she could say a word, Damon heard a voice behind them.

"Finally decided to show your face." His father stepped around Pam as if she wasn't there and nodded at the nurse.

"I wanted to make my peace with her," Damon replied.

"You have balls; I'll give you that. Won't get tested to see if you can save her, but you'll come to say goodbye." His father snapped through gritted teeth.

"I was tested. Doctor Burton sent me an email which said I wasn't a match." Damon managed to say, but it was hard when he was so close to his father.

"So, you're calling Doctor Burton a liar. Typical," his father spat.

"If Damon says he was tested, then he was. You have no right to say otherwise." Pam stepped in front of Damon.

His father didn't even acknowledge Pam's presence as she glared at him. He stalked away from the room without another word. Damon met Pam's eyes when she turned.

"I think you need to find out where those test results went," Nick whispered.

"I will, but I need to see my mother first." Damon peered into the room, but it was as if his feet were glued to the floor.

The thought that his mother was dying, and it might be the last time he'd ever see her alive, hit him like a ton of bricks. The last time he'd seen her, she was on the back porch of their estate with a glass of wine chasing a couple of pills.

Pam slipped her hand into his, and he clung to it as if it was his very own lifeline. The nurse motioned for them to follow her, and Pam gave his hand a gentle squeeze. It gave him the strength he needed to walk through the curtain to his mother's bedside.

Damon couldn't hold back the gasp of surprise at his first glimpse of his mom. The tiny woman in the hospital bed didn't look anything like the woman who raised him. An array of tubes and wires ran from his mother to machines all around her bed.

"Damon?" Pam whispered.

"I… I didn't realize she was this sick. I mean, they said she was dying but... she looks like a skeleton." Damon choked out the words as he tried to keep his composure.

"She doesn't hear very well, but if you move closer, she should hear you," the nurse told him as she pulled the curtain around them.

Damon clung to Pam's hand as he stepped next to the bed and stared down at the frail woman. Her skin appeared to have a yellow hue, and her lips were dry, cracked, and thin. As he swallowed the lump in his throat, his mom's eyes fluttered open.

"Da… Damon? Is it really you? Am I dreaming?" She lifted her hand and reached for him.

"Yes, Mother, it's me. You're not dreaming." Damon crouched lower so she could reach him.

"I… I can't believe you're here. I guess I must not have much time left." Her voice was raspy, and she had to swallow several times to finish her sentence.

Damon didn't know what to say. He only talked to her once a year since he returned from his deployment. He was angry and hurt because none of his family checked on him when he returned. It shattered his heart to have nobody care if he lived or died. Damon cut all ties with them after that.

"I must look a mess." His mother smoothed her hands over her dry, brittle, graying hair.

When he was growing up, his mother's hair, makeup, and clothing were always impeccable. Even when she was drunk or high, she still managed to look classy. As a little boy, Damon would watch her do her makeup for hours while she told him how a lady had to make sure she was perfect before she showed herself. Damon always thought she was perfect no matter how she looked, at least until he grew up.

"You look lovely." Pam moved to the other side of the bed.

A sweet smile appeared on his mother's face as she followed Pam with her eyes. When she looked back to Damon, a tear slipped from the corner of her eye.

"I'm so glad I had a chance to meet her." His mother sniffed.

"Meet who, Mom?" Damon was curious as to who his mother thought Pam was to him.

"Your beautiful wife." She reached for Pam and took her hand.

"Mom, Tri… Pam isn't my wife. Who told you she was?" Damon eased down on the side of her bed as she reached for his hand.

For a moment, she stared at Damon as if she didn't understand his words. She appeared confused as she worked out her thoughts. It was possible she thought he was Malcolm or someone else.

"Your brother said you might not be able to come because your wife was sick." His mother smiled up at Pam.

"Malcolm was mistaken. She and I are…" Damon glanced at Pam.

"You love her." His mother wasn't asking; she was making an observation.

"It's complicated, Mom." He forced a smile.

"Damon, you can't let your upbringing prevent you from finding happiness. Not all marriages end up like your father's and mine." His mother cupped his cheek.

"Mom, I know, and I'm happy," Damon lied.

"No, you're not. I see the sadness in your eyes, and I'm sorry. I wasn't a good mother to you." She coughed, and Pam reached for the cup of water with the straw.

After his mom took a couple of small sips, she smiled at Pam and turned back to Damon. It was heart-wrenching to see her like this. When he was a kid, she was an amazing mom, but the drinking and pills started, and she morphed into a different person.

"I've done this to myself." She pressed her lips together as another tear slipped from the corner of her eye.

"That was his fault," Damon growled as he gripped his mother's hand.

"No, Damon. I didn't have to turn to those things because I wasn't happy. It was my choice," she whispered.

"Mom, he treated you like shit and cheated on you all the time. Who could blame you?" Damon wasn't holding back.

"Damon, there's more to your father than just what you remember. He wasn't always that way, Warrick… let's just say, your dad had a lot of responsibility." She looked beyond Damon's shoulder as if she remembered something.

"It's not important, Mom." Damon cleared his throat and blinked back the tears forming in his eyes.

"Damon, it is important. Your father isn't the monster you believe he is. He was in pain too." His mother looked into his eyes.

"Mom, why do you defend him?" Damon whispered as he wiped a tear from her face.

"He's my husband." Her eyes fluttered closed.

Damon watched as she slipped off to sleep. He got lost in a memory of her reading to him and Malcolm when they were little.

They would sit in the living room in the large armchair and read. During the summer, they would sit on the back deck in the hammock. It was some of his best childhood memories.

Damon was brought out of his thoughts when a hand touched his shoulder. He turned around and looked into Pam's beautiful blue eyes filled with tears.

"You should stay. I'll head home with Nick," Pam whispered.

"No, you're stuck with me until we find out who abducted you." Damon stood up.

"Damon," Pam sighed.

"Trixie, someone took you because of me. Why? I've got no idea, but they aren't getting close to you again." He turned back to his mother.

She'd fallen back to sleep. Damon wasn't sure if he'd ever see her alive again, but he had to protect at least one woman in his life. He leaned down and kissed his mother's forehead.

"I do love you, Mom," he whispered into his mother's ear.

It felt odd to say the words to his mother since he hadn't contacted her no more than once a year since he'd left Newfoundland. He just couldn't watch her kill herself anymore and had to distance himself from her. Now he regretted it.

As Damon turned around, he froze at the sight of the woman behind Pam. Coming face to face with the woman who started the whole feud between his family made him want to roar out in anger. He was forced to pull Pam toward him because he was not comfortable with Gail so close to Pam.

"It's true. You are back." She stepped inside the drawn curtain and stood at the foot of the bed.

"Yes, I'm back," Damon replied with as little emotion as possible.

"I'm glad you got to see her before…" She pulled a tissue from her pocket and dabbed the corner of her eyes.

Damon had to muster every ounce of strength he could to control the anger that bubbled up inside at the sight of her fake tears. It wasn't possible for the heartless bitch to feel a bit of sadness for his mother.

"Your brother and the kids are so upset about all this." She sniffed.

Gail Small-Blackwood was his brother's wife. She was also the woman his father wanted Damon to marry in order to *close the deal* as his father put it. There was always an ulterior motive when it came to Alastair Blackwood, especially when his father needed to cover his ass.

"How are my… what are they to me?" Damon asked coldly.

"Damon, your brother's kids would be nieces and nephews." Pam seemed to sense the tension.

"Right. Sorry. How are my niece and nephew?" Damon locked eyes with Gail.

"They are trying to deal with the reality of losing Tabitha. We all are." Gail walked to the side of the bed and covered his mother's hand with hers.

"I'm sure it's hard." Damon tried to cover the detest for his sister-in-law.

"Will you be staying at the estate?" Gail asked.

Damon laughed. The woman had to be kidding or out of her mind. She knew damn well Damon would never set foot in his family home again. If she didn't, then she was insane. He was born and raised in that St. John's estate, but it had ceased to be his home the day he left for the Army.

"I don't think we'll be having another happy family dinner any time soon," Malcolm said as he walked through the curtain.

"Probably not. Did we ever have any?" Damon retorted and grabbed Pam's hand.

"You've got to work on your anger, Damon. It will eat you alive. Maybe the anger comes from a guilty conscious," Malcolm sneered as Damon tugged Pam out of ICU.

Before Pam could say another word, she was wrapped up in a pair of arms. Elaine might be her business partner, but she was one of her best friends. Elaine was Emily's younger sister. They were from a small town outside of St. John's called SummerBrook.

Most of the families who lived there were wealthy, and Elaine's family were no different. They'd become part of the O'Connor circle since Emily married Keith, and it was how Pam met Elaine.

"I'm so glad you're okay." Elaine hugged her tightly.

"Me too." Pam clung to her friend.

"I've packed you enough clothes for a week. Keith said we'd start with that. All your toiletries and essentials are in there as well." Elaine dragged the huge suitcase closer.

As usual, Elaine was impeccably dressed in a black pencil skirt and pale-yellow silk blouse. They were both paired with a pair of crocodile embossed, black, Jimmy Choo stilettos. Then there was her makeup which appeared as if it was professionally done, but Pam knew Elaine did it herself. Her long hair was pulled up into a stylish ponytail and hung down to her shoulders.

"Knowing you, I'm sure you have everything I need." Pam chuckled as she gave her friend another hug.

"I swear, I'm going to end up gray before my time with this family." Elaine groaned as she eased down into the chair on the other side of the table.

Damon didn't respond as he stomped down the corridor to the elevator. He didn't say a word because he wasn't sure he could control his rage until he was able to get away from his family.

"What happened?" Nick said as they stepped on the elevator.

"Hell, if I know." Pam shrugged.

Pam didn't need to know. His family were a bunch of screwed-up, over-privileged snobs and used their money to get people to do what they wanted. It was the reason he needed to get as far away from them as possible all those years ago. He wished he could've convinced his mother to leave with him, but he didn't try. She would never leave his father no matter what a bastard he was.

Damon closed his eyes and took several deep breaths. His therapist taught him a few techniques to control his rage and anxiety, and they worked most of the time. Deep breathing was one, and the other was to close his eyes and imagine a relaxing place. He'd always go back to the only time he felt completely calm. When he and Pam were in each other's arms.

Chapter 12

The drive back to Hopedale was uncomfortable, and the only sound was the soft country music playing on the radio. Damon sat in the front passenger seat, staring through the window. Pam sat in the back, wondering what the hell happened back at the hospital.

There was so much tension when his sister-in-law and brother entered the room that Pam was sure everyone on the unit could feel it. Several nurses passed by and stopped to look through the curtain.

It was hard for her to understand how any family could dislike each other so much. Maybe it was because hers were so close and were always in each other's pockets. As annoying as it could be, it was what she missed most when she lived in Toronto. She had great friends in Ontario, and she'd never forget her time with Damon. Still, none of it mattered if she couldn't share it with the people she loved the most.

"Pam, you'll be staying at *The Compound* until we figure this out," Nick said as he turned off the highway.

The Compound was what everyone called Keith's property. Keith and Emily owned more than six acres of land in Hopedale where he not only had his own home, but he also ran both his businesses from the property. His security company as well as the construction company.

The property also contained several smaller houses Keith used for employees or clients who needed a safe place to stay. The other building on the property included a full gym and offices.

Pam knew better than to argue about going back to her apartment because the truth was, she was afraid to be alone. She wasn't even sure if she still had a business. She'd been gone over a week, and when she was taken, Elaine was still away.

"I'm staying there as well," Damon spoke for the first time since they'd left the hospital.

Pam wanted to smack herself because of the way her body hummed at the thought of Damon being in the same house. No matter what she did, he still affected her the same way. She never stopped loving him, and she didn't know if she ever would.

"I need clothes," Pam whispered.

"Elaine is bringing over some things from your apartment. She's been worried sick about you," Nick told her.

Pam lifted her eyes to meet Nick's in the rearview mirror. He lightly motioned to Damon with his head. She didn't know what her cousin wanted to tell her, and she shrugged her shoulders.

"He's trying to tell you I was nearly out of my mind with worry too," Damon interjected without looking at Nick.

Nick pulled up to the security gate leading to Keith's property, making the uncomfortable moment easy to escape. Pam quickly jumped out of Nick's car and made her way up the steps to Keith's house. As she got to the top of the steps, a large orange cat jumped up on the rail and sauntered across to where Pam stood.

Keith had found the cat tangled in the burlap of one of the bushes several years earlier. He was just a kitten at the time, but Keith named the kitty Burlap, and now it was part of the family. He was a friendly cat and tended to greet any guests as soon as they arrived

"Hey, Burlap. Are you out trolling again?" Pam scratched the cat behind the ear.

The cat purred and jumped down to rub his body against Pam's leg. She laughed as he moved on to Nick when her cousin made his way up the steps.

"It seems he needs everyone to give him a scratch." Pam chuckled.

She gave the door a soft knock and walked into the house. Pam was immediately halted when a little boy flew into her and wrapped his arms around her legs.

"Auntie Pam, you're back," Patrick shouted as he hugged her legs.

Keith and Emily's middle child had become attached to Pam, and whenever she would visit, the little boy would be stuck to her like glue. He was three and always wanted Pam to play cars with him and watch the Disney movie, *Lilo and Stitch*. He loved the silly movie and knew every song by heart.

"Hi, buddy." Pam picked up the little boy so she could make her way into the house.

"He's been asking for you ever since the wedding." Emily smiled from where she stood bouncing little Scarlett in her arms.

"Probably because I promised to take him swimming the day after the wedding," Pam said as the little boy clung to her.

"Are you really okay?" Patrick murmured as he rested his little head on Pam's shoulder.

"I'm great, buddy." Pam was surprised he seemed aware she was missing.

"Daddy said you were sick and couldn't come to see me." Patrick lifted his head and held Pam's face between his little hands.

"I'm much better now." She smiled.

Pam knew she wouldn't get far from Patrick until he was satisfied she was okay. She sat on one of the kitchen chairs and placed the little boy on her lap while she talked with Emily.

"Is she having a fussy day?" Pam nodded toward the baby in Emily's arms.

"She's got a little gas and not really liking it." Emily continued to pat the baby's back while she lightly bounced up and down.

"Poor little thing." Pam looked up as Damon entered the house and walked right to the living room.

"He hasn't been sleeping at all," Emily whispered after Damon left the room.

"He never did sleep well," Pam said absentmindedly.

"Pam, Damon was out of his mind with worry. When Keith called him to tell him you were missing, he jumped on the first plane to St. John's." Emily sat next to Pam at the table.

"Why did Keith call him?" Pam sighed.

"You don't like Uncle Damon?" Patrick looked completely devastated.

"Oh, honey, of course, I do." Pam didn't like the look on the little boy's face.

"Good, 'cause he makes really good car sounds." Patrick nodded.

"Who wouldn't like a man who makes really good car sounds?" Pam tickled Patrick under the chin.

The little boy giggled and jumped down from Pam's lap. He gave Emily a hug and kissed little Scarlett on the cheek before running off to find his brother.

"He's going to be so upset when Noah starts school in September." Emily watched Patrick scamper up the stairs, screaming out to his older brother.

"I can't believe he and Brendan are already starting school." Pam shook her head.

Brendan was John and Stephanie's middle child and was the same age as Noah. When Pam would go to the monthly family suppers where their entire family got together, she was in awe at how quickly the kids were growing. In fact, Ian and Sandy's two older girls were starting high school. James and his wife Marina's two older boys were in junior high.

A twinge of jealousy hit Pam in the heart because she longed to have children, but it didn't look like it would happen. She was only a few years away from turning forty, and her biological clock was ticking loud enough for the world to hear.

"Me either. They're growing up way too fast." Emily sighed as she smiled down at baby Scarlett.

"I hope I'm not intruding," Damon said from the doorway of the kitchen.

Her heart started to pound in her chest just at the sight of him. He'd changed his clothes and was wearing a white t-shirt which accentuated his tanned skin. The sleeves strained around his muscled biceps and across his chest.

Damon still looked as sexy as he did the first time she met him. His dark eyes immediately locked with hers, and she found it hard to breathe. His hair was cut close just the way she liked it. It looked like he hadn't shaved in a couple of days, and it only made him look more irresistible.

"Not at all, Damon. You can keep Pam company while I put this little angel down for a nap." Emily gave Pam a little wink and quickly scurried out of the kitchen.

"She's not very subtle, is she?" Damon chuckled as he poured himself a cup of coffee.

"Not really." Pam rubbed her hands up and down on her thighs.

Without asking, he brought a second cup to the table and placed it in front of Pam. Then he sat in the chair Emily had vacated. Pam cupped her hands around the mug and stared down at the dark liquid.

"I put a little sugar in it," Damon said softly.

"You remembered." She lifted her eyes to meet his.

"I remember everything about you, Trixie." Damon's eyes dropped to her lips.

"Damon." Pam's voice was barely audible as he leaned closer to her.

"I could never forget how I feel about you." His eyes locked with hers as he pressed his forehead against hers.

"I'm sorry," Pam heard herself say before she could stop the words.

"For what?" Damon pulled back a little to look into her eyes.

"I shouldn't have left the way I did, and I should have told you my real name when we were dating." Pam shrugged.

"Yes, you should, but we can't change the past. I learned something from the kids in this house, *Hakuna Matata*." Damon smiled.

Pam burst out laughing at the words. She knew they were from the Disney movie, *The Lion King*. Emily's boys loved the film, and Pam had watched it with them more times than she could count.

"You aren't going to break out in song, are you?" Pam snorted.

When he began to sing, Pam couldn't help herself and started to sing along with him, although, he was more in tune than she was. Damon was a great singer and used to sing to her all the time when they were together. He even played the guitar.

"Dear Lord, that fucking song is contagious," Keith grumbled as he entered the house with Elaine behind him.

"No worries." Damon laughed.

Keith and Emily were deliriously happy, but it wasn't easy for them in the beginning. Keith had been hired by Emily's father to protect her after he'd received a threat against her. Emily hadn't liked the idea in the beginning, but it turned out great because she and Keith fell in love, even if Keith had almost died when he was shot. Everything worked out in the end.

"What's life without a bit of excitement?" Keith winked at Pam.

"I could do without the crazy," Emily said as she entered the kitchen.

"You love my crazy." Keith wiggled his eyebrows up and down as he tugged his wife into his arms.

"Your kind of crazy is the best, especially when…" Emily was interrupted by the groan from her sister.

"God, please stop. You two have three kids. How the hell can you still be like that?" Elaine shook her head.

"When it's good, you can't help it." Keith smirked.

Elaine gagged, but she still had a slight smile that told Pam her friend wasn't completely grossed out by Keith. Pam's eyes moved to where Damon sat next to her. He watched Keith and Emily with a grin. It brought back the memory of how she and Damon would tease each other at the club.

Pam would whisper dirty things to him when she would get close to him, and by the time they got back to his apartment, Damon was hard and ready to rock her world.

Was it possible they could have that again? She wasn't sure he'd be able to forgive her for running away from him. Could she tell her family what she really did all those years in Toronto? To some people it wouldn't be a big deal but to some it would be considered a step up from prostitution. Pam was terrified of which category her family would fall into.

Chapter 13

Damon picked up his phone from the night table next to the bed. It was a little after four in the morning, and he wondered why the hell Drake was calling him. The asshole had to know there was an hour and a half time difference between Newfoundland and Ontario.

"Hello," Damon answered groggily.

"Did I wake you?" Drake asked.

"It's four in the morning, genius. What do you think?" Damon sat up and swung his feet around to the floor.

"Sorry, but I wanted to see how things were going. Did you find Trixie?" Drake asked.

"Yeah, she escaped and managed to contact her family." Damon yawned.

"That's a relief. Who took her in the first place?" Drake had always cared about Pam and all the people who worked for him.

"Cops don't know, but they're working on it," Damon told him.

"Working on it, yeah. Fucking cops don't give a fuck about nobody." Drake scoffed.

"These cops do. Trixie's four cousins are police officers, and her uncle is the former chief. Trust me, they won't drop the ball on this one." Damon knew the O'Connors wouldn't rest until they got to the bottom of what happened.

"Wow, didn't know she had such a big family," Drake replied.

"You've got no idea, but they are good people." Damon said with confidence.

"Look, there's another reason I called," Drake said.

"I thought there might be." Damon chuckled.

"Are you coming back?" he asked.

For a moment, Damon didn't speak because the truth was, he didn't know. He had a feeling Pam wasn't leaving Newfoundland ever again, so if he wanted a future with her, he would have to give up his life in Toronto. It wouldn't be difficult because it wasn't as if he'd actually been living well over the last few years.

His life consisted of working at a gentleman's club as a bouncer and drinking until he could fall asleep. Hopefully, get enough sleep so he could function the next day. What kind of life was that?

"Damon, you still there?" Drake interrupted Damon's thoughts.

"Yeah, I was thinking," Damon admitted.

"Maybe you should see where things go," Drake said.

"Yeah, but I think no matter what happens, I won't be returning. I'm sorry to leave you short-staffed." Damon didn't want to hurt his friend, but his place was in Newfoundland.

"Don't worry about me, buddy. You take care of you and Trixie. Just make sure I get an invite to the wedding." Drake chuckled.

"Yeah, sure. By the way, her name isn't Trixie. It was the name she used for the club. Her name is Pam…" Damon was interrupted when Drake finished the name.

"Nightingale. I know," Drake finished.

"I guess you would since you were her boss." Damon returned.

"Look, you were so fucked up after she left, I couldn't tell you, and to be honest, as her employer I couldn't give out any of her information." Drake was right.

"I know, and it's okay." And it was.

After chatting about the club and how things were going with Drake, Damon ended the call and stood up. He scuffed to the window and looked outside. The sun wasn't even up, but he wouldn't be able to get back to sleep.

After he pulled on a pair of track pants and a t-shirt, he headed down to the kitchen as quietly as he could. Thankfully, Damon didn't have to pass any of the kids' bedrooms on his way down the hall to the stairs, but he did have to walk by the room where Pam slept.

He stopped momentarily in front of the door and had to use every ounce of strength not to open the door to check on her. She'd gone to bed just before he did and with good reason. Damon was sure Pam probably hadn't had a good night's sleep since she was taken.

Damon continued down the stairs and shuffled his way to the kitchen. It was always quiet early in the morning. Probably because the kids were asleep, but Damon didn't really mind the noise the little ones made. It was much better than the deafening quiet he lived with when he was in his apartment in Ontario.

"I see you still don't sleep in." Her voice was just above a whisper.

Pam stood in the kitchen doorway in a pair of flannel pajama pants and a tank top. Her choice in sleepwear had not changed over the years, although he preferred her to sleep naked when she was next to him.

"I probably would have, only Drake called to see how things were going." Damon leaned against the counter and watched her walk to the coffee pot.

While she prepared the coffeemaker, he pulled two cups from the cupboard and grabbed the sugar from the other side of the counter. They waited for the coffee to drip into the pot in comfortable silence for a few minutes.

"Damon, what did those people want from you?" Pam didn't look at him.

"I don't know, Trixie." Damon cringed at the name.

It was hard for him to get used to calling her anything else. He wasn't sure if he'd ever get used to calling her Pam. He was her Trixie, and it didn't matter what anyone else called her.

"I was thinking because, you know, sleep isn't my friend tonight, but could it be something to do with one of your missions when you were in the Army?" Pam turned to look at him.

Damon stared out the window for several minutes. The thought had never entered his mind because all his missions were overseas, and his identity was always hidden. It was his life as a sniper with the Joint Task Force Two, or JTF2, as they were known.

All his missions were to do with bringing down terrorists or rescuing victims who were kidnapped by extremists. Damon's job was to ensure anyone who interfered with the mission was eliminated and he did it more times than he cared to remember.

"I can't see how. Our missions were always confidential, and our identities were always kept secret," Damon explained.

"Oh. It was just a thought." Pam turned back and picked up the coffee pot.

"I guess that's probably the most I've ever told you about my job in the military." He would never tell her anything about his missions back then.

"I understood you couldn't talk about it." Pam filled the two cups and placed the pot back on the hot plate.

"Pam," Damon choked out her name.

She lifted her head, and her eyes met his. It was as if the world around them disappeared, and the only thing he could see was her. It was how it always was when they were together. He took a step toward her, and when she didn't move, he lifted his hand and cupped her cheek.

"How is it you can crawl out of bed and look this beautiful?" Damon whispered as he caressed her jaw with his thumb.

"Damon," Pam whispered as her tongue darted out to moisten her plump lips.

He lowered his head and brushed his mouth across hers. She didn't move and her eyes locked with his. Damon waited for her to push him away, but she only rested her hands on his hips. Damon cupped her face between both his hands and pressed his lips lightly against hers.

129

Their kiss was timid at first. Almost as if they were both unsure if they should continue, but when Pam moved closer and pushed her body against his, Damon slipped his tongue between her lips and kissed her the way he'd wanted to for so long.

Pam snaked her arms around him and smoothed her hands up the length of his back. She wanted it as much as he did, and he threaded his fingers into her soft hair. Damon tilted her head so he could get better access to her mouth and wrapped his other arm around her. He pulled her against him and continued to kiss her as if he needed her to live.

Pam moaned into his mouth, and it was all he needed to hear. Damon lifted her onto the counter and pressed his contained cock against her warm center. He pulled his mouth from hers and looked down to her breasts. He remembered vividly how her nipples would harden into sharp peaks when she wanted him. The sight of them straining against the thin cotton of her tank top made his cock throb, and he groaned with need.

When he raised his eyes, they stopped at her lips. She was biting her lower lip, and he could feel the moisture seeping from the tip of his dick. It always drove him crazy when she did it, mainly because he knew what she had in mind.

"Fuck, I've missed those lips." Damon groaned as he devoured her mouth.

He pulled her hips closer and ground his throbbing dick between her legs as he swirled his tongue around hers. She grabbed his biceps, and he grunted when she dug her nails in and sucked his tongue into her mouth.

He slid his hands around her waist and slowly slipped them under the bottom of her shirt. Her skin was still so soft against his calloused hands, and as he glided them up her sides, he felt the goosebumps rise on her body. He had almost made it to her breast with one hand when she pulled away.

"We can't do this." Pam panted.

Damon's heart sank, and it took all his strength to release her and back away. He turned away and adjusted his cock while he tried to clear his head. He hadn't meant for it to get so intense, but when it came to Pam, he'd lose all control whenever he put his hands on her. He loved her so much that he could never get enough of her, and it had been so long since he'd touched her.

"You're right. We were over a long time ago," Damon whispered as he turned around to face her.

He was confused by the smirk on her face. Pam tilted her head to the side and hopped off the counter. She took two steps and rested her hands on his hips. She raised her eyes to meet his and nibbled her lip.

"I meant we can't do this in Keith and Emily's kitchen." Pam stood up on her toes.

"But…" Damon stared into her eyes.

"We were never over, Damon. I ran away because I was afraid if you knew the truth, I'd lose you. You loved the fact I didn't have an intrusive family. I was terrified that if you found out just how nosey they were, you wouldn't want me." Pam dropped her head.

Damon put his finger under her chin and pulled up until she was forced to meet his eyes. The uncertainty in hers broke his heart. The last thing he wanted was for her to be unsure of how much he loved her.

"I know the truth now, and I'm not going anywhere. You're stuck with me, that's if you still want me." Damon pressed his head against hers.

"For what it's worth, I'm sorry I hurt you, and yes, I still want you," Pam whispered.

"We all make mistakes, Trixie. We learn from them and start over. Is it what you want? To start over?" Damon asked her.

"I know after seeing you, I still feel the same way, and after kissing you, I can't deny the chemistry we have. My feelings for you never changed, and nobody could ever make me feel the way you do." Pam brushed her lips against his.

"Nothing changed for me either, I still lo…" Damon's words were stopped when she pressed her finger against his lips.

"Don't say those words, yet. We've got a lot to work through first, but the difference is, now I want to be honest with you and my family." Pam ran a finger down the middle of his chest.

"I'll be with you when you tell them." Damon kissed her nose.

"Thank you, but right now, the only thing I want, is for you to come upstairs with me," Pam murmured.

Damon didn't need to be asked twice. He took her hand and practically dragged her down the hall and upstairs to her bedroom. It was closer than his, and he needed her more than he needed to breathe.

Chapter 14

Pam's heart pounded in her chest as Damon tugged her up the stairs toward the bedroom where she'd been sleeping. If she hadn't realized they were in the kitchen earlier, she would have let him take her on the kitchen counter.

He had his hand on the knob of the door when someone stepped out of one of the bedrooms. Pam and Damon spun around as Emily stepped out of her bedroom, holding a whimpering Scarlett on her shoulder.

"Umm…I… we…" Pam stammered.

"I'm sure it's none of my business, carry on." Emily grinned as she made her way down the stairs.

Damon turned the knob and tugged Pam into the room. He closed the door and pulled her against him. He was hard in all the right places, and she could feel an exceptional part of his anatomy rock hard and pressed against her stomach.

"I want you, Damon." She moaned as she wrestled his t-shirt up and off his body.

"Sweetheart, you got me." He groaned when she dragged her nails down over his muscled chest.

Damon hauled her tank off over her head while Pam slithered out of her pajama pants. Before she could slip out of her panties, Damon tugged her tight against his body. The heat from his bare chest and the light tickle of his chest hair had her body trembling with need.

He kissed across her jaw and down the side of her neck, causing goosebumps to erupt on her skin. Pam's head fell back to give him better access, and Damon's hands cupped her ass as he lifted her off the floor. Pam wrapped her legs around his waist as her lips found his again.

Pam kissed him like a woman starved as he lowered them both to the bed. His cock pressed against her warm center, and she thrust against him, aching to feel his bare shaft against her skin. He was still contained inside his track pants, but there was no hiding his arousal.

"Take them off," Pam murmured as she pulled her lips from his and nipped his lower lip.

"That would require me to let you go." Damon groaned as she thrust up against him again.

"Damon, I need to feel all of you." Pam reached between them and tried to shove down his pants.

After another hard kiss, he quickly dropped his pants to the floor, giving her a full view of his thick shaft. The tip glistened with moisture. Pam licked her lips, got up on her knees, and reached for his member.

"Trixie, lick it." Damon groaned as Pam lowered her mouth to the head of his dick.

Pam didn't make him wait. She swirled her tongue around the large head several times, and after a few seconds, she sucked him into her mouth. His deep groan made her core ache to have him inside her. As she pulled him deeper into her mouth, he thrust forward slowly.

"Fuck, baby. Your mouth is so damn hot." Damon said with a growl.

Pam hummed in response to his words and slid her mouth up and down his shaft a little faster. Damon fisted her ponytail and tugged it lightly which meant he wanted her to slow down.

She didn't normally enjoy performing blowjobs, but with Damon, it was as if she couldn't wait to taste him. Then again, everything with Damon was better than anyone she'd ever been with. He knew exactly how to make her moan and how to get her groaning in ecstasy.

"That's it, baby. Suck. Harder." Damon moaned, and she did until he pulled back from her.

"I was enjoying that." Pam pouted and sat back on her feet.

"Now you can enjoy this." Damon grabbed her knees and tipped her on her back.

He grabbed the sides of her panties and yanked them down her legs. After he tossed them to the side, he hooked his arms under her knees and tugged her to the edge of the bed as he dropped to his knees.

"You smell so damn sexy," Damon growled right before he ran his nose lightly across her bare pussy.

Pam gasped when he flicked his tongue once across her throbbing nub as he placed each of her legs on his shoulders. Damon was a man who took his time when he pleased her, and Pam had been thankful for it many times. She raised up on her elbows and watched as he traced her opening with his finger.

"Damon, more," Pam begged.

"I'm just getting started, sweetheart." Damon blew lightly against her skin, and she shivered.

Before she could say another word, he licked from the bottom of her opening to her clit. Pam inhaled sharply as he sucked her bundle of nerves and swirled his finger just inside her opening.

"Ah… yes." Pam thrust her hips up.

"You want my finger deeper, Trixie?" Damon whispered as he slipped it in a little more.

"God, yes." Pam moaned.

"More?" He teased as he pushed in a little more.

"Fuck, Damon, more, please," Pam cried.

Damon slipped his finger completely inside until his knuckle pressed against her folds, and his thumb circled her clit. Pam dropped back on the bed and arched her back as he continued to play her as if she was a musical instrument.

She could feel the first wave of her pleasure bubbling to the surface, and she fisted the sheets as he inserted a second finger and covered her nub with his hot mouth. Damon sucked until Pam's body convulsed in pleasure and she bit her lip to keep from screaming in ecstasy.

Damon sucked harder, and before she could catch her breath, he brought her over the edge a second time so fast she thought she would pass out. Pam tried to close her legs, but all she could do was squeeze his head between her thighs while she trembled.

"That was so fucking beautiful," Damon whispered a few minutes later.

He moved her legs off his shoulders and hoisted her to the center of the bed. Damon moved next to her and cupped one of her breasts in his hand as he swirled his tongue around her hard nipple.

Pam was weak from her orgasm, but the minute his hot lips sucked her nipple into his mouth, she arched her back and felt around until she could wrap her hand around his cock.

"I want you inside." Pam sighed.

"I don't have protection." He sighed.

"I do. Apparently, Elaine thought of everything when she packed my bag." Pam smirked as she hopped off the bed and scampered to where her suitcase lay on the floor.

"Thank you, Elaine." Damon chuckled as Pam hopped back on the bed and ripped open the foil package.

"I'll have to buy her a special gift," Pam straddled Damon's legs and proceeded to roll the condom down his hard length.

"Fuck, I love having your hands on my dick." Damon groaned.

"I can just keep using my hands if you don't want me to use anything else." Pam grinned.

"Hell no. I want to be deep inside you all night," Damon murmured as he flipped her over on her back and knelt between her legs.

"I know you've got stamina, but I don't think you will be there all night," Pam teased.

"I'll give it the old college try." Damon grabbed his shaft and positioned it at her opening.

Damon's eyes locked with hers as he slowly slipped inside her. His thick cock filled her as he pushed all the way in. He linked his hands with hers as he pulled back and thrust back inside her again.

"I've missed you so damn much. Every night I dreamed about you, and I'd wake up wishing you were next to me," Damon whispered as he continued to make love to her.

"Damon." Pam pulled him down on top and wrapped her legs around his hips.

Pam raised her hips to meet his every thrust. Damon found her mouth and kissed her as if he needed it to breathe, and the truth was, it was the first time in a very long time she felt whole. She loved Damon with all her heart and not being with him felt like she was missing a piece of her soul. Now he was here making love to her and giving her back the piece of her soul she'd lost. The only thing they needed now was to figure out what the people who took her wanted from Damon.

Chapter 15

Damon lay on his side and watched Pam sleep. He'd been next to her every night since she escaped a week earlier. The police had no leads on who took her, and the guy she'd knocked out wasn't talking. Even when Nick told the ass he'd be going away for a long time, he wouldn't cave.

The strange thing was the guy had no record, which meant even with his fingerprints, they couldn't identify him. The only thing they got out of the man was his name. It seemed as if Troy Cooper knew the law and refused to give any information, and when his lawyer showed up, all he did was smirk.

Now the bastard was out on bail, and they were still no further ahead. Nick had gone to John and asked about having the guy followed to see if they could find out anything, but it was against policy. Keith, however, didn't have any such rules, and he had two of his guys on Troy twenty-four hours a day. So far, the guy hadn't left his apartment, and nobody came to see him.

Damon had gone back to the hospital to visit his mother every day. Even running into his father, brother, and sister-in-law wasn't stopping him from being there for his mom. Doctor Burton finally found the test results which proved Damon wasn't a match for his mother, but there was something the doctor wasn't telling him.

His mother was sleeping more, and in the last five days he'd gone to see her, she only woke up for a few minutes while he was there. It was obvious to see she was not going to last much longer, and he had a feeling even if they did find a match, his mother would never make it through the surgery.

The only thing getting him through the days was being with Pam again. Even his nightmares were not as frequent, but unfortunately, Pam had them. He had to wake her a couple of nights and hold her until she stopped shaking.

She'd also made it clear she was returning to her shop on Monday. Damon, Keith, and Nick tried to talk her out of it, but it was no use, especially when she had her mother, grandmother, and female cousins backing her up.

He didn't know why she felt the urgent need to be there when Elaine agreed to run the shop until things were safe. Pam didn't like putting all the workload on her partner's shoulders.

She hadn't told her family about her past and had deemed she would do it during the weekend. Damon prayed they were as understanding as he believed, not that he thought what she did was so awful.

"You're so damn strong, Trixie," Damon whispered.

He brushed her hair back from her face and kissed her temple. Pam instinctively moved into his touch, and he pulled her into his side as he closed his eyes and tried to get some sleep.

He lay utterly motionless with his eye pressed against the scope of his C14 Timberwolf MRSWS. His team had gone into the bombed-out building to rescue the two young women captured by the Taliban soldiers. He couldn't think about what was happening to them, but he knew his teammates would get them out or die trying.

Damon's breaths were slow and steady as he focused on the entrance and counted as he listened for a sign of trouble. He would be invisible to anyone walking by, but if he had to show himself to protect his team, he would.

"Got them," he heard Adrian say through the earpiece.

"Get them out of there. Now. We've got company," another voice shouted.

Before Damon could turn to focus on the incoming enemy, a series of explosions echoed around him. He was tossed back, and it was as if someone stabbed him in the side of his head. His ear rang painfully, and he struggled to get to his feet.

He pulled the earpiece from his ear as he looked up. Two of his teammates were backing toward him with the women. It looked as if they were firing at something, but Damon barely heard it.

"They're dead," Adrian shouted, but the only thing Damon could see was four of his team lying on the ground.

Damon jolted up in the bed, soaked in sweat, and his heart pounded in his chest. The same memory floating back again, but there was something different about this one. He tried to remember what he saw in the dream, but as usual, it all faded into a blur.

"Are you okay?" Pam's quiet whisper helped him calm enough the trembling slowed.

"Just a dream." Damon wiped his hands down over his face.

"Those are never just dreams, Damon. I remember how bad your nightmares used to get." Pam crawled across his lap and held his face between her hands.

"They aren't as bad as they used to be, Trixie." Damon placed his hands on her hips.

"You know, Wade has a dog that helps when he has flashbacks in his sleep. Maybe you should look into it." She placed a light kiss on his cheek.

"I have you." Damon pulled her closer and hugged her to him.

"Are you calling me a dog?" She pinched his cheek.

"No. You're my calm and happy place." He brushed his lips across hers.

"You're the other half of my soul," Pam breathed against his mouth.

Damon pressed his mouth to hers and lowered her back to the bed. He didn't lie when he said she was his calm and happy place. Pam's presence made all the bad things seem not so bad. He'd never forget, of course, but with Pam, he could leave it.

Damon made his way down to the kitchen, leaving Pam asleep after they made love. Even after the restless night, he had more energy than he should, considering he only slept for two hours.

He stepped into the kitchen and into what seemed like a serious conversation between Keith and one of his employees. Ben 'Trunk' Murphy, like the other men who worked for NSS, lived close by and would drop into Keith's frequently.

Trunk was a pretty serious guy, and Damon hardly saw him smile. He always seemed to have the weight of the world on his shoulders, and he didn't speak much. The only time Damon ever saw any emotion out of the man was when Abbie Martin was close by.

"You know I can't," Trunk said and braced his fists against the kitchen counter.

"If you don't, you're going to lose your chance. What kind of life do you have now without her?" Keith dropped his hand on Trunk's shoulder.

"She deserves to be with someone who can give her what she wants. I just can't watch it. I need you to send me on the out-of-town job." Trunk's voice was shaky.

"I know how you feel about her, buddy," Keith said.

"Rusty, I want that mainland contract." Trunk spun around.

"I'm sorry, Trunk. I've already assigned someone. I need you here right now." Keith turned and locked eyes with Damon.

"Fine." Trunk stomped out of the house and slammed the door.

"I swear, if he woke the kids with that racket, I'll kick the shit out of him. If I don't Emily certainly will." Keith grumbled.

"What's wrong with him?" Damon made his way to the coffee pot.

"His life is a complete mess, and he won't fix what he has to fix in order to be with the one woman he wants to be with." Keith flopped down on the kitchen chair.

"Let me guess, Abbie?" Damon sat across from Keith.

"Yeah, she's seeing this dude in town and from what Billie tells Emily, they're getting pretty serious," Keith explained.

Billie was married to Keith's brother Mike, one of the younger O'Connor brothers. She worked with her friend Abbie, and they ran a Real Estate company in St. John's. Trunk had met Abbie when Billie was in danger and her friends had to be protected. Damon didn't know much else, but he'd heard the guys talk about it.

"Is that why he shaved his head?" Damon smirked.

"Maybe, or he wanted to look like Bull." Keith chuckled, referring to his business partner Dean 'Bull' Nash, who was also married to Keith's cousin Kristy.

Damon looked down to the cup he held between his hands. The only sound in the kitchen was the hum of the refrigerator and the soft tap of Keith's finger on the table.

"Keith, I'm worried about Pam going back to the shop. We still don't know who took her and if she's still in danger." Damon lifted his head to look at Keith.

"I know and I'd rather she not go back right now, but I learned a long time ago when the women in my family set their mind to something there's no changing it." Keith sighed.

"I don't understand how the house where Pam was held is the only one in that area not falling down. The town was abandoned years ago, or at least that's what Sandy said." Damon shook his head.

Sandy had investigated the ownership of the house where Pam was held. The only thing she could find was the owner died more than ten years earlier with no family. All the houses were either boarded up or ready to fall down.

"Even the power company wasn't any help. Sandy said it was under the deceased owner's name." Keith leaned back in the chair with his hands linked behind his neck.

"There has to be some way to figure out who's behind this." Damon was frustrated.

Even with all the resources at their fingertips, the person responsible was a ghost. Damon was also convinced his family wasn't involved. With everything going on, there was no way his father would go through so much trouble.

"Are you going to see your mom today?" Keith asked.

"Yeah, but Pam wants to talk to her parents first." Damon emptied his cup and brought it to the sink.

"Is she going to fill the rest of us in as well?" Keith asked.

"You'd have to ask her." Damon dropped his hand on Keith's shoulder. "It's up to her who she wants to tell."

"I hate secrets," Keith grumbled as Damon made his way back to the bedroom.

Pam was still sound asleep as he tiptoed into the room. Her auburn hair was scattered around the pillow, and she lay on her back with one arm under her head and the other at her side. It was a little after seven in the morning, and the sun was peeking through the blinds to light up the room.

Her skin glistened as the light skimmed across it, and she appeared angelic. His angel. The one person in his life he would move heaven and earth to protect. Damon didn't believe in love until he met her.

Pam taught him love was real. Even if she had left, he had no doubt what he felt in his heart was true love. He smiled as she sighed in her sleep. Her mother told him before he ran back to Ontario that Pam was the only woman to make him whole. She said nobody on the face of the earth was more suited for him.

Cora might be known as Cupid to her family, but Damon was pretty sure the woman was the real deal. When he thought about Pam's family, the woman had never been wrong.

Chapter 16

Pam paced her parents' living room as she waited for Damon to return from the hospital. He'd called ten minutes earlier and said he was on the way. She'd never been so nervous in her life because of what she was about to do.

Her father sat in his armchair while her mother and grandmother made tea in the kitchen. She knew she had to tell her whole family, but she wanted to start with the most important people in her life first. Which included her parents, grandmother, and Keith.

"Lois, you need to sit down. You're making me dizzy," Keith said from where he sat on the sofa.

Pam plopped down next to Keith and tried to keep her legs from jumping up and down. She realized she hadn't succeeded when Keith placed his hand over her knees.

"Is it really that bad?" Keith whispered.

"Yes. No. Depends on your perspective." Pam lay her head on Keith's shoulder.

"Nothing is going change how much we all love you." Keith kissed the top of her head.

"Thanks, Superman." Pam smiled.

A few minutes later, her mother and Nanny Betty walked into the living room with Damon behind them. Her mother placed the teapot on the coffee table, and Damon put the tray of teacups next to it.

"Let's all sit back and have a cuppa tea while Pam tells us da big secret," Nanny Betty said.

"I don't drink tea, Nan." Keith sat forward and placed his elbows on his knees.

"You'll drink it taday." Nanny Betty handed him a cup.

"I guess I'm drinking tea." Keith snorted and took the cup from Nanny Betty.

After everyone had been given tea, Pam placed her cup down and stood up. She took a deep breath and walked around the coffee table and turned to her family. Damon stood next to her, and she clung to his hand.

"You're pregnant." Her mother looked almost giddy with happiness.

"No, Mom." Pam sighed.

"It's not long enough for her to…" Keith stopped when Pam glared at him.

"Sweetheart, just tell us," her father urged.

There was no other way to do it but to tell them straight. Her heart thudded in her chest as she imagined how they would react or how they would look at her. She hated to see the disappointment on their faces or worse, disgust, but she wasn't hiding her past anymore.

"You've all asked me how I met Damon and why he calls me Trixie. The truth is when we met, I introduced myself to him as Trixie Knight." Pam took a deep breath.

"Why would you give him a fake name?" her mother asked.

"Because where I worked, our boss didn't want us to tell the patrons our real names," Pam went on.

"Dat's strange," Nanny Betty said as she sipped her tea.

"Not really. I worked as a bartender at a gentleman's bar." Pam said it so fast she wasn't sure if they understood what she said.

"Gentleman's bar?" Keith narrowed his eyes.

"Yes," Pam replied.

"Wat in heaven's name is a gentleman's bar?" Nanny Betty asked.

"Some people call them strip clubs," Keith explained.

"Oh," her mom replied.

"Yes, but this wasn't a dive. It's an upper-class place. The dancers are never naked." Pam swallowed hard.

"What's the big deal about you bartending at a club like that?" Keith's expression told her he knew what she was about to say next.

"I also designed costumes for the dancers and…" Pam glanced up at Damon, and he nodded. "I was also a dancer part-time."

Pam gripped Damon's hand so hard she was sure she probably hurt him, but her parents, grandmother, and Keith sat silently, and she didn't know what else to do. In reality, it was only seconds before someone spoke, but it seemed like hours.

"You put on a sexy outfit and danced on stage for customers," her mother said slowly.

"Yes," Pam replied.

"They were never allowed to touch her," Damon interjected.

"You were there with her?" her father said, but Pam couldn't read his expression.

"I worked there as security," Damon explained.

"How often did you dance?" her mother asked.

"Maybe one or two days a week. Mostly to fill in for other dancers. My main job was bartending, and I used the money from designing the costumes to open my shop." Pam's legs felt like they were about to give out.

She didn't like the way this was going, and she was sure they were about to give her an earful on doing what she did. Her grandmother had not said another word as she sat back and sipped her tea. When she placed her cup on the table and stood up, Pam held her breath as she waited for a lecture.

"I'm not a bit surprised. Pam was always good at makin' stuff for her dolls when she was a youngster." Nanny Betty walked over to Pam and cupped her face between her hands. "We all do stuff we have ta in order ta make a future fer ourselves."

"You aren't disgusted at what I did?" Pam choked as a tear slipped down her cheek.

"Lassie, dere isn't a person in dis world dat hasn't at one time or anudder done somethin' dey aren't proud of. Ya didn't hurt anyone and so wat, ya gave a couple of lads a trill fer a night. Ya were always a good dancer." Nanny Betty kissed her cheek and made her way back to the kitchen with the tray of empty cups.

"You weren't forced to do anything…" Her mother stopped.

"No, Mom. The guy who owns the club treats the dancers very respectfully, and he doesn't stand for anyone mistreating them," Pam assured her mother.

"I can vouch for Drake. I've seen him toss guys out on their ears if they even talked down to any of the dancers," Damon interjected.

"Look, I don't want any of you to be upset with me. One of the reasons I left Damon was because I didn't want my life up there to get back to all of you, but if I want to have a life with him, you need to know everything," Pam explained.

"Look, cuz, I don't care what you do, I'll always love you. Nothing will ever change that." Keith made his way toward her and pulled her into a hug.

"Thanks. I love you too." Pam wrapped her arms around his waist and rested her head on his chest.

Keith was always her best friend growing up, and no matter what, he would always have her back. She just hoped her parents and the rest of her family handled it as well as he did.

"I got to head out, but I'll see you later." Keith gave another quick hug before he left.

Her parents weren't looking at her, and she wished she could read their minds. Pam didn't want to push it, but she had to know what they thought of her. Her father looked up from where his hands were folded in front of him, and Pam swallowed hard, waiting for his response.

"Why did you keep this from us?" he asked.

"Dad, I didn't want you both to be ashamed of me." Pam blinked back the tears.

"Pam, I'm ashamed you would believe our feelings for you would change because of your job. I want you to listen to me, little girl. There is nothing you could ever do that would make us love you any less than we do. Do you understand me?" He dropped his head and looked out over the top of his reading glasses.

"Yes, Dad." Pam nodded.

"I can't believe you were able to keep this from us for so long. We visited you and never had a clue. I am angry." Her mother shot to her feet.

"Mom, I'm sorry." Pam bit her lip to keep it from quivering.

"Not at you. At myself for not figuring it out." Her mother smiled and held out her arms.

Pam immediately hurried into her mother's arms and closed her eyes as her mom wrapped her up in a hug. She was so relieved they weren't disgusted with her past that it was overwhelming, and tears rolled down her cheeks.

"Maybe you can show me a few dance moves to do for your father." Her mother chuckled.

"Mom!" Pam cringed at the thought of her mother dancing like the women in the club.

Pam could finally relax a little. She still had to tell her cousins, but she wasn't nervous about it anymore. Her worries weren't over since they didn't know who kidnapped her, but Pam felt stronger with the weight of her secret off her shoulders.

"Now all that is out of the way, I'm Damon Blackwood." Damon stepped in front of her.

"What are you doing?" She laughed as she took his hand.

"We were never introduced with your actual name." Damon smirked.

"Really?" She scoffed.

"Really," he returned.

"Fine. Hello, Damon. My name is Pamela Nightingale, but everyone calls me Pam." She shook his hand.

"Nice name, but just so you know, you're still my Trixie." Damon grinned as he wrapped his arms around her waist and pressed his forehead against hers.

"I can live with that." Pam sighed when he kissed her cheek.

"By the way, why Trixie?" Damon pulled back and looked at her with curiosity in his eyes.

"When I was a kid, I used to love these detective books. There were a few different authors who wrote the books, but the main character's name was Trixie Belden. It was the first name I thought of when Drake told me to pick out a pseudonym." Pam shrugged.

"I used to love the Hardy Boys." Damon chuckled.

"I know. You had a ton of those books on your bookshelves when we were together." Pam ran her hand over the top of his head.

"Yeah, I'm kind of a book hoarder." Damon laughed.

"You can never have too many books. I'm pretty sure all my Trixie Belden books are still up in the attic here." Pam remembered packing a lot of her things when she moved away and stored them up in her parents' attic.

"Are you two staying for supper?" Her mother stuck her head into the living room.

"If you're cooking, Cora, I'm staying." Damon winked.

"Actually, Mom is cooking, but I'm sure that's okay with you too." Her mother laughed.

"More than okay." Damon wrapped his arm around Pam, and they made their way to the kitchen.

Later in the evening, Pam was in her room folding clothes. Keith and Emily had gone out to pick up groceries, and Damon and Pam agreed to watch the kids. Not long after their parents left, the boys sucked Damon into watching a Disney movie. That's when Pam escaped to fold her laundry.

She was almost finished when Emily came into her room with a huge grin. She put her fingers to her lips and motioned for Pam to follow her. The two women tiptoed down the steps and peeped into the living room.

Damon and the two boys were in the middle of the living room with their backs to Pam. He was singing along to a song by Elvis Presley from the movie *Lilo and Stitch*. The boys were laughing while Damon did his impression of the King of Rock 'n' Roll.

Before he was finished, Keith walked into the room from the other entrance. Pam thought he would make fun of Damon, but a few seconds later, both men were singing and swiveling their hips. Pam and Emily covered their mouths so the men wouldn't hear them laugh.

Pam thought it was the cutest thing she'd ever seen as the two men picked up Noah and Patrick and danced with them. Before the song ended, the dance was interrupted.

"Why the hell didn't I record this with my phone?" Sandy said as she stepped into the living room

"You speak a word of this to anyone, and I'll fire you," Keith threatened.

"No, you won't." Sandy smirked.

"Fine, I won't, but I'll tell Ian to cut you off in the bedroom." Keith grinned.

"He doesn't have the willpower." Sandy placed her fist on one hip.

"You're a pain in my ass," Keith grumbled.

Pam and Emily entered from the other doorway, and when Keith saw them, he rolled his eyes. Damon didn't seem the least bit concerned about being caught singing with the kids.

"If you two are finished with your hunka, hunka, burning love, I have something to show you." Sandy motioned for them to follow her.

When Pam walked into the kitchen, Sandy opened her tablet and tapped the screen a few times. When she looked up, she motioned for Damon to come closer.

"Do you know this woman?" Sandy held up the tablet.

Damon stared at the picture for several minutes, but Pam didn't see any recognition. He shrugged, and Sandy turned the tablet back and tapped the screen a couple more times before turning it back to Damon.

"What about this man?" Sandy asked.

"Yes, that's my grandfather, Warrick Blackwood, but it's an old picture. He died when I was really young," Damon told her.

"Sandy, what's this all about?" Keith asked.

Sandy held up her finger and then proceeded to tap the screen several more times with her other hand. Pam met Damon's eyes, and he shrugged as Sandy continued to tap and swipe.

"There is a marriage license for Damon's grandfather and this woman. Her name is Greta Blackwood." Sandy showed them a picture of the certificate.

"She's too young to be married to my grandfather. He died when I was little. She doesn't look much older than I am," Damon said as he brought the picture back up again.

"She's actually eighteen years older than you," Sandy told him.

Pam could tell by the look on Sandy's face that she was bursting to tell them more. It appeared like she wanted Damon to get his head around the first piece of news before she continued.

"Sandy, this is all great for a family history lesson for Damon, but why is all this important?" Keith asked.

"It's important because Greta's maiden name was Yugov," Sandy explained.

"I still don't…" Damon started, but Pam interrupted.

"As in Vladimir Yugov?" Pam didn't know what her creepy client had to do with everything, but the guy appeared out of nowhere, and it made the hair on the back of her neck stand up on end.

"That's the customer you were supposed to see the night you went missing," Keith said.

"Yes, but he said he didn't know anything, and we have no proof he did," Sandy reminded them.

"Maybe you could talk to his wife," Pam suggested.

"That's just it. He's not married," Sandy told her.

"Then who has he been getting all the clothes for?" Pam asked.

"I have no idea, but I got the feeling it was a ploy to get close to you," Sandy told her.

Pam turned to Damon. He still hadn't spoken, and he was staring at the picture as if he remembered something. She walked behind him and placed her hand on his arm.

"I don't know why, but there's something familiar about her. I just don't ever remember meeting this woman," Damon said the words, but it seemed mostly to himself.

"Your dad has to know." Pam wasn't sure it was a good idea for Damon to have any discussion with his father, but she had a feeling Greta was the link to everything.

Chapter 17

Damon refused for the tenth time, but it was no use. Pam wasn't going to back down. He needed to talk to his father and find out who Greta was, and he didn't want Pam anywhere near his father when the shit hit the fan.

"I'm going, and you can shake your head until all the rocks in there fall out. You are not going to see him alone." Pam stood in front of him all five-foot-three of her, arms folded across her chest and hip jutted out as she tapped her foot.

Keith, Crash, and Trunk were useless because they only stood aside and watched this tiny woman argue with him. All they did was smirk. Damon could predict he wasn't about to win the argument.

"I'm not going alone, Trixie. Trunk is coming with me." Damon motioned toward the big bald man on the other side of the kitchen.

"Yes, and so am I." Pam raised an eyebrow as she waited for his response.

"Lad, yer not gonna win, so ya mite as well take her wit ya." Pam's grandmother walked into the house with Tom behind her.

"Listen to my darling, young man. The most beautiful women are the most stubborn." Tom chuckled as he placed a box on Keith's kitchen counter.

"What's this?" Keith asked.

"Some homemade bread your grandmother made yesterday. We are on deliveries today." Tom smiled.

Damon shook his head because here was Tom, eighty-seven years old, and he was out delivering bread just to make Nanny Betty happy. Since the day he met them, Damon never heard them raise their voices to each other, and Tom usually ended all his sentences with *yes, dear*.

Damon turned back to Pam and sighed. He knew he was fighting a losing battle because if Pam didn't go with them, she'd only get someone else to go with her or worse, go off by herself when they still didn't know who took her. Damon dropped his hands to his sides.

"Yes, dear," Damon muttered as he turned around and headed out the door.

"Atta boy," Tom shouted behind him.

They made their way to the hospital first. Chances were if his father wasn't there, the nurse could let them know if and when he would be there during the day. Damon knew he went there because he'd run into him a couple of times on his visits. They usually didn't speak, and he would leave when Damon arrived.

The good thing was, it was more peaceful for his mother. Her last days didn't need to be filled with listening to harsh words between her husband and her son. Damon cared too much about her to put her through the stress.

"Are you okay?" Pam asked as she took his hand and walked into the hospital.

Both Trunk and Crash had gone with them and were following close behind as they made their way toward his mother's room. He stepped inside and was surprised to see his mother awake, and she smiled at him.

"Damon, I'm so glad to see you." She reached for him.

"You're looking terrific today." Damon kissed her cheek.

"They're trying me on some new medication, but I don't think it will do any good." His mom glanced around him, and her smile grew when she saw Pam.

"Oh, look, you brought your beautiful girl with you," his mom said.

"Hi, Mrs. Blackwood." Pam smiled.

"For heaven's sake, call me Tabitha, honey." His mother brushed her hair back over the top of her head.

"Okay, Tabitha." Pam sat in the chair in the corner of the room.

His mom had been moved to a private room, and it looked homier than the standard hospital rooms. She seemed more relaxed since she was moved. Damon was glad in her final days she could be comfortable.

"Mom, I was wondering if Alastair was here today or if he's coming by?" Damon wanted to get right to the point.

"Damon, I don't like you calling him by his name." His mother shook her head.

"I'm sorry. Has he been here today?" Damon pushed.

"I don't think so, but I'm in and out so sometimes I forget." She lowered her eyes.

"It's okay, Tabitha. I'll ask the nurse." Pam stood up and stepped outside the room.

He didn't worry since Crash and Trunk were on the other side of the door. There was no way anything would happen to Pam with those two watching her.

"She's lovely." His mother folded her hands on her lap.

"She is." Damon sat on the side of the bed.

"You look distressed." His mom tilted her head as she studied him.

"Nothing to worry about. Just a lot on my mind." Damon winked at her.

Before his mother could speak again, Damon heard his father's voice outside the door. His mother sat up straighter when his father raised his voice.

"Who the hell do you think you are?" Damon's father said as he stepped into the room with his phone to his ear.

"Heavens, Alastair. Keep your voice down," Damon's mother whispered.

"Sorry, just a bad business call," Damon's father said as he ignored Damon to give his wife a kiss.

"Aren't you going to say hello to Damon?" his mother motioned toward him.

"Tabby, I'm here to see you." His father smiled down at her, and for the first time in a very long time, Damon could see the affection between his father and mother.

Maybe things had changed since he left, but it didn't mean he would be able to forget all the years he'd watched his mother slip into depression and addiction.

"I do need to talk to you, Father." Damon stood up to his full height and stared at the back of his father's head.

"I don't have time for your poor-me attitude, Damon." His father didn't even turn around.

"It's important. Someone I care about is in danger, and you may be able to give me some answers," Damon explained.

His father stood up and turned slowly to face Damon. His face was red, and his hands were fisted at his sides. Damon had pissed him off, as usual, but he appeared to want to control the rage.

"If you're talking about, your girlfriend's abduction, I had nothing to do with it, and I don't appreciate you sending law enforcement to my home to question me about something I would have no way of knowing." His father's voice was monotone, but Damon saw the tick in his jaw, which meant he was furious.

"I had nothing to do with them talking to you. She was taken because someone wants something from me and they are checking all angles. Don't take offense." Damon used the same controlled tone his father used.

"Then what do you want?" Damon's dad seemed to calm a little.

"Who's Greta?" When Damon said the name, his father's eyes widened, and his mother's face turned ghostly white.

"Where did you hear that name?" his father snapped.

"It came out in the investigation. She was married to your father." Damon's eyes flicked back and forth between his parents.

They both seemed on edge, but he had no idea why his mother would be uneasy. Greta seemed to strike fear in his mom and anger in his father.

"Don't bring her name up again in front of your mother. There is no way she would be involved in anything to do with your girlfriend or you." His father sat next to his mom and wrapped his arm around her shoulder.

His mom lay her head on his dad's shoulder and closed her eyes. All her color was gone, and she seemed so frail again that Damon wanted to kick himself for even bringing up the name.

"Alastair, you have to tell him," his mother whispered.

"Tabby, there's nothing he needs to know about that woman. She's not in any of our lives anymore." His father kissed the top of his mother's head.

"He deserves to know. They both should know before I die." His mother lifted her head and looked into his dad's face.

A tear slipped down her cheek as she reached up to cup his father's face. His dad looked torn as he shook his head, but when his mom nodded, he closed his eyes and took a deep breath.

"He deserves to know." His mother lay back on the bed and closed her eyes.

"Why would you bring this up now? She doesn't need this." His father stood up and stomped around the foot of the bed.

"Who is this woman?" Damon asked.

"Keep your voice down. I'm not talking about it here, so if you want to hear the whole story, come to the estate tonight. If I'm going to tell you about this, then I'll talk to you and your brother at the same time. I don't want to have to talk about this more than once, but be prepared, this isn't going to be pleasant." His father walked out of the room, leaving Damon alone in the doorway.

"What did he say?" Pam asked.

"He wants me to go to the estate tonight. Whoever Greta is, he wants to tell Malcolm and me together." Damon watched his father disappear into the elevator at the end of the corridor.

"Why couldn't he just tell you here?" Pam linked her fingers with his.

"From the look on his face when I mentioned Greta, I don't think this is going to end well for any of us." Damon had a feeling his life was about to be turned upside down.

Chapter 18

Pam sat in the living room of Ian and Sandy's house while Keith, Damon, Sandy, and Aaron tried to find more information on Greta and what Damon's dad could possibly have to tell his sons.

It tore at her heart to see him look so anxious over what he could potentially hear from his dad. Alastair had sent Damon a message to be at the house by seven. He'd asked her not to insist on going with him because he didn't know what would happen.

She wanted to go, but how could she make a meeting with his father and brother more uncomfortable? Of course, Shadow and Trunk made it clear Damon wouldn't be going alone. Although he didn't believe it was necessary, he didn't argue. Especially since Keith told him it wasn't up for negotiation.

"Aunt Pam, are you okay?" The soft voice of Ian's daughter Lily drew her attention.

Lily was fifteen years old and one of Ian and Sandy's two oldest children. She was brilliant, and like Keith, had an eidetic memory. Aaron and Nick teased Ian all the time about the boys who were going to come knocking for Lily and their other daughter Evie.

Pam was sure Ian wasn't too worried, considering he was a black belt in karate and Sandy not only worked for Keith as a computer analyst, but she was also a police officer. Still, Pam could see the boys flocking to the door if in fact, they weren't already.

Lily and Evie were the complete opposite in their looks. Lily had the O'Connor blue eyes and strawberry-blonde hair. Although her hair was naturally wavy, since she'd gotten older, she kept it straight and long. Evie was the mirror image of her mother, black curly hair, dark brown eyes.

The girls were inseparable and even though they weren't sisters biologically, they were as close as two sisters could be. Between the two of them, Ian and Sandy had four children. Lily and Grace were Ian's from a previous relationship, and Evie was Sandy's daughter with her ex. When they got together, they had Alexander, but it didn't matter, all the kids were treated the same.

"I'm hanging in there, Lily." Pam forced a smile.

"Good." Lily gave her a sweet smile.

Evie sat on the floor in front of Pam and Lily, but the two teenagers seemed to be talking without actually using words. Pam glanced back and forth between them, and when she finally couldn't take it anymore, she sighed.

"Okay, girls. What's up?" Pam asked.

"There's a semi-formal at the community center for the people who helped out during the summer," Lily began.

"We sort of got invited." Evie blushed.

"Oh?" Pam smiled.

"Yeah, but Mom doesn't know anything about fancy clothes. She's a jeans and t-shirt girl." Evie rolled her eyes.

"Or yoga pants and tank tops." Lily nodded toward where Sandy sat on the floor.

"I still don't know how Dad got her into a wedding dress." Evie laughed.

"Actually, I helped her pick out her dress," Pam told the girls.

Pam had still lived in Ontario then, but she helped Sandy over facetime to pick out the perfect dress. Pam headed back to Newfoundland shortly after.

"You girls are asking me to help you pick out dresses for the dance?" Pam chuckled.

"We don't have to actually go shopping. You have great dresses in your shop." Evie moved up onto her knees.

"I do, and we do have sizes to fit you girls." Pam nodded.

"Especially since Lily has massive boobs," Evie whispered.

"Evie." Lily gasped and crossed her arms across her breasts.

"Honey, it's an O'Connor curse." Pam wrapped her arm around Lily's shoulder.

"Evie doesn't exactly lack in that area either." Lily narrowed her eyes and glared at her sister.

"Are you two complaining about your boobs again?" Grace appeared next to Pam and rolled her eyes.

"Hush, Gracie," Evie whispered as she scanned the people on the other side of the room.

"You two are so weird." Grace grabbed the remote.

The news popped up on the television, and before Grace had a chance to change the channel, a picture popped up on the screen. Pam gasped as Grace turned the volume up on the television.

"*He was arrested after being found in the house where Hopedale business owner, Pam Nightingale, was held for several days until she escaped. Troy Cooper was found in his apartment, deceased from an apparent overdose. Police are investigating the death as suspicious*," the reporter said as Pam looked up to see everyone had now surrounded the television.

"I guess we aren't getting any information out of him," Keith grumbled.

"How come Nick didn't tell us?" Damon turned to where Aaron was on his phone.

"Maybe because it's not linked to Pam's abduction." Sandy shrugged.

"That's no coincidence." Shadow sat on the arm of the couch.

"It's not," Aaron said as he joined them.

"What did Nick say?" Keith asked.

"He said they found the guy…" Aaron stopped when he noticed Lily, Evie, and Grace staring up at him.

"Girls, why don't you go upstairs and clean your rooms?" Sandy motioned with her head.

"Ah, we never get to hear the good stuff." Grace stomped out of the room.

"I'm sure it's not stuff we need to hear." Lily urged her younger sister out of the living room.

Sandy checked to make sure the kids were out of earshot and nodded to let Aaron know to continue. Pam understood, trying to keep the kids out of all the chaos. They'd all seen way too much in their short lives, and it started with the murder of Lily and Grace's mother.

"Go on, A.J.," Sandy urged.

"The guy was found on the floor of his apartment with foam around his mouth. He was already dead, so the Narcan didn't work. They are going to do an autopsy to find out for sure, but it looks like an opiate overdose." As Aaron explained what happened, Pam caught Damon out of the corner of her eye.

His hands shook, and he was staring off into space. She knew what was happening, and she immediately went to his side. Damon was having an anxiety attack. She'd seen him have them a few times but much to her dismay, he'd started trying to control them with alcohol. It was the one thing she worried about with him, but she hadn't seen him take a drink at all.

"Damon." Pam touched his arm gently.

"I'm okay, Trixie. Just didn't realize how much I depended on the booze until now." His voice cracked.

"What do you need?" Pam whispered as the rest in the room went back to what they were doing before the news came on.

"A drink." He snorted.

"Maybe a walk on the beach would be better." Pam took his hand.

"I'm not in the best state of mind to take you for a walk on the beach alone." Damon pulled her into his arms and kissed the top of her head.

Pam could feel his body tremble, and he hugged her tighter than was comfortable, but she knew it was what he needed to get through the anxiety. At least she hoped it helped because she wasn't sure how else to help him through this.

It was hard to know if it was the pending conversation with his father, the loss of the only person connected to her kidnapping, or memories from overseas that brought on the episode. Maybe it was a combination of all of it. Pam would do anything to help him and she prayed he knew.

"You look like you need a drink," Aaron said as he stepped next to them.

"To tell you the truth, I actually don't. I've done way too much drinking over the last few years, and I need to deal with life without the help of alcohol," Damon told Aaron.

"They say the first step is to admit there's a problem. We're all here if you need anything, Damon. You're family." Aaron placed his hand on Damon's shoulder, and Pam had to close her eyes to hold back the tears.

Aaron's statement was one of the reasons she loved her family so much. They accepted anyone into the family no matter what issues or flaws they had. Nobody was ever left out in the cold.

"Thanks, A.J." The emotion in Damon's voice was evident to anyone who heard the way he choked out the words.

"We got you." Aaron nodded and walked out of the living room.

"Trixie, you're one damn lucky woman." Damon kissed her temple and tucked his head into the crook of Pam's neck.

"I know. I have you," Pam whispered.

"Sweetheart, I'm the lucky one because someone upstairs was looking over me the day I met you." He sighed in her embrace.

The time for Damon to leave came way too soon for Pam. She'd resigned herself to not going with him, and it was more for Damon's peace of mind than anything. She also had Trunk's assurance he wouldn't let anything happen to Damon or let him do anything stupid.

Since she had nothing else to do but worry, she talked Keith and Sandy into bringing her to her shop to help the girls pick out dresses. Another of Keith's security guys and one of Damon's best friends met them at her shop. Adrian was glad to help out.

It was a great distraction to have Lily and Evie model dresses. Sandy seemed to enjoy it as well, even though the woman hated shopping. The only time Pam saw Sandy in the shop was when there was a wedding, or she wanted something sexy to wear for a night with Ian.

Before she knew it, two hours had passed, and both girls had picked out the perfect dress for the dance. Much to Ian's dismay, both girls had strapless dresses, and he threatened to sew straps on the dresses himself.

"Dad, you don't know how to sew." Evie laughed.

"You'll be surprised what I can do when I put my mind to it, little girl." Ian narrowed his eyes at his daughter.

"Yeah, I think I'll be hiding my dress at Nanny and Poppy's house." Lily laughed.

"I grew up in that house. There's no place you can hide it where I won't find it." Ian chuckled.

"We'll put them in Nanny Betty's room." Evie smirked.

"Ha, you won't get them in there, Dad." Lily laughed, and both girls ran out of the kitchen when Ian jumped to his feet.

"They're growing up too damn fast. I don't like it," Ian grumbled.

"It's okay, Doc. You'll always have me." Sandy plopped down on Ian's lap and kissed his cheek.

Pam took that moment to make her way to the living room and check the time. It was almost ten at night, and she hadn't heard from Damon, Trunk, or Shadow. She was ready to leave Ian's place and Crash told her he and Adrian would bring her back to Keith's place.

She prayed on the way back to *The Compound* that Damon was okay and whatever his father had to tell him didn't destroy the man she loved.

Chapter 19

Damon stood on the bottom of the stone steps leading to the house where he was born. It appeared smaller than he remembered, but still looked cold. He felt an icy chill run up his spine as he knocked on the door.

"Nice house," Trunk said.

"Too damn big for my liking," Shadow murmured as Damon knocked again.

When the door opened, Gail glared at him as if he were a piece of dirt. Damon didn't care how the woman felt about him, but she wasn't going to keep him from finding out what he'd gone there to do.

"I'm surprised you didn't just come barging in with your friends," Gail said snidely.

"Where's Alastair?" Damon wasn't letting her get to him as he stepped inside the house.

"Wow, calling your father by his first name." Gail rolled her eyes.

"Gail, I don't have time for your shitty attitude. Where is he?" Damon snapped.

"Watch how you speak to my wife," Malcolm growled as he walked down the marble stairs.

"Tell your wife to keep her snarky opinions to herself," Damon returned.

"She has a reason to be snarky with you, doesn't she?" Malcolm asked.

"I'm not here to argue with you two." Damon got more irritated the longer he stood there.

"He's in his office. You do remember where that is, right?" Gail sneered as she tossed her hair over her shoulder and walked away.

"Was she born a bitch, or did she go to school for it?" Trunk whispered in Damon's ear.

"I think it's her natural state." Damon smirked.

"I'll let him know you're here." Malcolm stalked down the long hallway.

"I think we better follow." Damon made his way toward the large oak door at the end of the long hall.

He ignored all the familiar pictures and pieces of furniture which had been in the house as long as he could remember. Since his father was an only child, he'd inherited the entire estate when Damon's grandfather died.

"Is that the queen of England in that picture?" Trunk pointed to a photo of his grandfather with the head of the monarchy in Great Britain.

"Yeah." Damon shrugged.

Damon stepped inside the large office. Nothing had changed. The Edwardian mahogany antique desk his grandfather once owned still stood in the center of the room. If Damon remembered correctly, the desk was over a hundred years old. The walls behind the desk were floor-to-ceiling bookshelves and were filled with more books than anyone could ever read in a lifetime.

"Your friends can wait outside," his father snapped as he walked into the room.

"Sorry, sir. We are here as security for Damon. We stay." Shadow stood next to the door.

"This is family business," he roared at Shadow.

Damon was impressed with Shadow's composure. The man didn't even flinch. He simply tilted his head and glanced at Trunk, then back at Damon's father.

"Again, we are security for Damon, and we sign privacy contracts so we wouldn't be permitted to say anything we hear while on duty," Shadow replied.

Damon's father glared at Shadow for several minutes before he turned and slammed the office door. Trunk took a spot on the other side of the door, but Damon saw the slight glint in the man's eyes as if he wanted to give Shadow a huge pat on the back. Damon did too.

"Sit." His father pointed to the two chairs as he made his way around to the large leather office chair behind the desk.

"Dad, what's this all about? I have things to do and don't have time for Damon's theatrics." Malcolm unbuttoned his suit jacket and sat down.

"I'm doing this because my wife asked me to do it. Considering it's probably the last thing I'll be able to do for her before she leaves us, then I'm going to do it." His father's voice quivered, but his demeanor didn't change.

"Damon, you asked me who Greta is." His father met Damon's eyes.

"Yes," Damon replied.

"She was my father's second wife." His father returned.

"I know that, Dad." Damon sighed.

"She's also…" His father looked down at the desk for a moment and then back up again. "She's also the woman who murdered my father."

"What?" Damon and Malcolm said together.

"I thought Grandfather died because he was drunk and fell down the stairs?" Malcolm asked.

"He did die from the fall down the stairs, but she pushed him. He'd told her he was taking her out of his will because she'd been unfaithful to him." His father was very uncomfortable.

"I guess it runs in the family," Damon muttered.

"So, what happened to her?" Malcolm said as he glared at Damon.

"With all the drama that the family was dragged through when my father married Greta, we had to protect the family image. She was family. It's why my father's death was ruled an accident. The problem was, Greta tried to leave, but we couldn't let her until we had her sign some legal documents. We couldn't let her take what she wanted." His father stood up and walked to the window.

"What did she want?" Damon asked.

"Her children," his father replied.

"I don't understand." Malcolm sounded irritated.

"Greta wasn't stable. Even her brother warned my father about her when they got married. Dad brushed it off as an overprotective older brother because his sister was marrying a man thirty years older than her." His father turned around.

"Thirty years?" Malcolm gasped.

"Yes." His father nodded.

"So, I'm guessing she ended up with her children since we've never met them." Malcolm shrugged.

Damon watched his father's expression change from stoic to sadness. It suddenly hit Damon. Greta must have done something to her kids, and it was why his father felt so guilty. Either way, he couldn't see what it would have to do with Pam.

"No, she didn't." His father sat down.

"Did she hurt them?" Damon asked.

"No, one was just a baby, and the other was a toddler. We couldn't let her take them." His father sighed.

"Dad, where are her kids?" Damon had a sick feeling in his stomach.

"They were adopted," his father continued.

"Is it why we were sent that message?" Malcolm asked.

"What message?" Damon asked.

"Dad got an email with a woman tied to a chair with a message. We thought it was a prank because we didn't know who the woman was." Malcolm opened the email on his phone.

Damon took it, and his blood ran cold. It was Pam. Damon wasn't the only one who'd gotten the message, but it didn't make sense. His father and brother didn't know Pam was involved with him, and he was pretty sure they wouldn't care either way.

"That's Pam." Damon pulled out his own phone and showed them his message.

"I don't understand." Malcolm wasn't the only one.

"Her kids think by taking Pam, you would give them what they want. What is it they want? Money?" Damon could feel the rage bubbling up inside.

"It's not her kids. I can assure you of that," his father returned.

"How do you know?" Malcolm asked.

"They wouldn't because they don't know about any of this." His father stood up again. "They don't even know who they are."

"You mean they don't know they're adopted." Damon glanced at Malcolm.

"Dad?" Malcolm stood up and walked to where their father stood by the window.

"I'm sorry, but we had to keep this from getting out." His father turned, and his eyes glistened with tears.

"Dad, will you just tell us what's going on?" Malcolm snapped.

"Greta Yugov Blackwood had two sons. She named them Damon and Malcolm." His father's voice cracked.

Malcolm flopped back into the chair, and his expression probably mirrored Damon's own. He wasn't sure if he understood what he heard and shook his head in disbelief.

"Are you saying you and Mom…" Damon couldn't finish the sentence.

"No. No, we must be named after them. You wouldn't keep something like that from us for our entire lives." Malcolm shot to his feet.

"You weren't named after them. You are them." His father looked heartbroken.

"No. No. If it's true… why would you… no. This is bullshit," Malcolm shouted.

"It's not, and I'm sorry, but we needed to protect you." His father reached for Malcolm.

Malcolm slapped Alastair's hand away and stomped out of the room. Damon tried to get his head around what he'd been told. If what Alastair said was true, then he and Malcolm were raised by their half-brother.

"Is all this why Mom drank and popped pills?" Damon asked.

"Damon, it started long after we adopted you two. You must remember how great she was with both of you when you were little. Tabitha and I tried for years to have a child of our own with no luck. When we had the chance to take you and Malcolm away from such an unstable woman, we took it. I've never seen Tabitha so happy. When you were ten, she found out she was pregnant for the fourth time." His father swallowed.

Damon couldn't remember his mother being pregnant. It was then it hit him; she wasn't his mother. What a completely fucked-up situation. His mother wasn't his mother, and his father was his half-brother.

"She was almost seven months when she lost the baby, and they had to do an emergency hysterectomy. She was devastated. Damon, I know what you thought about me, but the truth was, I became a bastard after that too. My heart shattered, watching her sink into depression and not let me help her. I couldn't leave her, but she wasn't the woman I married. It's not an excuse to be unfaithful, I know, but there's nothing I can do to change it now." His father lifted his head and met Damon's eyes.

"No, it isn't an excuse," Damon snapped.

Damon turned his back to Alastair. He had to stop thinking of this man as his father, because he wasn't. It made sense why Tabitha would get so upset when Damon would call her husband by his first name. She feared the truth coming out.

He glanced at Shadow then Trunk. Both men hadn't moved, and their faces didn't show any reaction to what they heard. Damon didn't know what he was supposed to do, and he and Malcolm might be estranged, but he was concerned about how his brother reacted.

Malcolm had been such a jovial young man before Damon left. He begged Damon not to leave after the huge blow-up with Alastair. It was hard to believe that while he was in boot camp, Malcolm would be convinced to step in and marry Gail.

His brother had been madly in love with the daughter of one of their housekeepers. The week before Damon left, Malcolm told him he was planning on proposing to the girl. Damon found out about Malcolm's marriage to Gail through an announcement sent to the basic training camp in Nova Scotia.

It had been the last time Damon walked into his family home. He had to find out what happened. When he arrived, he found a cold and angry brother who blamed Damon for walking out on his responsibilities.

"I've got to go talk to your brother. There's more he needs to know." Alastair started to leave the office.

"How much more could you have hidden from him?" Damon shouted.

Alastair stopped right outside the office door with his back to Damon. Gail had seated herself outside the room, and for the first time since Damon had known the woman, her smug, arrogant look was gone.

"You can't tell him." Gail stepped in front of Alastair.

"No more. I must do this. For everyone involved. It's Tabitha's last wish." Alastair tried to step around Gail.

189

"Why, because you love her so much? I didn't hear you declare your love for her while you were…" Gail stopped when she met Damon's eyes over his father's shoulder. "Don't do this to Malcolm and the twins."

"Alastair, what is she talking about?" Damon asked as Malcolm appeared behind Gail.

"Yeah, Dad. Or do I call you Alastair now? What is my beloved wife talking about?" Malcolm snarled.

Damon stepped around his father and went to be next to Malcolm. For the first time, his younger brother didn't step away or make a cruel remark. The only thing he did was glare at the man who had raised them.

"It's nothing, Malcolm. Your father…" Gail's words were stopped when Malcolm shouted at her.

"Shut your lying mouth. You think I don't know what goes on in this house? We may be married, but I'm the only one of the Blackwood brothers you haven't screwed. At least when I cheated, I didn't do it inside our home." Malcolm shook with rage.

It took Damon a moment to register what his brother said. He grabbed Malcolm's arm so he could see his brother's eyes. If what his brother just said was true, then a whole barrel of shit was about to hit the fan.

"What do you mean the only brother not to sleep with her?" Damon asked as calmly as possible.

"Like you don't fucking know. I had to give up my happiness for you because you didn't have the balls to do what was right. You ran away to the Army to get away from your responsibilities. I was guilted into making sure I covered for you. I lost everything," Malcolm shouted.

"What did he tell you, Mal?" Damon's own rage started to bubble up.

"I told him Gail was pregnant," Alastair interjected.

"What would that have to do with me?" Damon glanced at his father.

"Because you knocked her up," Malcolm roared.

"Malcolm, keep your voice down. The kids will be home from their friends soon," Gail snapped.

"You're going to leave them in the dark. What are you going to do? Wait until their lives are completely screwed up before you tell them I'm not their father? Tell them their father ran off to the Army to escape…" Malcolm's rant was interrupted by Alastair's roar.

"I'm their father," Alastair wailed.

"You told Malcolm I got Gail pregnant and ran off. Let me guess; you told him it was up to him to protect the family name. The only thing you were doing was covering your own ass, you, self righteous bastard." Damon grabbed Alastair by the suit jacket and slammed him against the wall several times.

191

"Stop it. You're going to hurt him." Gail grabbed Damon's arm and tried to pull him off Alastair.

"Damon, step aside." Malcolm pulled Gail away and stepped next to Damon.

"Malcolm, I'm so sorry." Alastair appeared sincerely apologetic.

"Sorry? Sorry? You ruined my fucking life. You sent away the only woman I've ever loved and made me think I was doing something to protect the family because my brother was a coward. The funny thing is it was the truth, but you were the cowardly brother. You're the bastard who couldn't keep his dick in his pants, not Damon." Malcolm's voice grew louder and colder with every word.

Before Damon knew what happened, Malcolm raised his fist and slammed it into Alastair's face over and over as he ranted about how selfish Alastair was.

Damon and Trunk seized Malcolm by the arms and pulled him back, but not before he'd did some severe damage. Alastair was barely conscious as he slid down the wall and slumped over on the floor.

"My God, Malcolm, you could have killed him," Gail screamed as she knelt next to Alastair.

"No. I deserved it," Alastair mumbled.

"You deserved that and more, you, selfish prick," Malcolm bellowed as he struggled to free himself from Damon and Trunk.

"Mal, he's not worth it." Damon moved in front of his brother and forced Malcolm to look him in the eye.

"He made me hate you. He turned me against you, and I spent years despising you because of him. I lost Kelsey because of him." Tears streamed down Malcolm's cheeks.

"I know, and we can't change any of it now. I would like to beat the living shit out of him right now too; it's not going to help. The only thing it's going to do is upset the kids you've raised. The boy and girl who think *you're* their father." Damon placed his hands on Malcolm's shoulders and gave him a little shake.

"I love them like they were my own. You should see them, Damon, they're fifteen years old and Melody, she's so smart and the sweetest girl. Marshall is such a great athlete. He reminds me so much of you when you were his age." Malcolm mimicked Damon's stance and placed his hands on top of Damon's shoulders.

"I'm looking forward to meeting them." Damon nodded.

"You aren't going near them," Gail snapped. "Either of you."

"I'd keep your mouth shut if I were you," Shadow stepped in front of Gail.

"Look, as much as I would like to let him suffer, you don't want the kids coming and seeing the man they believe is their grandfather bleeding on the ground. We need to get him upstairs and cleaned up. Maybe call his doctor." Damon released Malcolm and turned to where Gail tried to help Alastair to his feet.

"The last thing I want to do is hurt them." Malcolm started to step toward Alastair.

"Maybe we should let Trunk and Shadow help him up to his room." Damon nodded.

"Yeah, I might let him slip over the stairs." Malcolm stepped back as the two security guards guided Alastair up the stairs.

For several minutes, Damon, Malcolm, and Gail stood in the foyer without speaking. He could see the fury on her face, and it was apparent to anyone, Gail wanted to say something. Damon had a feeling part of the reason Alastair pulled what he did, was because Gail must have found out the family secret and blackmailed him.

"I can't believe you two. He raised you and took care of you." Gail dabbed her fingers under her eyes to wipe away nonexistent tears.

"I'm going to say this once and once only. You're no longer welcome in this house. I want you packed and out of here by the end of the day." Malcolm spoke in a calm, controlled tone.

"You can't kick me out of here. This is Alastair's house." Gail scoffed.

"See that's where you'd be wrong. Alastair turned the house over to me two months ago. He was planning to retire and move him and Mom, I mean, Tabitha, to the lake house. Which means, dear *wife*, I can kick you out of here, and I think you better call your father. Maybe he knows a good divorce lawyer." Malcolm stalked off toward the office.

"He can't do that." Gail turned to Damon.

"Apparently, he can." Damon smirked as he followed Malcolm to the office.

It was time he and his brother had a long talk to see if they could find out what Pam's kidnappers wanted from his family before they came after Pam again. He wasn't about to let his family drama put her in anymore danger.

Chapter 20

Pam breathed a sigh of relief when she received a text from Shadow to let her know they were on the way back to Hopedale. He didn't explain why they'd taken so long, but he did say Damon had been thrown a curveball. Pam knew it was something huge. Especially when he told her Damon's brother was coming with his son and daughter.

Pam asked about Malcolm's wife, but Shadow told her it was way too much to explain in a text. She had to wait until they returned to hear the whole story.

With the news they would be expecting extra guests, Keith sent Crash to one of the bunkhouses to make sure everything was ready for company. Emily wanted to make sure Malcolm and the children were comfortable since they weren't sure how long they would be staying.

By the time they arrived, it was a little before midnight. Damon seemed drained, Malcolm was obviously angry, and the kids looked lost. Since it was late, Emily escorted the kids to the rooms where Pam and Damon had been sleeping. Pam figured it was mostly to give the adults a chance to discuss the situation. When Emily returned to the kitchen, she assured Malcolm the kids were comfortable and resting.

"Are you sure we aren't intruding?" Malcolm asked as Emily put a cup of coffee in front of him.

"Not at all. You're not the first surprise house guest we've had over the years, and I'm sure you won't be the last." Emily smiled and touched Malcolm's shoulder.

Once the introductions were done, Damon, Malcolm, Trunk, and Shadow told them everything. The reason Malcolm left with the kids was because Damon didn't want to leave his brother alone in the house with Gail and Alastair. Not because he was worried about them but because he was concerned about what Malcolm might do if Gail pushed too hard.

Unfortunately, Gail's kids overheard everything that happened. Nobody knew they'd come in through the back door just before everything blew up. Since nobody knew they were home, it was a complete shock to everyone when they insisted on going with Malcolm.

"I just don't understand what all this would have to do with Pam's kidnapping." Emily sat across the table from Pam and Damon.

"Dad, I mean Alastair… We got an email with a picture of a woman we didn't know. It turns out it was Pam, and whoever is involved thought we knew her." Malcolm shrugged.

"Obviously, they don't know much about our family if they thought we were in contact. Plus, when she was taken, Pam and I weren't together," Damon interjected.

"Have you been able to get in touch with Vladimir Yugov?" Pam asked Nick.

"No, he's out of town, but there's a woman housesitting for him. She said he didn't say when he would return. At first, I thought she was his wife, but her name is Kelsey Oliver," Nick explained, but Pam was distracted by Malcolm's reaction.

"I'm sorry? Did you say Kelsey Oliver?" Malcolm's voice quivered.

"Yes, do you know her?" Nick asked.

"She…" Malcolm pressed his lips together.

"If it's the same girl, she and Malcolm were in love before Alastair talked him into marrying Gail," Damon said with more distaste than Pam had ever heard from him before.

"Do you think it's merely a coincidence that she's at a house of the person of interest in Pam's abduction?" Keith asked.

"No. No." Malcolm shouted and shot to his feet. "She'd never do that. Not her. Kelsey was one of the sweetest people I've ever known."

"Do you still talk to her?" Nick asked.

"Not since the day I told her I was marrying Gail. I'll never forget the agony in her eyes." Malcolm stood in front of the window with his back to everyone.

Damon wrapped his arm around Pam's shoulder. He probably knew what it was like to have someone run out on a relationship. After all, Pam left him with no explanation. Granted she didn't run off and marry someone else, but he still had to know the hurt.

"Heartbreak can do strange things to people, Malcolm," Keith said.

Pam's family had seen several people who lost their minds because they felt betrayed or hurt. It could drive someone to do horrifying things to get revenge. Maybe Kelsey waited all this time to get retaliation on Damon's family.

"Not with Kelsey. She could never hurt a fly. When I told her it was over between us, she didn't yell or scream; she just told me to be happy," Malcolm murmured.

Pam could see the agony in Malcolm's expression. His tone told her Malcolm never stopped loving Kelsey, and it would be hell for him if it turned out she was involved.

"I hope you're right, but the fact she's in Yugov's house doesn't make it look good." Nick turned to Damon. "I'm going to head home and give Lora a break with the baby. Sam has started waking up at two in the morning, and he doesn't go back to sleep until daylight. Lora is exhausted."

Nick and Lora had two children; Molly was Lora's daughter from a previous relationship. She was eight years old, and Nick adopted the little girl when he and Lora got married. Samuel, or Sam, was born a little over a year after they got married and was almost four months old.

"Sounds fun." Keith chuckled.

"Yeah, it's a regular barrel of laughs. I don't remember the last time Lora and I slept in the bed together." Nick sighed.

"Aww, poor Nicky not getting his dicky wet," Emily teased.

"Goodnight." Nick ignored Emily's comment and sauntered out of the house.

Shadow and Trunk headed back to their own places, and Keith and Emily went to bed. Leaving Pam, Damon, and Malcolm alone in the kitchen. Malcolm hadn't moved from the window, and Damon seemed lost.

"She had the most beautiful smile," Malcolm murmured.

"Mal, we don't know if she's involved," Damon insisted.

"I know, but who could blame her. I hurt her more than I ever thought I would." Malcolm turned around, and his entire focus was on Pam. "I'm sorry you were taken. It must have been terrifying for you."

"It's okay, Malcolm. I'm okay, and it's not your fault," Pam assured him.

"She's a tough lady. She took down a guy twice her size." Damon grinned.

"I wouldn't piss her off then if I were you." For the first time since he'd come into Keith's house, Malcolm smiled.

"I try not to." Damon winked at her.

"How about we head down to the bunkhouse and let Malcolm get some rest? Emily made up the day bed in Keith's office for you." Pam stood up and yawned.

"I can put the kids in the same room and you two can take the other room," Malcolm suggested.

"It's fine. I think they need a good night's sleep as much as you do. Besides, it's only down the path." Pam hugged Malcolm.

"Thank you." Malcolm's voice cracked.

"Get some sleep, Mal." Damon slapped his brother on the back.

"I don't know if it will happen, but I'll try. Thanks." Malcolm disappeared into Keith's den while Pam and Damon headed out.

"He's going to be okay." Pam and Damon started the short walk to one of the bunkhouses at the back of Keith's property.

"I hope so, and I hope to God Kelsey isn't involved in any of this. It will kill him if she's responsible." Damon linked his fingers with hers.

"He loved her that much?" Pam asked.

"When I was going to boot camp, he had planned to propose," Damon told her as they entered the small house.

"I feel so sorry for him." Pam knew how it felt to walk away from love.

Damon closed the door, and when he turned around, Pam took his hands. She gazed into his hazel eyes and wondered how she was able to walk away from him back then. Looking at him, she knew she would never be able to walk away from him again.

"Damon, I love you. I've always loved you," she whispered in the dim light of the room.

"I told you once I didn't believe in love. Mostly because of what happened with my family. You made me believe it was real and I've loved you with all my heart since the first time I saw you behind the bar. Even when you left, I couldn't get you out of my heart. You are my heart." He held her face in his hands as he spoke.

"I'll never leave you again," Pam whispered against his lips.

Damon moved his mouth against hers and his tongue glided across the seam of her lips. Pam opened, and he slipped inside as he slowly swirled his tongue with hers, making love to her mouth.

Pam grabbed the bottom of his shirt and lifted it as he opened the front of her blouse. The whole time they undressed each other, they made their way to the small bedroom at the back of the house. She needed to be close to him and forget the world at least for the night.

By the time they stood in the bedroom, they were down to nothing. Damon's hands smoothed from her hips and up her sides, sending shivers of desire through her body. His thumbs grazed against the underside of her breasts as he lowered his head to pull her peaked nipple into his hot mouth.

Pam fisted his hair, and her head fell back as he sucked one then the other. His hands cradled her breasts as he knelt in front of her and continued to suck and tug on her nipples. Pam pulled his hair; it was as if she couldn't get him close enough.

Damon's hands slowly moved around to her back as he nipped the tip of each breast. He caressed her back as he kissed down her stomach and circled her navel with his tongue.

His hand continued to move lower until they covered both of her ass cheeks. He squeezed and caressed as he licked down to the top of her sex.

Pam forced her eyes open and looked down as his tongue slipped between her folds and swirled around her clit. Damon took his time tasting every inch of her opening and moving back to her sensitive bud.

"Ah, yes." Pam moaned.

"I love how you taste," Damon whispered and proceeded to hum as he gently sucked each lip of her pussy into his mouth.

Pam thrust her hips forward to meet the rhythm of his tongue. Damon slipped one hand around her hip and ran a finger between her folds while he flicked and teased her clitoris. She was so wet his finger slid easily inside her, and he pushed it in deep as he pulled her nub into his mouth.

"God, yes." Pam gasped as he thrust a second finger inside her.

Her legs shook as the orgasm built, and she panted as Damon brought her over the edge. Pam's body shuttered in pleasure, and she had to brace her hands on his shoulders to keep from falling to the floor.

Damon must have sensed she couldn't hold herself any longer because he stood and lifted her into his arms. He gently placed her on the bed and moved between her legs as he linked their fingers together.

Pam pulled him down on top of her, and their lips met in a desperately passionate kiss. Damon pushed her arms above her head as he ground his erect cock against her wet sex. It pressed against her clit, bringing her close to another explosion of pleasure, and he hadn't even entered her yet.

Pam wiggled under him as she ached to feel him thrust inside her. He wasn't having it as he swiveled his hips against her. Pam groaned into his mouth as she felt the wave of pleasure rush through her body, and she convulsed in ecstasy.

"Jesus, I love when you do that." Damon hummed when he pulled his lips from hers.

"My turn," she said with a growl as she freed her hands and pushed him over onto his back.

"I'm not gonna argue." Damon grinned.

Pam straddled his legs as she dragged her fingernails lightly down his muscled chest. She smiled as he groaned with pleasure when she circled the head of his cock with her finger. He was hard, and precum seeped from the tip.

Pam locked her gaze with Damon as she slowly lowered her head until her tongue could flick out and lick the tip. Damon grunted once, and she gave him another lick, but this time, she ran her tongue around the head of his cock in slow and deliberate circles.

"Fuck, baby." Damon moaned.

"You want to fuck, or do you want me to suck?" Pam purred and gave him another quick lick.

"Suck first then I'm going to…" Before he could finish, Pam wrapped her mouth around his thick cock.

Damon groaned as she slowly sucked him deeper inside her mouth. Pam moved with unhurried up and down motions, and every time she moved back to the head, she would swirl her tongue around it, then back down again.

"Yes, that feels so fucking good," Damon said through his teeth.

Pam continued to pleasure him for several minutes, relishing the sounds he made and the look on his face every time she'd slide her lips down his length. He thrust up and down in rhythm with her while she cupped his testicles and gently rolled them in her hand.

"Baby… oh. Fuck… I want to be inside you." Damon stumbled over his words.

Pam pulled her mouth from his shaft with a pop, making him grunt when she released him. He sat up and pulled her closer until her opening hovered over his dick.

"Shit, we don't have a condom," Damon grumbled.

"Do you really think I'd be silly enough to be alone with you and not have protection?" Pam moved off the bed and hurried out into the room where they'd dropped their clothes and her purse.

She pulled out the strip of condoms as she walked into the bedroom and held them up. Damon chuckled as she tore one off the strip and tossed the rest on the nightstand.

"Are you planning on being up all night?" He smirked as she handed him the foil package.

"If you can stay up all night, I'd be game." Pam grinned.

After he slipped the condom over his cock, Pam got more turned on by the second as she watched him slide it over his thick shaft. He grabbed her around the waist and hoisted her onto his lap. Pam lowered herself down over his length, both of them moaning when he was entirely inside her.

"You're so damn hot," Damon whispered as she started to ride him slowly.

Damon squeezed her ass as she rode his cock, and they kissed with such desperation their teeth knocked several times. It didn't slow their passion as Pam rose up and slammed down on him again. Damon groaned into her mouth, and the next second, Pam was on her back with Damon slamming into her over and over.

"God, yes. That's it. Harder," Pam begged as Damon lifted her legs and drove deep inside her.

Pam's body quivered as another orgasm built slowly and Damon picked up speed. Before she could do anything else, Damon pinched her clit between his thumb and finger. It brought her over, and she cried out his name as he slammed inside one more time and roared out her name.

His body twitched, and she could feel him jerk inside her. With every pulse of his cock, Damon would let out a little grunt.

Damon sighed and rolled them both, so they were on their side, but he was still inside her. Pam snuggled into his bare chest, wrapped in his arms as they caught their breath. After several minutes, Damon kissed the top of her head.

"I love you, Trixie," Damon whispered.

"I love you too." Pam pressed her lips against his chest.

"Baby?" Damon's voice cracked.

"Yeah?" Pam tipped her head back so she could look into his eyes.

"I'm sorry you got dragged into my family shit." Damon ran his hand up and down her arm.

"It's not your fault, but I believe things happen for a reason." Pam firmly believed what she said.

"Maybe you're right. Malcolm knows I wasn't the bastard he thought I was." Damon smiled, but she could tell it was forced.

"Let's not worry about it tonight. I just want to forget the world and be with you," Pam said honestly.

"You got it." Damon wrapped her in his arms.

Pam closed her eyes and imagined their world was only in that moment and in the tiny house. She wanted them to pretend that there wasn't someone out there trying to hurt Damon. Someone that seemed set on getting revenge for some unknown reason. No, all that needed to be set aside for one night. A night where she and Damon could be happy with being together.

Chapter 21

Damon hurried behind Malcolm through the hospital corridor. It had been three days since the truth came out, and Malcolm and the kids had not returned to the estate. However, they'd gone to the hospital every day to check on Tabitha.

No matter what she'd gone along with, they didn't blame her for any of it. Alastair could be compelling when he wanted something. As far as they were concerned, she was a woman who hadn't been able to have a baby of her own, and when given a chance to raise the children she ached for, she took it. Damon knew she loved them.

When Malcolm got a frantic call from her, saying she was being moved to a home, he and Damon got to the hospital as quickly as they could. Damon was the first to rush into her room and stopped when he saw the empty bed.

"Where is she?" Malcolm checked the bathroom, but she was gone.

Damon ran out to the nurses' station with Malcolm close on his tail. There wasn't anyone there, and they looked frantically up and down to find someone to give them some information.

As they were running to the next nurse' station, they ran into one of the medical staff who had worked with Tabitha. Damon grabbed the woman by the arm, and she gasped as she tried to yank her arm free.

"Let me go," she demanded.

"Look, I'm sorry, but where is Tabitha Blackwood?" Damon asked the woman as he released her.

"She's been moved home at your father's request." The nurse looked from Damon to Malcolm and back again.

"He was here?" Malcolm asked.

"No, he sent a couple of male nurses to pick her up. He emailed the correct paperwork, and since he's her next of kin, there wasn't an issue. We did warn against it because of her delicate health," the nurse explained.

"He didn't come himself?" Damon repeated.

"No, is something wrong?" the nurse asked.

"I hope not. We got a call from our... mother. She seemed frantic," Malcolm told her.

"I'm sorry, but she was sedated at the request of the doctor. By the time I came on shift she was gone." The nurse motioned for them to follow her.

She showed them a paper with the signature of the doctor as well as his printed name. Malcolm acknowledged it was Tabitha's family physician and quickly made the call since he was a family friend.

Several minutes later, Damon felt sick. Doctor Burton said he didn't know anything about moving Tabitha, and he had not signed the release form. Malcolm had put a call in to the housekeeper and asked her to check to see if Tabitha was at the estate. She wasn't.

"We've got to go to the estate and see if Alastair knows anything about this," Damon told Malcolm.

"As long as Trunk and Shadow are with us, I'm sure he will be safe from me," Malcolm groused.

"We've got to keep our heads; Mal. Mom needs us right now." Damon said as he nodded for Trunk and Shadow to follow them to the truck. "We've got to go to the estate."

Damon jumped into the vehicle and for a few seconds neither Trunk nor Shadow moved. Damon was about to call out to them when Shadow stuck his head in through the open window.

"You think that's a good idea?" Shadow asked.

"Don't know, but we have to see if she's there because if she's not, and the old man doesn't know about her being moved, then she's in danger." Damon sat back in the seat with his legs jumping up and down.

It seemed to take forever to get to the mansion. Luckily, Alastair hadn't changed the code on the main gate, and Malcolm was able to get it open. Damon didn't even know if Trunk had stopped the truck when he opened the door and leaped out.

He and Malcolm were up the stone steps, and before they could enter the house, the door opened. Gail blocked their entrance with several suitcases next to the door.

"Did you pay the housekeeper to call you when I was leaving?" She snarled at Malcolm.

"Where's Mom?" Malcolm sneered, so Damon quickly stepped between Gail and his brother.

"She's at the hospital and in case you forgot, she's not, Mom." Gail put air quotes around the word *mom*.

"Someone moved her out of the hospital. Where's Alastair?" Malcolm yelled.

"He's in the office. He wouldn't move her out of there. She won't survive without medical care." Gail's face paled, and for the first time, Damon saw concern on her face.

"What are you doing here?" Alastair shouted as he hurried into the foyer.

Damon was startled when he looked at the man he'd always thought was his father. Alastair had fading bruises on his cheek, and his eye still looked slightly swollen. It was black, and there was a healed cut across his nose and another on his forehead.

"You really did a number on him, Malcolm," Shadow whispered behind them.

"Did you have Mom moved from the hospital?" Damon asked.

"What? Of course not. She needs to be where she can get constant medical care." Alastair pulled his phone from his pocket.

"There's no use calling the hospital. They said you emailed them with documents to say she was being moved to a home. She's not at the hospital." Damon watched all the blood drain from Alastair's face.

He stumbled and grabbed the wall to steady himself as he stared at Damon. It was noticeable he had no idea where Tabitha had been taken, which meant whoever took her was probably the same person who took Pam.

"She won't survive without care," Alastair croaked.

"We have to find her." Gail sobbed.

"Like you give a fuck about her," Malcolm shouted.

"I don't care what you think of me, but I care about Tabitha. She was a huge help when the twins were born. As screwed up as she was with her addiction, she always made time for the kids," Gail shouted back.

"I'm going to call Sandy and see if she can get into the hospital's surveillance videos. Maybe these guys will show up somewhere, or we will see them take her out." Trunk stepped outside with his phone to his ear.

"I'm calling John O'Connor. He'll get people on this right away too," Shadow told them as he made a call.

"Damon, why would someone take her?" Alastair had moved to the bottom of the stairs and sat there.

"This has to have something to do with what happened to Pam. Did you get any more messages?" Damon asked.

"I haven't checked today. I've been… I've been getting some things in order." Alastair dropped his head.

"In other words, making sure we don't get a look at his father's will. Well I should probably say, our father." Malcolm snapped.

"Whatever you think of me, my son, I never did any of this to hurt either of you." Alastair lifted his head.

"I'm not your son," Malcolm retorted.

"Sandy's on it," Trunk said as he stepped into the house again.

"Give me your phone, Alastair." Damon held out his hand.

For a few seconds, he thought Alastair would refuse, but he reached into his pocket with a trembling hand and tapped in his passcode.

Alastair handed him the phone, and Damon opened the email app. He scrolled through the emails and wasn't surprised to see dozens related to business. Damon was about to give up after he'd opened a few that appeared different from the others.

Damon took one more chance and scrolled once more and saw an email with *Tabitha* in the subject line. Damon opened the email, and the first thing he saw was the link to a video. He tapped it and saw Tabitha sat in a bed looking ghostly white.

"Alastair, I don't know what they want, but they said if you want to see me before I die…" Tabitha choked on the words and then continued, "Help me, please."

The video ended, and Damon lifted his head. Alastair's face was pale, and his eyes were wide with fear. It was at that moment he realized no matter what the man did, Alastair loved Tabitha.

"What do we do?" Alastair said after he cleared his throat.

"We'll find her." Damon tried to sound confident, but the truth was he wasn't sure if they'd find her before it was too late.

A little over two hours later, Damon stood in the living room of the family estate, watching Alastair struggle to keep from falling apart. As angry as Damon was, it was hard not to empathize with

Alastair. The man looked like he hadn't slept in days and his clothes were disheveled.

Malcolm was able to keep his anger in check with Alastair but was unable to remain civil with Gail. She'd been brought to her father's house and warned not to leave town. Everyone in the family was still under suspicion.

Damon was on edge because Pam insisted on joining him at the estate. He hated to be away from her, but he felt uneasy with her in the mansion. Probably because most of his memories in the house were not good.

Damon scanned the family room. He was surprised to see so many pictures of all of them as kids. School pictures, and a couple of family photos taken at the lake house on their last family vacation. It was right before Tabitha sank into the pit of addiction. He picked up the picture and studied the people as if they were strangers. All smiling and holding fishing poles as they stood on the private dock behind the house.

"That's the last time I remember all of us going there together," Malcolm said from behind Damon.

"I remember you fell out of the boat." Damon smirked.

"You pushed me out of the boat, you mean." Malcolm chuckled.

"She lost the baby two weeks later." Alastair's voice was barely audible.

Damon focused on Tabitha. It was the first time he noticed the slight bump of her stomach and the way she laid her hand against it. He never noticed it before, and he couldn't remember ever being told she was having a baby.

"Why didn't you tell us she was pregnant?" Damon asked.

"She wanted to wait until she was over the seventh month. She was so scared of losing another baby." Alastair sighed and flopped against the back of the chair.

"We've got a video of two men putting her into the back of an ambulance." Sandy ran into the room with her tablet.

Damon stepped behind her as she showed everyone the screen. There, in full color, was Tabitha on a stretcher being loaded into the back of what looked like an ambulance. It sent a chill through his body, but when Pam gasped his senses really went on high alert.

"Pam, what's wrong?" Nick asked.

"That's two of the goons." Pam pointed to the tablet screen.

"Their faces are not clear. Are you sure?" Damon asked.

"Trust me, I'd never forget those guys." Pam shivered.

"What the fuck do they want?" Malcolm spun around and shouted at Alastair.

"Don't you think if I knew, I'd give them everything they wanted? Do you think I want her last days to be spent with strangers and scared?" Alastair jumped to his feet and flailed his arms around as his eyes filled with tears.

"Alastair, think. Is there any other buried secrets? Maybe something that would make someone believe the family owes them?" Damon grabbed Alastair by the shoulders and gave him a little shake.

"No, I've told you everything. Everything," he croaked.

Damon caught Alastair as he dropped to the floor on his knees and shook. The sobs coming from the man didn't sound as if it was coming from a human, but it was. Damon stepped back from Alastair as he stared in shock. When he glanced at Malcolm, Damon saw the same look of surprise.

"I'm going to search the plate number, but I've got a feeling it's stolen or a fake." Sandy didn't even seem to notice Alastair.

"I've called Ian. He's going to come and give something to Alastair to help keep him calm," Pam whispered.

"Thanks. I've never seen him like that. Ever." Damon shook his head.

"Neither have I." Malcolm whispered.

"You have to find her." Alastair rocked as he hugged a picture of his wife.

Damon was sure if Tabitha wasn't found quickly, Alastair might completely crack. If it was too late when they did find her, it meant they wouldn't get a chance to say their final goodbyes. Damon wasn't sure how any of them would deal with that. It would be hell for everyone.

Chapter 22

The O'Connor family had taken over the Blackwood mansion along with the police. Pam stood in the kitchen and watched Nanny Betty, her mom, and Aunt Kathleen. They'd shown up a couple of hours earlier along with John, James, and Aaron.

They did what they did best, put together a feast fit for a hoard of people. Nanny Betty was slicing up roast beef and placing it on a platter while Pam's mother mashed potatoes and Kathleen scooped up the peas and carrots.

"Pam, make sure Alastair eats. Dat man is gonna drop if he don't get a bit 'a grub in his gut." Nanny Betty handed Pam a plate.

Alastair sat behind his desk clinging to a photo of Tabitha smiling. Pam quietly approached him and placed the plate on the desk in front of him. He didn't look up, and he didn't put down the picture.

"They think I'm a cruel bastard, and maybe I was, but my heart broke when she lost the baby. I not only lost a daughter that day, but the Tabitha I loved died too. For years, I tried to bring her back, but she was broken by the last loss." Alastair's words were quiet in the large room.

"They'll find her, Alastair." Pam touched his hand. "Nan wanted me to bring you this. You should eat so you'll be strong when they bring her home."

For the first time, he lifted his head and she saw the tears. He didn't look like the stern father Damon had described to her. He seemed like a man scared of never seeing the woman he loved ever again. Her heart went out to him.

"You really think they'll find her?" He hugged the picture to his chest.

"I do." Pam tried to sound confident, but the truth was she'd seen how ill Tabitha was and without the proper care, she might die before they found her.

"Damon's a lucky man. I may have alienated my sons, I mean, my brothers, but I pray they both find happiness." He placed a hand on top of Pam's arm.

"Eat, Alastair. Then try to get some sleep, my mom brought you some blankets from upstairs and put them there on the couch." Pam gently removed the photo from his other hand and placed it on the desk next to him.

The sedative Ian gave Alastair helped calm him, and he wasn't as hysterical. Pam breathed a sigh of relief when he picked up the fork and put some food in his mouth. She left the office, relieved to see him eat.

"He doesn't seem like Alastair right now." Pam turned at the female voice.

Gail stood just outside the office door with her arms wrapped around herself. She looked sad and almost seemed scared to let Alastair see her. Pam didn't know she'd come back to the house and was a little worried seeing her might set Malcolm off on a rampage.

"I thought you went home?" Pam asked as she stepped out of the office.

"I did, but I needed to come back to pick up some things I left." Gail's eyes never moved from Alastair.

Pam could see the affection Gail had for Alastair. It was written all over her face, but what she didn't understand was how the woman could marry Malcolm when she didn't love him.

"I loved him and was so happy when he said I'd be moving into the mansion after he found out about my pregnancy. I thought I'd be with Alastair. I didn't know until I got here that he wanted me to marry Malcolm. I had to lie about who the father was." Gail turned and rested her back against the wall.

"I'm sorry you had to live like that." Pam didn't know what else to say to her.

"I had a great life until Damon showed up. Malcolm never questioned anything. He'd go to work, come home, and then spend time with the kids. He's a great father, but I was never attracted to him. I only wanted Alastair." Gail pushed off the wall.

Pam watched her as she glanced into the office once more before she turned and sauntered down the hall toward the front door. How could someone marry one man while she was in love with another? It had to be a sad life for all concerned.

"Are you okay?" Malcolm walked toward her.

"Yeah, I was just making sure your dad... I mean Alastair ate something," Pam told him.

"As angry as I am with him, I can't help but feel for him. I've never in my life seen him like this." Malcolm loosened his tie and shoved his hands into his pants' pockets.

"He really loves Tabitha." Pam didn't doubt it for a second.

"I guess I can sort of understand why he turned to other women. Mom...Tabitha wasn't exactly in her right mind over the last twenty years." Malcolm dropped his head back and looked up at the ceiling.

"I can't pretend to know what all of you are going through, but don't let the anger overpower you. Life is too short for holding on to hate or grudges." Pam touched Malcolm's arm and then made her way back to the kitchen.

Pam was exhausted and curled up on the massive armchair in the living room. She glanced around the room and out into the large foyer. It was a scene she'd seen several times over the years, and they'd all turned out good. She was hopeful this would too.

"Trixie, why don't I take you upstairs to get some sleep?" Damon crouched down next to her.

"You need to sleep too," Pam whispered as she cupped his face between her hands.

"I don't know if I could sleep. We finally got Alastair to lie down." Damon pulled her to her feet. "I'll bring you up to my old room; the housekeeper said she put clean linens on the bed."

"I don't want to sleep without you." Pam yawned as Damon escorted her up the marble stairs.

"I'll lie down with you." Damon wrapped his arm around her shoulders as he pushed a large oak door opened.

"This used to be your room?" Pam gasped as she slowly spun around in the oversized room.

"Yeah." Damon shrugged.

Damon seemed as if it was no big deal to be in a room her whole apartment could fit into. On the far wall was a king-size poster bed between two windows. There were two steps up to the bed and a huge chandelier hung down in the center of the room.

"This room is gorgeous." Pam walked to one of the windows and looked out at the stunning grounds on the back of the house.

"It's a room, Trixie. I'd sooner sleep in the little room at the bunkhouse or in your apartment." Damon walked up the steps and sat on the bed.

"I get it, but you can't deny this room is incredible." Pam climbed up on the bed and began to rub his shoulders.

"That feels amazing." Damon sighed.

"You need to sleep," Pam whispered in his ear as she continued to work the tight muscles of his neck and shoulders.

"You keep doing that, and I'll fall asleep sitting up." Damon moaned.

"Then, my plan is working." Pam pulled him back until he lay across the bed.

She curled up next to him and laid her head on his chest. As Damon pulled her into his arms, he pressed his lips against the top of her head, and she closed her eyes. The steady beat of his heart lulled her into a deep sleep within minutes.

Pam opened her eyes and glanced around the room. For a moment, she forgot where she was and started to panic. It was like being locked in that room again. She jumped off the bed and almost tumbled down the two steps.

She rushed to the door and grabbed the doorknob. Pam fumbled with it but couldn't get it to turn, and her heart started to race. Pam stepped back and tried to calm herself before she reached for the door again. She was about to try once more but before she could, the door opened, and she jumped back in surprise.

"Trixie, what's wrong?" Damon asked as she flew into his arms.

"I...I couldn't get...the door opened." Pam couldn't control the way her body trembled.

"It's okay, I've got you." Damon kissed the top of her head.

"I don't know why I was so freaked out." Pam forced a small chuckle.

"It's normal after an ordeal or a trauma," Damon whispered.

"Is this like some form of a post-traumatic stress thing?" Pam lifted her head and looked up at him.

"It could be. Maybe you should speak to someone. You probably haven't dealt with everything." Damon tucked a stray piece of her hair behind her ear.

Maybe he was right. She hadn't really talked to anyone about what happened after the first few days. She'd tried to bury it so nobody would worry about her, especially Damon.

"I'm okay. I guess I wasn't completely awake." Pam gave him a quick kiss on the lips and straightened up.

"Trixie, you were probably triggered when you woke up in a strange place. It happens." Damon held her head in his hands, so she had to look up at him.

"You make me sound like a gun about to go off." Pam rolled her eyes.

"In a way, you are. Just like I am. Sweetheart, sometimes the tiniest thing brings me back to Iraq or Afghanistan. It happens before I even realize it. I'm ashamed to admit it, but up until I came back to help find you, I was using booze to dull the memories." Damon kissed her forehead and turned his back to her. "I still want to drink, but I found an Alcoholics Anonymous group here, and I've been going once a week. You know, when I tell you I'm going for a drive."

Damon turned back around and gave her a guilty smile. She didn't mind that he didn't tell her, after all, it was anonymous. She hadn't realized Damon's drinking had gotten so bad, but she was happy to see he realized he had a problem before it got out of control.

"I always thought my tendency to use a drink to deal with things was inevitable because of my mother, but since Tabitha is not my biological mother, it didn't come from her." Damon grasped both of her hands. "I've struggled the last twenty-four hours, but I didn't slip."

"That's great." Pam sighed.

Her heart finally slowed, and she didn't feel as if she couldn't breathe. The panic had eased since the door was open. Pam never realized it until that moment, but she was no longer comfortable when she was in a room alone with the door closed, unless Damon was in the room with her.

"By the way, Nick and John are going back to Yugov's house. Malcolm and I are going with him. They're hoping if Kelsey is there and sees us, it might get a reaction out of her," Damon told her.

"Okay, I'll stay here with Alastair," Pam said as they walked out of the room.

"Actually, Trunk is bringing you and Alastair back to Keith's place. The kids asked to see him," Damon told her.

"Do you think they'll be okay? I mean, it's a shock for you and Malcolm. They must be so confused." Pam didn't know how she'd handle it if she was put in their situation.

"I think with the right help, and we promise to be honest from this point forward, the kids will be okay. We'll make sure the kids get everything they need." Damon kissed her cheek as they got to the bottom of the stairs.

Trunk seemed lost in his thoughts as he stood next to the door. Pam could see the man was stressed, and she had a feeling it had something to do with Abbie dating a very successful real estate developer. Although Billie, Lora, and the rest of the girls in the family gave her a hard time about giving up on Trunk.

Pam couldn't blame her, Abbie had been waiting for years for Trunk, and the only thing he did was frustrate her or piss her off.

Abbie told them she resigned herself that a relationship with Trunk wasn't going to happen and she was moving on.

Pam remembered vividly the first time Abbie went to her aunt's diner with her new man. Trunk looked like his head would explode, and every time the guy touched Abbie, Trunk would clench his teeth together so hard, Pam was surprised he had a tooth left in his head.

Still, he didn't do anything, but Sandy told everyone Trunk had his reasons. She wouldn't elaborate on the vague statement. As much of a busy-body as Sandy could be, she was loyal to the guys who worked for Keith. They were like her brothers, and she would never betray them.

"I'm ready whenever you are, Ben." Pam still couldn't call the guys by their nicknames.

"Just waiting for Mr. Blackwood to grab a few things." Trunk gave her a forced smile.

Pam nodded as she watched Damon hop into the vehicle with Nick and Malcolm. She prayed they would find the poor woman. Tabitha may not be Damon's mother, but he loved her. He would never forgive himself if she didn't make it before they got her home.

Chapter 23

Damon glanced at his brother as they drove down the highway. Malcolm looked ready to jump out of his own skin, but Damon could understand why. He might be about to come face to face with the woman he'd hurt so many years ago.

They might even be confronted with the very person who kidnapped his mother and Pam. It still didn't make sense to him why Pam was dragged into their family drama. Pam had never been in contact with his family and as far as he knew, they wouldn't have known about her.

"It's been more than a day since Mom was taken. I mean, Tabitha." Malcolm sighed. "I don't know if I'll ever get used to calling her anything but Mom."

"I know what you mean," Damon murmured.

"Look, I've kept quiet about your family drama, but to me, whether she was your biological mother or not, she still raised you. To be a parent, you don't always have to be blood-related." Nick glanced at Damon through the mirror. "I may not have fathered Molly, but she's as much my kid as Sam is. James is as much a father to Danny as he is to Mason, Colin, Hope, and Faith. Jess loves Ocean as if she was her very own daughter. Ian loves Evie exactly the way he loves Lily, Grace, and Alexander. You don't have to be blood-related to be a dad or a mom."

Nick was right, Damon saw it over and over with the O'Connor family. There was an old saying that said, *blood was thicker than water*, but it didn't apply to the O'Connors. To them, everyone was family.

Still, his situation was different. All the O'Connor kids knew about their true parentage. Damon and Malcolm didn't. They'd lived their lives not knowing they'd been adopted by their brother and his wife. That was the difference.

The house came into view, and Damon tensed. It appeared like any ordinary home found in the city. It was well-maintained with a large dogberry tree in the front yard.

The only peculiar thing was all the windows were closed, and the curtains were drawn. There wasn't an air conditioner anywhere he could see, so unless nobody was home, having the windows closed was a little unusual. After all, it was mid-August, and even in Newfoundland, it could get pretty hot.

"It looks the same as it did the other day," John said as Nick parked the car next to the sidewalk.

"All the cars are there." Nick nodded toward the van and SUV in the driveway.

Damon followed Nick and John as they made their way up the front door. Malcolm lagged behind, almost as if he was afraid to get too close. It was easy to see the apprehension in his expression.

Nick knocked on the door and stepped back while John casually walked to one of the windows and tried to look inside. It seemed like they'd been stood there forever when Nick knocked a second time.

"Maybe nobody is here." Malcolm turned around to glance behind him.

"You might be right," John replied.

"We can sit on the house for a bit and see if anyone comes home." Nick shrugged.

"Okay, we'll sit here for an hour or so and if nobody shows, then I'll get an unmarked to sit on the house." John stepped back and glanced up at the second level windows.

As they turned to head back to the car, the door of the house opened. A tall slim woman with short dark hair stepped into view. She was older, but Damon recognized her right away. If he didn't, Malcolm's reaction would have confirmed it was Kelsey.

"Can I help you?" Kelsey said.

"Ms. Oliver, I was here last week. Do you remember? I'm Inspector Nick O'Connor." Nick held up his badge. "This is our Chief, John O'Connor."

"Yes, I remember you," Kelsey answered.

"We were wondering if Mr. Yugov has returned?" John asked.

Kelsey was about to say something, but she stopped when she locked eyes with Malcolm. Her face turned pale, and she took several steps back and almost tripped over the step leading into the house.

Nick caught her before she fell, and she quickly pulled her arm from Nick's touch. She glanced back into the house several times and seemed ready to bolt.

"I... I'm...sorry. He's not here." Kelsey's hand trembled as she reached for the doorknob.

"Kelsey, are you okay?" Nick asked.

"No, I mean yes. I'm busy," she whispered.

"Kelsey, we're looking for a woman who was abducted. She's very ill, and she needs medical care." John sounded pissed.

"Kelsey, it's my mother." Malcolm made his way up to where Kelsey stood.

"Why would I care about you or your mother?" Her voice trembled, and she wouldn't meet Malcolm's eyes.

"Kels, why are you here?" Malcolm ducked his head to look into her eyes.

Damon wasn't sure Kelsey would answer Malcolm's question. She seemed scared, but Damon didn't know if it was Malcolm she was afraid of or something else.

As a sniper, Damon was trained to observe his surroundings. Someone wanted the house to look as if nobody was home. Damon could see inside through the slightly open door, and he knew someone else was there.

He could see slight movement through the crack of the door where it was hinged to the doorjamb. He crept up the step and stood behind Nick as Malcolm tried to get some information out of Kelsey.

"Someone is behind the door," Damon whispered close to Nick's ear as he reached for the handgun he'd brought.

Damon knew he probably should have let John know Keith had given him a revolver to take with him, but he figured they would've been against it. He had a license, but since he no longer required it for his job, he technically shouldn't carry a weapon. He just wasn't taking any chances.

"I fucking knew you had one," Nick whispered as he looked down at Damon's hand.

"Sorry, but I just didn't want to get caught unaware." Damon hadn't moved his eyes from where he saw the movement.

"You're sure you saw something?" Nick stepped closer to where Malcolm was still talking to Kelsey.

"My hearing may be fucked, but my eyes are perfect."
Damon saw John move closer to him and Nick in his peripheral
vision.

"What's wrong?" John asked.

While Nick explained things to John, Damon hid his weapon
behind him as he moved closer to the door, out of the vision of
whoever was hiding.

"Kelsey, are you sure there is nobody in the house?" John
asked as he stepped next to Malcolm.

She glanced back at the door and then back to John with her
head shaking frantically. Damon had taken position next to the
entrance where the person behind the door wouldn't see him.

"There's… no one here. Just me," Kelsey said as she
continued to glance back at the door.

"Could we go inside and have a look around?" John asked as
he motioned to Damon to move closer to the door.

"I can't. It's not my house. I'm just…I'm…" Kelsey
stumbled over her words, but she didn't get a chance to finish the
sentence.

John grabbed Kelsey and pulled her away from the entrance
as Nick yanked Malcolm out of the line of vision from the person
hiding. At the same time, Damon ducked into the house and
slammed the door back against the body behind the door.

Damon heard a grunt, and he moved behind the door, holding his weapon on the man pinned against the wall. The guy was dressed in jeans and a t-shirt that barely covered a huge beer belly. He'd dropped his bat and was about to reach for it.

"Unless you want a hole between your eyes, I'd leave the bat alone," Damon said between his teeth.

"I got this, Damon." John stepped next to him with his gun pointed at the suspect. "Get up slowly with your hands on your head and don't make any stupid moves or I'll give you a hole between your eyes."

Damon and John stepped back as the man struggled to get to his feet. He fell to his knee a couple of times, and Damon rolled his eyes because the guy didn't any balance. John seemed to get annoyed at the length of time it took the guy to stand and reached for the man's arm to help him to his feet.

"Who are you?" John asked as he frisked the man.

"I want a lawyer," the guy spat.

"Weird name, but okay." John smirked as he placed handcuffs on the man and read him his rights.

"Wait, why am I being arrested?" the guy shouted and struggled as John pushed him out through the door.

"For being a dick," Damon mumbled.

"For attempted assault." John shoved the guy.

"I didn't assault anyone," the guy screeched.

"Damon, didn't he attempt to hit you with a bat?" John asked.

"He sure did, Chief O'Connor." Damon grinned.

"He's a fucking liar." The guy tried to pull out of John's grasp.

"Settle down, or I'll add resisting arrest," John replied as he shoved the guy into the back of the police cruiser.

Damon glanced to the side of the step where Kelsey stood wide-eyed with Malcolm at her side. He had his arm wrapped around her shoulders, but her eyes were glued to the police cruiser where the guy glared out of the window at her.

"Kelsey, he can't hurt you now." Nick stepped in her line of vision.

"You don't understand," Kelsey whispered.

"Then you need to tell us." Damon walked next to his brother as several police officers stormed the house.

"You need a warrant." Kelsey looked up at John.

"Not if we suspect someone is in danger," Nick explained.

"Are you in danger, Kels?" Malcolm asked.

She turned and looked up at Damon's brother. It was as if for the first time she saw who was next to her. Tears filled her eyes, and she began to tremble as her legs buckled, but Malcolm caught her before she hit the ground.

"I didn't have a choice," she sobbed.

"Were you kept here against your will?" Nick asked.

Kelsey nodded.

"Do you know who that man is?" Damon crouched in front of Kelsey and Malcolm.

Kelsey shook her head.

"How long have you been here?" Malcolm's voice cracked.

"A while." She lifted her head.

"Why were you not reported missing?" Nick asked.

"Kelsey has no family left. Her mother passed away shortly before I left for the Army. Her mom was our housekeeper for years." Damon remembered it was one of the reasons Alastair didn't want Malcolm with her.

"You must have friends who missed you?" Nick asked her.

"They made me send a text to my two close friends and tell them I was leaving Newfoundland because…" She glanced up at Malcolm and then down at her hands.

"Because?" Malcolm covered her hands with his.

"I didn't want to have to see the woman you married every day." Kelsey didn't lift her head.

"How would you see Gail every day?" Damon asked.

"She goes to the restaurant where I work every day for lunch. She always sits at one of my tables, and it's just hard for me to see her. It was as if she was taunting me." Kelsey lifted her head and closed her eyes.

Damon and Malcolm locked eyes. Was Gail going there on purpose, or did she not know who Kelsey was? Knowing his sister-in-law, Damon knew it wasn't a coincidence.

"Did she say anything to you?" Damon needed more information.

"Not directly. She'd make snide comments to whoever she was having lunch with, which was usually another snooty woman. It never bothered me except when she'd mention her husband." Kelsey turned and looked up at Malcolm.

"Let's get you out of here." Malcolm helped her to her feet.

"I'll get a car to bring you to Keith's compound. I don't want any of you going back to the estate," John explained.

"Are you sure that's a good idea? Shouldn't you take her to the station?" Damon was a little confused.

After all, Kelsey could be part of the whole situation, and she could just be trying to cover her ass. Damon watched her as Malcolm helped her into the cruiser. If she was faking, she should be in Hollywood.

"Sir, the house is clear," a police officer told John as he walked out behind several other cops.

"Thanks. Let's get forensics in there now and see what we can find," John told the young man.

"Damon, maybe you should go back with Malcolm. Keith's going to be there, but let's be cautious." John waved to the officer who was about to leave with Malcolm and Kelsey.

"Tabitha's not in there?" Damon glanced back at the house.

"No, but we'll find her." John dropped his hand on Damon's shoulder as they walked to the cruiser.

The drive back to Hopedale was relatively quiet. The only noises were the calls coming over the police radio. The young officer was courteous and assured them he'd get them safely to Hopedale.

Kelsey sat in the back, practically clinging to the door. It was as if she wanted to sit as far away from Malcolm as she could possibly get. Malcolm sat stoically staring forward with his hands folded in his lap. Damon had no doubt that his brother's emotions hit him like a punch in the gut.

Trunk was outside the gate when they pulled up in front of the compound entrance. He nodded as he opened the gate and followed the car onto the property. Damon, Malcolm, and Kelsey were dropped off at Keith's house, then the cruiser left.

"Who lives here?" Kelsey stood at the bottom of the steps.

"The chief of police's brother." Damon motioned for her to go ahead of him.

She looked ready to bolt, and Damon looked to Malcolm for help. His brother stood at the top of the steps and nodded to Kelsey. She still didn't move, and when the door opened, she took a step back.

The minute Kelsey saw Pam, her face turned completely white. Damon saw a look of recognition on Pam's face as well, but he didn't understand how they would know each other.

"She's the maid." Pam walked toward them.

"The maid?" Damon asked.

"When I was held in the house. She was the woman who came in to clean the room." Pam pointed to Kelsey.

"I…I didn't have a choice." Kelsey looked directly at Pam.

"She was being held against her will too," Malcolm told Pam.

"You don't understand how horrible those men are." Kelsey shook her head. "The first week I was there, they didn't talk to me. I was just kept in a room. They brought me food and clothes, but they never talked."

"It's what they did with me too." Pam touched Kelsey's arm.

"After the third week, I wished they would stop talking to me. They made me do things I knew were wrong... I... they hurt me." Kelsey dropped her head.

"Maybe we should take her to the hospital." Malcolm was at Kelsey side in a second.

"I'll call Uncle Sean and Ian. One of them can come over and check her out." Pam pulled out her phone and walked toward the house.

An hour later, Sean O'Connor assured them Kelsey was physically healthy but did have several sets of healing bruises on her body. He'd also made it clear she was mentally and emotionally abused. He recommended they encourage her to talk to someone as soon as possible.

"Was she... assaulted? Sexually, I mean," Malcolm had asked.

"She says she wasn't, and it was the only thing she was adamant about," Sean told Malcolm.

"You believe her?" Damon asked.

"I do. She was honest with all the questions I asked. Her bruises are all in the arms and upper body. There is also a faint bruise on her left cheek. She had most of it covered with makeup." Sean held out his phone.

"Jesus," Damon growled.

"I'll send these pictures to John. Pam and Emily are in with her now. She asked if she could take a bath and they are giving her something to change into." Sean dropped his hand on Malcolm's shoulder.

"Thanks, Sean." Damon shook hands with Keith's father.

"That's what family is for." He winked at Damon and pulled a piece of paper out of his pocket. "I've written a prescription for a sedative, just in case she needs it to sleep. She said she didn't want to take anything right now. She may be safe at the moment, but she'll probably have some nightmares for a while."

"I know the feeling." Damon nodded.

"I'm sure you do. It's probably good you can relate to her." Sean shook Damon's hand, and Keith gave his father a quick hug.

"Thanks, Dad." Keith waved as his father left.

"I'm trying to figure out why they would take Kelsey." Malcolm lowered himself into one of the kitchen chairs.

"I don't know. Have you two been in contact over the years?" Keith asked.

"No. I wouldn't do that to her. I hurt her so badly when I agreed to marry Gail." Malcolm folded his hands on the table.

"Alastair, have you had contact with her?" Damon asked.

Alastair had been sat at the table since they arrived but hadn't spoken a word to anyone. He seemed to find his cup of coffee very interesting when Damon asked his question.

"No," Alastair answered.

"Why don't I believe you?" Damon sat across from the man who raised him.

"I never had contact with her." Alastair lifted his head and looked directly into Damon's eyes.

"But you had contact with someone." Damon narrowed his eyes because he wasn't asking.

Alastair's gaze went back to the cup he grasped between his hands. It wasn't like the man to be so quiet. Damon had a feeling Alastair knew about Kelsey's abduction.

"Out with it, old man," Damon snapped.

"I thought she was trying to worm her way into Malcolm's life again. I couldn't let her ruin everything." Alastair shook his head.

"Spill it," Malcolm growled.

"I got an email a few months ago," Alastair began.

"A few *months* ago?" Malcolm shot to his feet.

"It didn't seem legitimate." Alastair didn't lift his head.

"No, nothing with Kelsey ever seemed important to you. Including how I felt about her." Malcolm slammed his hands down on the table.

"She wasn't good for you." Alastair finally looked up at Malcolm.

"Why, because you needed me to cover your fucking ass? You needed someone to be there to cover up your fucking mess, and because Damon wouldn't bow down to you, I was guilted into picking up my brother's mess, but it wasn't Damon's mess. It was yours, and I had to marry the one woman who made my skin crawl." Malcolm's voice got louder.

"Mal, keep your voice down. The kids are upstairs," Damon reminded his brother.

Malcolm paced the kitchen, but he didn't seem to be any calmer than he was five minutes earlier. Damon was worried his brother was about to explode, and who could blame him.

"I didn't think it was true." Alastair shook his head.

"I want to see the email." Damon held out his hand.

Alastair placed his phone in Damon's hand after he unlocked it. Damon opened the email and scrolled down through the dozens of business emails but didn't see anything mentioning Kelsey.

"It's in the confidential folder," Alastair finally told him.

Damon clenched his teeth as he tried to control what little patience he had left. When he finally found the email, he opened it and began to read.

You will give me what I want, or I'll end her life, and I won't make it quick. The longer you take to answer, the more she will suffer.

Damon opened the picture attached to the email and shook his head. Kelsey sat in the same room and was secured to the chair in the same way Pam had been.

"If you had taken this fucking email seriously, none of this would have happened. Your wife would not be missing, and Kelsey and Pam would never have had to suffer." Malcolm grabbed Alastair by the shirt and pulled him up out of the chair.

"Dad?" A soft gasp stopped Malcolm's tirade cold.

"Melody, it's okay. Dad is just a little upset." Damon assured his niece.

"What did Grandfather do now? Or do we start calling him Dad and you Malcolm?" She leaned against the doorjamb and folded her arms over her chest.

"Melody, regardless of who fathered you, Malcolm is the man who raised you." Pam stepped into view.

"Is that true, Dad?" The young girl looked at Malcolm as if she was about to burst into tears.

"Melly, you're my little girl. No matter what your DNA says. I'll always be your dad." Malcolm had quickly calmed himself and pulled Melody into his arms.

"That means you still consider him your dad?" Melody nodded toward Alastair.

"It's a little more complicated, baby." Malcolm hugged her.

"I don't see how. He did wrong, but he still raised you." Marshall appeared behind his sister.

Damon watched his brother struggle with what his son had said. It was true. Alastair had raised them, and for a while, he was a good father. Everything got screwed when it wasn't possible for her to have any more children. It seemed like that one moment in their lives changed everything.

"You're right, Marsh. It's just going to take me a while to forgive him for what he did." Malcolm pulled his son into a hug.

"Should we hold a grudge against you too? I mean, technically, you did the same thing. Even if you did think, Uncle Damon was our dad," Marshall said.

"Why don't we just forget the grudges and try to move on from this?" Pam stepped into the kitchen. "Life is too short, and we still need to find Tabitha."

For several minutes, nobody said a word. Damon glanced from Malcolm to Alastair and then back to Pam. She was right.

Anger didn't help solve anything, and regardless of what happened, they were all still family.

"We are going to need some major family counseling." Melody sighed.

Damon couldn't hold it in. He started to laugh, and within minutes, Alastair, Marshall, Melody, Malcolm, and Pam were all laughing hysterically. Significant family counseling was an understatement.

Chapter 24

Pam was so glad to be back at her apartment and in her own bed. It took some major convincing, but Nick and John finally agreed to let her go back to her place. Since Damon would be with her, and Trunk would be bunking down in the back of her shop.

Pam had spent the day going through her sales and was surprised to see all her books were up to date. Elaine had told her she stole Sabrina away from Pam's aunt's pub and the girl had been heaven-sent.

Apparently, Sabrina had a background in retail management and was happy to help out until Pam could get back to the shop full-time. Looking at how organized everything was and how great the shop looked, Pam started to think Sabrina should stay permanently.

"I'm going to ask your Aunt Alice if she needs me back. I hope she does because I really need the work," Sabrina said as they closed for the day.

"Don't jump on that yet. I want you to stay here at least until things are back to normal," Pam said as they locked the main door.

"Really?" Sabrina looked so thrilled, Pam could only smile at the sweet woman.

"Really. You've been a great help to us. I may just keep you." Pam gave her a little side hug as she walked her out through the back where Sabrina's car was parked.

"I would be happy to stay." Sabrina made her way down the back steps but came to a halt when she saw the man getting out of a truck.

Hunter 'Crunch' Crawford was at the bottom of the steps and Pam couldn't deny the guy was deliciously yummy. He had just returned from a job on the mainland after being gone a few weeks. He worked for Keith, and he had a crush on Sabrina.

"Hey, Hunter." Pam waved at him as he waited for Sabrina to get in her car.

"Hey, I'm covering for Trunk tonight," Crunch told her as he watched Sabrina drive off.

"When are you going to bite the bullet and ask her out?" Pam smirked as he stepped inside the shop.

"I did. She said no." Crunch shrugged.

"Really?" Pam was surprised, especially since Hunter was not only a good-looking man, but he was also one of the sweetest guys she'd ever met.

"No, not really." He smirked. "She doesn't seem interested, and I'm not going to get my ego slammed by getting rejected."

"Like you've ever been turned down." Pam nudged him with her shoulder.

"You'd be surprised." Crunch closed the rear door and secured it.

"I think her mother is rubbing off on her." Damon leaned against the counter in the central part of the shop.

"My mother is a wonderful woman." Pam smiled.

It had been two days since Kelsey had been rescued. Pam had several conversations with her and learned she'd been kept in the same house for the first two weeks of her abduction. She'd been impressed when Pam told her how she escaped.

Kelsey was intelligent but had never been able to do anything past high school. It was quite evident she never got over Malcolm, and according to her, she hadn't dated anyone seriously since him.

Still, there was something off with her. Pam couldn't put her finger on it, and since Kelsey was still pretty fragile, Pam couldn't push anything. Malcolm, however, had been hovering over the woman, but Kelsey tried to keep her distance.

"No word on Tabitha yet?" Crunch asked.

"No, Alastair is beside himself. If we don't find her soon, I'm afraid he may not get over this." Damon sighed.

"Nick said they didn't find anything at the house where I was held." Pam wrapped her arms around Damon and snuggled under his arm.

"They also can't find Vladimir Yugov. It's weird how he just vanished." Damon squeezed her close.

"Have they tried to find your mother?" Crunch asked.

"Tabitha has vanished," Damon replied.

"No, I mean your biological mother. Trunk told me all about it." Crunch plopped down on the small couch Pam had put there for the security who stayed overnight.

"I'm not sure Alastair knows where she is." Damon shrugged.

"If he doesn't, Sandy can find her." Crunch winked as he put the phone to his ear.

"Do you think she could be involved?" Pam whispered as Crunch spoke to Sandy.

"I don't know. Alastair said she was unstable." Damon shook his head.

"Why don't we go upstairs to see if we can distract ourselves? I heard there's a *Three's Company* marathon on tonight." Pam cupped his cheek.

"I think it sounds like a great plan." Damon covered her hand with his and kissed her palm.

"Sandy said she's already on it. John asked her to look into Greta, but the last known address for her is the house where Kelsey was found," Crunch told them.

"So where are Greta and her brother?" Damon murmured.

"Go up and watch your marathon. If there's anyone who can find them, Sandy will." Crunch propped his feet up on the small table in front of the couch as he pulled out his iPad.

Damon made a couple of sandwiches, and Pam poured them both a glass of milk. Neither of them liked pop, and it was too late for coffee or tea. As they settled in front of the television, Pam tried to keep her attention on the show. She couldn't stop thinking about Tabitha and how scared she must be.

As strong as Pam tried to be when she was abducted, she was scared most of the time. In Tabitha's condition, she had to be terrified. That was if she was still alive. You didn't have to be a doctor to know she was on borrowed time.

The last couple of days, Damon had been doing his best to keep his emotions in check, but Pam knew he wasn't sleeping well. He'd be up several times during the night, and some of it was probably because of his time overseas, but he'd called out to Tabitha several times in his sleep.

He'd also been going to several AA meetings a week, and she knew it had to be difficult for him. Damon used to drink in excess sometimes, but Pam never thought much of it. She'd mentioned it to him once, and he'd only shrugged it off.

"Why don't they make shows like this anymore?" Damon chuckled.

"I don't know, but I'm glad for reruns." Pam snuggled into Damon's side.

Pam woke suddenly, but she wasn't sure what had woken her. Damon was sleeping peacefully next to her. She glanced around the dark living room as she sat up. She wasn't surprised they'd fallen asleep on the couch, but she was confused when she woke up to complete darkness.

She stood up and almost tripped over where she and Damon took off their shoes. She made her way to the door leading to her shop. It was possible Crunch came up and saw them asleep.

When she got down to the bottom of the staircase, she didn't see Crunch on the couch. The emergency lights were on, and she stumbled into the shop looking for Crunch. She found him scanning the street through the large picture window.

"Hunter?" Pam wrapped her arms around herself.

"Everything okay?" Crunch turned around.

"Yeah, I just woke up and everything was dark." Pam walked to the window.

"I think the thunderstorm knocked out the power." Crunch motioned to the dark street.

"I didn't even hear the thunder. It looks like the rain is really coming down out there." Pam hopped back from the window when a bright light lit up the shop.

"Thunder is about ten seconds away," Crunch told her.

Before she could speak, the loud rumble of thunder sounded overhead. She looked at Crunch, and he smirked.

"Been going on now for about twenty minutes. It's probably what woke you." Crunch sauntered back to the couch. "I should have downloaded the movie I was watching."

"There are some movies upstairs." Pam shrugged.

"Just how would I play them?" Crunch laughed.

"Oh, right. Well, I guess I'm going to head to bed." Pam started to make her way up the stairs.

When she got to the top, the door to the apartment opened, and Damon stood there with a look of complete panic on his face. When he saw her, he blew out a breath of air and pulled her into his arms.

"Jesus, I woke up, and you were gone," Damon choked out as he tucked his face into the crook of her neck.

"I'm fine. I think the thunder woke me and I went down to see if Hunter turned off the television. The power is out." Pam tried to pull back from his embrace, but he held tightly.

"It sounded like a bomb. I woke up and…" Damon trembled as he spoke.

"It was thunder, Damon. I'm okay." Pam hugged him tightly.

"You're okay." Damon pulled back and looked down at her. "We're okay."

"Let's go to bed." Pam closed the door, and they made their way to the bedroom.

"We aren't going to find her. At least not before it's too late," Damon said as they stepped into the room.

"Don't think like that." Pam straddled his legs and wrapped her arms around him.

"You don't understand. She was in my dream, and she told me she was finally happy. She was with her babies." Damon sobbed into Pam's chest.

"It was a dream, baby. You know as well as I do our fears come out in our dreams," Pam whispered.

How was she supposed to convince Damon things would be okay if she couldn't get herself to believe it? They were quite the pair. Damon with his PTSD and family drama, and Pam with her own secrets that she'd kept from everyone and now her nightmares on top of it.

"My past comes out in nightmares. Things I did. Things I should have done." Damon's body was tense, but he clung to her as he spoke. "I killed people, Trixie. They weren't good people, but I still took lives. It was my job."

"I know, baby." Pam held him and let him get out his thoughts.

"The day of that explosion, I lost friends. My brothers. Men I was supposed to keep safe." Damon trembled, and Pam felt the front of her shirt dampen from his tears.

"It wasn't your fault," was all she could think to say to him.

"Their eyes haunt me. Adrian and I were the only ones to walk away with minor injuries. Pop was burned over a third of his body and spent months recovering. The rest didn't make it." Damon's voice had become a whisper.

"Pop?" Pam leaned back so she could look at him.

"Alvin Popov, we called him Pop. He was older than most of us, but he was a damn good guy. I couldn't face him after. I talked to him a few times, but I could never..." Damon stopped.

"It's okay. I'm sure he understands." Pam kissed the side of his face.

"I haven't talked to him in years. Adrian hasn't either. I don't even know if he's still in Ontario or if he went back home to the west coast," Damon continued.

"We can get Sandy to find him if you really want. Let's try and get some sleep." Pam pressed her lips to his temple and waited for him to release his embrace.

After several minutes, he finally blew out a breath, and his arms dropped to his sides. He wiped his hands down over his face as Pam stood up.

"You sure you want to deal with all this crap with me?" Damon looked up at her as he took her hands in his.

"As long as you can deal with my crap too." Pam smiled.

"I love you, Trixie." Damon stood up and cupped her face in his hands.

"I love you too," Pam whispered.

Damon lowered his head and gently brushed his lips across hers. She slipped her arms around his waist as she deepened the kiss. He lowered them to the bed and for a little while they got lost in each other, blocking out all the bad memories and terrible dreams.

Pam spent the next day lost in her memories of what Damon said the night before. It was hard for her to think about what could have happened to him over there. If things had gone another way, she never would have met him, and the thought gave her a knot in the pit of her stomach.

Damon went with Nick to check out another address Sandy had found connected to Yugov family. Pam killed time waiting to hear from them, sketching behind the counter.

"You're so talented," Sabrina said from behind her.

"Thanks, I've always loved to draw, but I found drawing sexy undies to be my greatest talent." Pam winked.

"As long as you love what you do." Sabrina smiled as she started to unbox the shipment which arrived that morning.

Pam's phone vibrated in her pocket, and she smiled when she saw her cousin's number. She made her way to the back of the shop. Maybe leaving Sabrina and Crunch alone in the front would get them talking.

"Jesus, I'm starting to sound like Mom," Pam mumbled to herself as she tapped the screen. "Hi, Isabelle."

"I'm so sorry I haven't had a chance to drop by." Isabelle sounded as if she was about to cry.

"Pregnancy hormones getting to you, cuz." Pam chuckled.

"Maybe but I've just been crazy busy trying to get everything in place for when the baby comes in November. Roman keeps telling me to slow down, but I've got to make sure my restaurant isn't going to fall apart." Isabelle inhaled loudly, and Pam laughed.

"I hope this little boy isn't a rambler like you," Pam teased.

"Don't make me say bad words, Pam," Isabelle grumbled.

"I've been busy too, Isabelle. Plus, I'd rather you take care of you than get in the middle of whatever I'm in the middle of." Pam eased down on the bottom step.

"Would you like a distraction tonight?" Isabelle asked.

"What kind of distraction?" Pam laughed.

Knowing her family, it would include either a trip to Roman's club, *The Rock*, or the family pub, *Jack's Place*. She knew it would never happen because the person who took her was still out there.

"I know I can't get my wedding dress yet because we're waiting until the baby is born, but I'd like to get some ideas on dresses and bridesmaid dresses," Isabelle explained.

"Good idea," Pam admitted.

"Are you busy tonight?" Isabelle asked.

"No, but wait until after seven. It's better after we close to do that stuff," Pam told her.

"Sounds perfect." Isabelle sounded so excited.

"Who'll be coming with you?" Pam asked.

"Do you really have to ask?" Isabelle laughed.

"Let me guess, Jess, Kristy and Aunt Alice for sure." Pam knew Isabelle's sisters and mother would never miss picking out dresses.

"Yep, and Nan, Aunt Kathleen, your mom, Stephanie, Marina, Emily, Lora, Bethany, Billie and of course your partner Elaine." Isabelle listed off most of the women in her family.

"What? Sandy is going to miss it?" Pam laughed.

"Nope, Sandy's already here." Sandy called out from the front door.

"Yeah, she said she'd be over there most of the day." Isabelle laughed.

"What about the kids?" Pam asked.

"I think Lily and Evie are coming with Jess, but the younger ones will be a little later," Isabelle explained.

"Sounds like a party." Pam chuckled.

"Yeah, Kristy's bringing the wine." Isabelle laughed.

They chatted for a few more minutes, and then Pam ended the call. Sandy had set up her computer in the back and was doing some research on Damon's family.

"Nick called me. There wasn't anyone at the house. I keep wondering how many damn houses are connected with that family." Sandy spoke as she tapped the keys on her laptop.

"Damon's family is wealthy; it's possible she got a settlement when they adopted Damon and Malcolm." Pam shrugged.

"Yeah, I thought about that, but Alastair said she didn't get a dime, but her family was well off," Sandy explained.

"What a mess." Pam shook her head.

"As Bull would say, it's a fucked-up can of worms," Sandy said, referring to Kristy's husband.

Pam nodded in agreement as she made her way back to the front of the shop. She sighed when she saw Crunch still leaned against the wall on the other side of the room, and Sabrina was still unpacking boxes. Maybe she should get her mother to talk to them, but then again perhaps they were not a match in her mom's eyes.

The store was unusually busy all day, and Pam was relieved when she locked the door at six. Elaine was sorting dresses to show Isabelle, and Sandy was complaining about having to wear another frock.

"Pam, when you get married, you should demand everyone wear jeans." Sandy grunted as she tugged the rack of dresses out to the front of the shop.

"Sorry, Sandy. Pam is a girly girl when it comes to dressy stuff." Kristy laughed as Elaine let her in.

"Where's Jess? She'll go along with me." Sandy tossed her hands up in the air.

"Didn't Jess wear a beautiful Justin Alexander A-line ball gown?" Elaine asked.

"Only because I was bullied into it." Jess stepped into the shop.

"Ha, see. Come here, my best friend." Sandy wrapped her arm around Jess' shoulders. "We'll stick together."

While the girls tried on dozens of bridesmaid's dresses, Isabelle skimmed through the rack of wedding dresses. Damon and Crunch sat next to the main door, watching them in amusement as each dress was modeled on the platform.

"It's going to be a January wedding. Pale colors aren't the way to go." Elaine placed a book of fabrics in various colors next to Isabelle.

"I'm thinking hunter green or emerald. Most of you are redheads, and the color will look amazing on all of you. Steph and Marina are blonde, but the color is still flattering to them," Elaine explained.

Isabelle just looked confused and overwhelmed. Being almost seven months pregnant didn't help her make decisions. Emily must have seen Isabelle's discomfort and wrapped her arm around Isabelle's shoulders.

"I think the hunter green is the way to go." Emily smiled.

"I agree," Pam interjected.

"Hunter green it is." Isabelle smiled.

"I've got another idea," Emily said. "You and Pam are the same build. Maybe Pam can try on some of the styles you picked out, and you can narrow down what you would like?" Emily glanced at Pam.

"You wouldn't mind?" Isabelle asked.

"Only for you, cuz." Pam hugged Isabelle, then followed Elaine into the dressing area.

"Damon, you'll get an idea of what she'll look like coming up the middle of the church," Sandy shouted loud enough Pam could hear her in the dressing room.

"I'll pay attention," Damon yelled.

"Good, lad. Ya knows wat ta say." Nanny Betty laughed.

"It's not like it's a big secret. They'll be there soon." Her mother stood next to the entrance of the dressing room

"After Pam, ya need ta get workin' on the lads dat work fer Keithy," Nanny Betty told Pam's mother.

"Nan, you stop putting idea's in Cora's head," Crunch shouted.

Pam shivered at the thought of one day being Damon's wife. It was a pleasure she'd never thought would even be possible, but with the way things had been going, she could see it in her future.

Pam slipped into the sixth dress, and Elaine adjusted it to fit. Pam lifted the bottom of the off-the-shoulder ball gown. It was ivory with lace around the bodice and satin from the waist to the floor. Pam always thought it would be the type of dress she would choose.

"It's so beautiful." Kathleen gasped.

"I think so too." Marina nodded.

"It is, but it's not Isabelle." Emily tilted her head back and forth as if checking it out from a different angle would help her decided.

"I like it, but Emily is right, it's more Pam than Isabelle." Kristy sat back and sipped her wine.

"What's that?" Lora pointed at Pam.

"What?" Pam glanced down at the dress.

"What's the red dot on the chest?" Stephanie sat forward.

Pam glanced down to see a red light flicker around the front of the dress she wore. She lifted her head and as if in slow-motion, Damon flew through the air toward her as he and Crunch shouted.

"Get down on the ground. Now," Damon yelled as he slammed against Pam and brought her hard to the floor.

In what seemed less than a second, the picture window shattered, and the distant sound of what sounded like fireworks echoed outside.

"Stay low and get to the back of the store." Crunch crouched behind the display case at the front of the store.

"Can you see anyone?" Sandy yelled as she pulled out her service revolver and knelt behind one of the chairs.

"No, get the women in the back," Crunch told her.

Pam gasped as she tried to catch her breath. When Damon knocked her to the ground, he'd knocked the wind out of her, and it was tough to get a breath with him still on top of her.

"Stay down, Trixie," Damon ordered her.

"I…can't…breathe." Pam grunted out the words.

"Sit up and breathe slowly," Kristy told her as Damon pulled her into the back.

"Everyone stay here," Damon ordered as she crawled out front.

Pam managed to start breathing normally with the help of Kristy. She was never so thankful to have a nurse in the family. Pam glanced around to see all the women in her family crouched down on the floor.

Pam's stomach churned to see her family huddled together. Pam didn't need anyone to tell her someone just shot at them. What if her grandmother, mother, or one of her aunts got hit? If any of her cousins' wives were hurt or worse, they'd never get over it. James already lost one wife and he barely survived.

"Well, that's the second time I've been behind a window shattered by bullets," Stephanie grumbled.

"Is everyone okay?" Pam asked.

"I'll let you know when my heart slows down." Bethany blew out a breath.

Several minutes later, Damon and Crunch appeared in the doorway. They made sure nobody had been hit and brought the chairs from the front of the store back for the older ladies.

"I called Nick. He's on the way, but I imagine the rest of the family will be here too." Crunch barely had the words out of his mouth when someone pounded on the rear door.

"Alice?" Uncle Kurt's panicked voice came from outside.

Sandy opened the door, and Kurt, Sean, and Pam's father rushed into the shop. They immediately went to the women to confirm they were all okay.

"I give it five seconds and the rest…" Crunch finished his statement when all her cousins filed in through the back door.

"Are all of you okay?" Nick asked as Bull, Roman, and Wade walked in behind him.

"Nobody was hit," Sandy assured them as Ian wrapped her in his arms.

"No, but if whoever did it hadn't use a laser sight, Pam would have been hit right in the chest," Damon's voice cracked.

"I've got guys out looking around the area." John kissed the top of Stephanie's head.

"Can we just have one month go by where someone doesn't want to kill one of us?" Marina sighed and tucked herself under James' arm.

"Someone's watchin' over us." Nanny Betty grasped the locket she wore around her neck.

The necklace was given to her grandmother by her father when she was a young girl. She kept pictures of her parents, brothers, and Pam's grandfather in it.

"I think you may be right." Tom sat next to Nanny Betty.

"I'm going to have someone talk to everyone before you all leave. I'll have a couple of the guys come in and start so we can get you all home." John motioned for three officers to come in.

An hour later, Keith had someone come and board up the shattered picture window. The police collected several bullets that were lodged in the walls, and one by one everyone began to leave.

"I think you should come stay at home." Her father wrapped her up in his arms.

"Dad, Damon is here, and I think Crunch is staying." Pam closed her eyes as she allowed her father's hug to make her feel safe like it did when she was a little girl.

"Plus, it would be safer for her to go back to Keith's compound." James walked next to them.

"I want to stay in my apartment," Pam complained.

"Cuz, you were shot at." James smoothed his hand over the top of her head.

"But I didn't get shot. I'm not letting whoever this is force me out of my home," Pam snapped.

"I'll keep her safe." Damon stepped behind her.

"You better. My niece is in trouble because of something to do with your family, Damon." Kurt said.

"You think I don't know that? Do you think I want her to stay here? She's as stubborn as the rest of you. I've had my head slammed against a wall, and I don't feel like doing it daily by arguing with Pam." Damon smirked.

"You may just fit in this family better than I thought." Kurt smiled.

Pam sat in the middle of her bed while Damon went around the apartment and made sure all the windows were locked and blinds closed. It was the third time he'd done it since they got upstairs.

"Damon, can we go to sleep now?" Pam huffed when he returned to the room.

"I'm sorry. I just can't relax. When I saw the laser set in the middle of your chest…my heart stopped." Damon crawled on the bed and knelt in front of her.

"I'm safe." Pam ran her hands down the sides of his face.

"I know." Damon tucked her hair behind her ears and pressed his lips against her forehead.

"You protected me," Pam whispered.

"You saved me." Damon brushed his lips across hers.

Pam sighed against his lips as he lowered her down to the bed. His hand ran from her hip up to her waist and across her stomach. The heat of his palm against her skin set her on fire as he slipped under the waistband of her panties and slipped his finger between her folds.

Pam groaned as his finger moved in small slow circles around her swollen clit. She felt his erection grow against her hip, and he moaned as he humped against her. He groaned as she reached between them and cupped his hard cock.

"Fuck," Damon growled and slipped his finger inside her.

"Yes," Pam gasped.

Damon thrust his cock forward, and Pam wrapped her hand around it. She slowly stroked him as he plunged his tongue into her mouth and swirled it against hers. Pam pushed up against his hand as he slowly fucked her with his fingers and stimulated her clitoris with the palm of his hand.

Damon kissed across her jaw and moved down the side of her neck as he pumped his hand in and out. Pam was so close to falling over the edge and felt the familiar tingle slam through her body.

"Oh...oh...Damon." Pam shuddered as he continued to stimulate her until another orgasm hit her like a freight train.

"That's it, Trixie. Come in my hand." He growled into her neck.

Pam squeezed his cock gently, and he groaned in pleasure. He lifted his hips enough to slip out of his boxers and yanked her panties down her legs. When he knelt between her legs, she licked her lips.

He was gorgeously naked. His thick cock pointed up and jerked as she ran her finger around the purple head. Before Pam could wrap her hand around it, Damon flipped her over on her stomach and yanked her hips up.

"I need to get deep inside you." Damon whispered in her ear then he bent her over.

"Yes." Pam groaned as he pressed his cock against her backside.

"Condom," Damon grunted as Pam swiveled her hips against his erection.

She fumbled in the night table drawer and handed him the gold foil package. A few seconds later, she felt the head of his dick at her opening. He thrust slowly as he held her hips and pushed deep inside her.

"Holy fucking hell." Damon roared as he filled her completely.

"Fuck me, baby," Pam begged.

"Hold on." Damon grunted as he pulled out and slammed into her.

Once, twice, and then she lost count. When his hand slipped around her, she drew in a surprised breath when she felt something vibrate against her clit.

"What…what is that?" Pam gasped in pleasure.

"I found it in your drawer. You were holding out on me." Damon grunted and slammed into her again as he kept the small finger vibrator against her throbbing nub.

"God, don't…baby, don't stop." Pam panted as she gripped the headboard and allowed him to bring her to the height of ecstasy.

"I couldn't stop now if my life depended on it," Damon growled through his teeth.

"Damon, I'm…" Pam couldn't finish the words as her body convulsed in pleasure.

She squeezed her eyes closed, and she could swear she saw stars behind her eyelids. She was so lost in her intense orgasm she almost didn't hear Damon roar out as he pushed hard inside her and shuddered.

"Baby, fuck." Damon gasped for air as he gripped tight to her hips and she felt him jerk inside her.

Pam wasn't sure if she had the energy to move and fell flat on her stomach with Damon on top of her. His hot breath blew against her neck, but the buzzing against her hip forced her to move.

"Damon, you didn't turn off Nubby." Pam giggled.

"I'm sorry, Nubby?" Damon snorted.

"It's what I call it." Pam turned her head so she could see his face.

"You named it?" Damon chuckled.

"Yes, I did. Would you rather I call your dick that?" Pam raised an eyebrow.

"My junk is a little bigger than a nubby." Damon rolled over onto his back, and Pam turned onto her side.

"Maybe a little." Pam held up her thumb and index finger about a hair apart.

"It makes you scream." Damon rolled over and pinned her to the bed.

"I like it when you make me scream." Pam grinned

"Give me ten minutes, and I'll do it again." Damon wiggled his eyebrows up and down.

"Hmm, you think you got it in you, soldier?" Pam smirked

"My little soldier can come to attention pretty quick." Damon dropped his head and sucked her nipple into his mouth, making her gasp.

"I guess I better pull out the strip of condoms then." Pam arched her back as he licked and sucked both her nipples into hard peaks.

"Let me toss this one first." Damon hopped up and disappeared into the bathroom.

Pam threw her hands up over her head and smiled. It might have been a scary start to the evening, but the rest of the night was going to be hot.

Chapter 25

Damon woke to the shrill chirp of his cell phone. He grabbed it off the night table and tried to focus on the screen. Malcolm's number appeared on the display, and he tapped it.

"Hello." Damon yawned.

"She's back at the hospital." Malcolm practically shouted.

"Who? Mom? Tabitha?" Damon didn't know if he'd ever get used to calling her by her name.

"Yes, they found her this morning in a chair at the entrance of the emergency room," Malcolm explained.

Damon was out of the bed and half-dressed before he realized Pam was looking at him like he was crazy. Malcolm told him he was on the way, and he'd meet him there.

"What's wrong?" Pam asked.

"Tabitha was dropped off at the hospital." Damon yanked a t-shirt over his head.

Pam jumped out of bed and threw on clothes. He wasn't sure if she should go, but it had been two days since the shooting, and he didn't have time to argue with her about staying out of sight.

In less than ten minutes, they were in one of Keith's bulletproof SUVs. Trunk and Crash sat in the front seat of the vehicle, and Damon was in the back with Pam. Trunk seemed even more solemn than he'd been weeks earlier.

Damon's leg shook as he grasped Pam's hand and wondered why the road to St. John's seemed to have gotten longer. He was about ready to jump out and run the rest of the way when Trunk pulled up in front of the ER.

"I'll go with them." Crash hopped out and followed Damon and Pam.

Damon ran into the ER department, practically dragging Pam behind him. He stepped up to the reception and tapped at the window to get the woman behind the barrier to notice him.

"Just a minute, sir," the woman snapped.

"I don't know if I have a minute. I'm here to see Tabitha Blackwood, and I'm not going to wait," Damon returned.

"Was she brought in an ambulance?" The woman looked at him as she chewed her gum.

"No, she was left at the entrance." Damon clenched his teeth together.

"So you dropped her off?" The woman tapped the computer keys with her way-too-long nails.

"Look, my…mother has been missing for over a week. She was left here, and she's in liver failure. Do you think you could pull your head out of your ass long enough to speak to someone who has half a brain?" Damon snapped.

The woman stared at him, and her mouth dropped open as if she'd never been told off before. Pam pulled Damon back and stepped in front of him.

"I'm sorry for his abrupt demeanor, but he is concerned for his mother. We just got a call from his brother to let him know she was here. Could you check, please?" Pam spoke with such a polite tone Damon had to roll his eyes.

"Sure," the woman said as she stood up and disappeared through the door behind her.

"Damon," Malcolm called from the door leading to the patients.

Damon, Pam, and Crash hurried through the door, ignoring the woman behind the reception desk as she yelled to them. He didn't really hear what she said, and he didn't care.

"Is she okay?" Damon asked Malcolm.

"She was asleep when we got here. Alastair hasn't moved from her side," Malcolm told them.

"They aren't going to let us all in the room together," Pam told Damon.

"There aren't enough people here to stop me and you from going into her room," Damon grumbled as they stepped into the room behind Malcolm.

"It's okay. I told the nurses we wanted a room where we could all be in here," Malcolm explained. "They weren't happy about it, but when Doctor Burton showed up, they tripped over themselves."

Damon walked next to the bed and looked down at Tabitha. She seemed the same as she did the last time he saw her. She was pale, thin, and her skin had a slight yellow hue.

"She hasn't woken up yet." Alastair held her hand between his with his lips pressed against her fingers.

"What did the doctor say?" Damon asked.

"He did blood work, and she's hooked up to all the medications she was on before she was taken. The only issue is, she hasn't woken up." Malcolm stood at the foot of the bed.

"What did they do with her?" Alastair whispered as he gazed at his wife.

"She's back, and we'll go from there." Damon smoothed her hair back from her face.

The room was quiet except for the rhythmic beep of the monitors. Alastair had his head rested on the bed next to Tabitha's hand. They tried to get him to go back to Hopedale to rest, but he wouldn't budge. Pam did manage to get him to eat a sandwich and an apple.

Malcolm sat in the corner, his head back against the wall and eyes closed. Damon knew he wasn't asleep because anytime a nurse entered the room or someone moved, Malcolm would open his eyes. Pam sat in the armchair, reading on her phone because she also wouldn't leave.

The doctor sent his intern to tell them all Tabitha's tests came back and it didn't look promising. She only had a matter of days, possibly hours before she would slip away. The doctor was convinced Tabitha would never regain consciousness.

Since Tabitha signed a paper months earlier to say she did not want to be resuscitated, they weren't permitted to use CPR if her heart stopped. Alastair almost lost it when the doctor reminded him of the document.

"She just looks like she's asleep." Damon glanced toward Malcolm.

"Yeah," Damon agreed.

"Do you remember how she used to tell us we were her special boys because we were chosen for her and Alastair?" Malcolm whispered.

"Yeah, she would say she was so lucky God brought us to her," Damon remembered.

"It makes me wonder if she was trying to tell us back then we were adopted." Malcolm leaned forward and rested his elbows on his knees.

"Maybe." Damon stretched his arms over his head.

Another hour passed, and Damon was now the only one not asleep. Crash and Trunk had been relieved by Shadow and Crunch, and they stood outside the darkened room.

They'd been there all day, and it was almost ten in the evening. A nurse brought in another recliner, and Alastair finally moved into it and fell asleep again.

Malcolm was sprawled out on two of the chairs with his head propped against the wall, and Pam was curled up in the armchair. Damon yawned and closed his eyes for a moment to ease the burning. His arm was rested on the bed next to Tabitha, and he started to drift off.

He jumped when someone brushed against his hand. Damon woke with a start to see Tabitha's eyes were open. Her hand moved, and she covered Damon's hand with her own.

"They…" She took a deep intake of air and swallowed.

"Don't talk," Damon whispered.

Tabitha shook her head as she gripped Damon's fingers. She licked her lips and swallowed again as she glanced around the room. She used her other hand to tap her lips, and Damon hopped up to grab her a moisture swab the nurse used earlier to moisten her lips.

"I can't give you anything to drink right now, but this will take the dryness out of your mouth." Damon slipped the swab into her mouth, and she screwed up her face.

The doctor didn't want her eating or drinking anything until all the blood work came back. They didn't know what she'd been exposed to and if she had to be rushed into surgery, it was better if her stomach was empty.

Alastair jumped to his feet when he saw Damon and grabbed Tabitha's other hand. He kissed it over and over as she swallowed several times.

"Honey, I'm so glad you woke up." He sobbed. "You're gonna be okay now."

Tabitha shook her head and turned back to Damon. He could see she wanted to tell him something, but she was having trouble getting it out.

"Do you think you could write what you want to say?" Pam whispered from next to Damon.

Tabitha nodded slowly, and Pam asked Crunch to get paper and a pen. Malcolm had woken as well and sat at the foot of the bed.

A tear slipped out of the corner of Tabitha's eye, and Alastair tried to soothe her as Crash handed Damon the clipboard and a pencil.

Tabitha shakily took the pencil and started to write while Damon held the board steady. It seemed to take forever for her to finish, but when she did, Damon turned the paper where he could read it.

"They want revenge?" Damon looked at Tabitha to confirm what she had written.

She nodded and motioned for the clipboard. She started to write again but dropped the pencil several times. Damon tried not to get frustrated, but when he handed her the pencil for the third time, he saw her eyes roll up into her head, and she started to gasp for air.

"Nurse," Malcolm shouted as the machines started to alarm.

Damon had to pull Alastair away while the medical team surrounded the bed. Damon and Malcolm held Alastair up as they watched.

Damon knew the minute it was over. One nurse reached above the bed and turned off the monitor, and the team started to remove gloves. Then the doctor made the announcement.

"Time of death, eleven twenty-one pm." The doctor turned and stepped in front of Damon, Malcolm, and Alastair. "I'm sorry."

Damon heard the words, but it didn't seem real. Tabitha was gone. Alastair scuffed across the room and dropped into the chair next to the bed. He picked up her hand and softly murmured to her.

Malcolm was motionless next to Damon and seemed to be barely holding it together. Damon stared at Tabitha in the bed for several seconds until she started to blur in his vision. His eyes filled with tears, and his gaze dropped to the floor.

The clipboard had been kicked under the bed, and Damon crouched next to Alastair to retrieve it. He looked at where she'd started to write before she dropped the pencil.

"Revenge. Al?" Damon whispered.

"Someone wants revenge on Alastair?" Pam asked.

"Well, I hope they're happy because the bastards just got that," Alastair choked.

It was the first time he'd ever seen how much Alastair actually loved Tabitha. It was confusing to know how much he screwed around and to see him so distraught over his wife.

"I need to go break this to the kids," Malcolm whispered as he wiped his hands over his face.

"Alastair, we need to leave." Damon crouched next to the chair.

"She'll be afraid here by herself." He sobbed.

"Alastair, she won't ever be afraid again. She's happy now and all her pain is gone." Pam stepped next to Damon.

"I should never have let this happen." Alastair stood up and bent down until he could place a kiss on her lips. "Be well, my darling."

On the drive back to Hopedale, Damon held the clipboard tightly between his hands. *Revenge? Al? Do they want revenge?* Was it Alastair she'd been referring to? Damon stared at the shaky writing and tried to will the answers to pop off the page.

"We'll figure it out," Pam whispered as she linked her arm into his. "Right now, Alastair needs us all."

Damon nodded. Was he a hypocrite? He'd despised Alastair for so many years, and he still wasn't sure how he felt about the man. He lied to them for most of their lives, and he'd cheated on Tabitha for years with Malcolm's wife. How was Damon supposed to forget that? How could any of them?

Chapter 26

It had been a week since Tabitha had passed. It took extra time to release her body because the police wanted an autopsy. Now they stood in the graveyard surrounded by police and security.

Alastair had placed the urn down into the hole and stepped back. Crash caught him before he fell to his knees sobbing. He remained there while the priest performed the burial service.

Malcolm was barely holding it together as he held a crying Melody. Marshall stood next to them, trembling while tears ran down his cheeks, and Damon seemed as if he was in a daze.

Pam was worried about Damon. He hadn't said much the entire week, and he seemed focused on the clipboard. Too focused. It was almost as if he'd become obsessed with figuring out what Tabitha tried to tell them before she died.

The priest finished the service, and as the family dropped roses into the opening with the urn, Aaron and Nick sang the hymn *Amazing Grace* as Damon had requested.

A lump formed in Pam's throat as the beautiful harmony between her cousins echoed in the air while Damon and his family laid Tabitha to rest.

Her Aunt Alice had opened the pub for the reception after the funeral. Damon, Malcolm, and Alastair greeted people as they entered and offered condolences, but Damon was anxious. She could see it by the way he moved back and forth from foot to foot.

"He looks ready to explode," Billie said from next to Pam.

"He is. He has to grieve, but he's obsessed with what she wrote," Pam said as she met Damon's gaze.

"He'll do it in time. Grief hits everyone differently." Billie gave her a side hug.

"I guess. I just wish we knew who was responsible for all the crap. It's the only way he's going to finally let go." Pam sighed.

"They'll show themselves eventually," Billie said.

Pam wasn't so sure. These people were all over the place. Kidnapping Kelsey, Pam, and Tabitha. Then there was the shooting and was this all related to Greta and her brother? It made no sense. Pam had five police officers, two data analysts, a former police officer, and the mayor of Hopedale at her disposal. There had to be some way to find out who was after Damon's family.

"He's tough, ya know?" Adrian said as he plopped down next to her.

"I know." Pam forced a smile.

"He survived a lot when we were deployed," Adrian continued.

"So did you," Pam reminded him.

"Yes, but it affects him more." Adrian turned to look at her.

"Weren't you both on the same mission?" She was sure she hadn't misunderstood Damon.

"Pam, he was our lookout, so to speak. Nothing ever got by him, which was why he was on this mission." Adrian cleared his throat.

"He blames himself." Pam heard him scream it many times in his dreams.

"He does, but it wasn't his fault. We should have gotten out of there faster. Pop thought he heard another woman, but we had only been sent in to rescue two. We listened, and by the time we ran out of the structure, they were on our asses." Adrian shook his head as if to escape the memory.

"He still has nightmares," Pam told Adrian.

"We all do, honey. We all do." Adrian gave her a gentle tap on the knee with his hand.

Melody sat on the edge of the stage and appeared to be lost in her own thoughts. She looked as if she was ready to burst into tears, and Pam's heart went out to the girl.

"Did you get anything to eat or drink?" Pam asked as she sat next to her.

"I'm not really hungry." Melody shrugged.

"It's been a long day, huh?" Pam looked around the bar.

"Yeah." Melody kicked her legs and her heels drummed against the edge of the stage.

"If you want, I can get someone to take you back to Keith's house," Pam suggested.

"I already asked. Dad said no." Melody dropped her head.

"Maybe he'd be okay if my cousin's daughters went with you. Have you met Lily and Evie?" Pam nodded to where the two girls sat talking with some of the other younger cousins.

"Yeah, Emily introduced me." Melody gave a little smile.

"Let me see what I can do." Pam winked and headed to where Malcolm and Damon were talking to someone with their back to her.

"Excuse me, Malcolm. I was wondering if it was okay for the kids to go back to Keith's. I'll ask Lily and Evie to go back with them for company." Pam stepped next to Damon.

"Melody does look miserable." Damon nodded to where his niece still sat on the stage.

"I guess it's okay. I'm sure they'll be safe there." Malcolm nodded.

Emily was more than happy to volunteer to go back to her house with Melody, Marshall, Lily, and Evie. Keith went with them and took most of the older kids with him. The younger ones went home with their respective grandparents, leaving Pam's family, some friends, and the Blackwoods.

Pam didn't pay attention to most of the people she'd been introduced to. All she wanted to do was to go back to her apartment with Damon and relax. Damon seemed reluctant to leave Malcolm and Alastair.

"I'm so sorry for your loss." The voice was familiar.

When Pam turned around, Gail was behind her dressed in black. All her focus was on Alastair, not Malcolm. Pam could feel the tension in Malcolm's body from across the room and hoped Damon's brother would be able to control his rage.

"What. Are. You. Doing. Here?" Malcolm's voice was cold as he pronounced every word.

"We're family." Gail squared her shoulders and blatantly linked into the crook of Alastair's arm.

"You, conniving little bitch." Malcolm took a step toward her.

"Malcolm, let me handle this." Alastair turned to face Gail.

"You look tired, Alastair. Why don't I take you out of this dreary little town and back to the estate?" She reached up to touch Alastair's face.

Damon stepped in front of Malcolm as he started to lunge toward Gail. Pam motioned to Crash and Shadow to come closer, but it was Alastair who surprised Pam.

"You really believe with Tabitha gone you'd step in and become the lady of the house, don't you?" Alastair grabbed her wrist.

"She was the only thing keeping us from living as a couple." Gail smiled.

"Listen to me and listen carefully. You never meant more to me than an easy lay. I have no interest in living with you or any other woman. Now the truth is out, I don't ever want to see you again. You can't blackmail me anymore." Alastair released Gail's wrist, and she slapped him.

He didn't even flinch. Gail stood there for several seconds glancing between Alastair, Malcolm, Damon, and Pam. When none of them showed her any support, she turned to Malcolm and smiled.

"You'll be getting a letter from my lawyer." She spun on her heel and stomped out of the pub.

"People here must think I'm a complete bastard." Alastair dropped his head.

"Doncha worry. We're all here ta help. Ya can't change da past. It's wat ya do from here on out, dat counts. Holdin' grudges never helped anyone." Nanny Betty gently patted her hand on Alastair's shoulder.

"Nan is right, Alastair." Damon wrapped his arm around Pam. "Tabitha never wanted this anger between us."

"It's gonna be hard to forget the past," Malcolm began, "but I'm willing to try. I've got to look ahead for the kids' sake. I'm not letting Gail get her hands on them."

A tear slipped out of the corner of Alastair's eye, and he held out his hand to Malcolm and Damon. The three men clasped hands and words didn't need to be said.

"At least something good came out of losing her," Alastair choked.

"Tings happen fer a reason." Nanny Betty nodded then scurried away.

What was the reason someone had sworn revenge on Alastair and what was their next move? Maybe it was something else but what?

Chapter 27

Damon sat on the edge of the bed and stared at the picture of the clipboard he'd taken before he handed it over to Nick. It wasn't like it would help. Damon was actually going cross-eyed from studying it.

Nick dropped by the day after the funeral and told him Sandy had Smash tracking the emails sent to Alastair as well as the one sent to Damon when Pam was taken.

The only thing they knew was they all came from the same email, and it was sent from the city library. Of course, whoever sent the emails managed to keep hidden from the security cameras. Since the library only had one in the main area, it wasn't hard to do.

"Guess what?" Pam smiled as she sat on the bed next to him.

"What?" Damon smiled back.

"Lily got Melody and Marshall invites to the semi-formal at the community center tomorrow night." Pam grinned.

"That's great. Those kids need to have some fun." Damon kissed Pam's cheek.

"They do." Pam took his phone and tossed it on the bed as she crawled into his lap.

"What are you doing?" Damon smirked.

"I want you to stop driving yourself crazy with the note your mother wrote." Pam threaded her fingers through his hair.

"I can't help it. It's staring me right in the face, and until we figure this out, you're not safe, and neither is Kelsey. Malcolm says he hears her crying all night." Damon knew his brother was anxious about Kelsey.

"She was with the kidnappers a lot longer than I was, and they hurt her." Pam shivered.

"I hope she gets help." Damon looked into Pam's blue eyes.

"Me too." Pam snuggled into him and rested her head on his shoulder.

He loved having her in his arms. It calmed him and helped some of his anxiety subside. Damon's cravings for alcohol had diminished as well, but he knew through his meetings it would probably never go away.

"Damon, Pam, are you in there?" Nick's voice echoed from the living room.

"Yeah, we're coming," Pam shouted as they made their way out of the room.

"Sandy found Greta," Nick told them.

"Let's go." Damon headed for the door.

"Damon, she's not the one who's been doing all this." Nick handed Damon a piece of paper.

"What is this?" Damon looked down and froze.

"She passed away almost a year ago." Nick sounded apologetic.

"Jesus. Why didn't you find this sooner?" Damon snapped as he slapped the certificate against his hand.

"Because we didn't know she'd married again," Nick explained. "Technically, she wasn't married because there was no official certificate, but she was buried under her married name."

He looked down at the name and shook his head. Greta was a dead end, literally. Apparently, she'd ended up in the psychiatric hospital. It gutted him because they were no further ahead by finding his biological mother.

"You're sure this is her?" Damon held up the death certificate.

"Yeah, the birthdate matches, and there's a photo on her file at the hospital," Nick answered.

"What about her brother?" Pam interjected.

"He's vanished." Nick sighed and flopped down on the sofa.

"I could try to contact him. Ask him if he will need any more clothing for his wife," Pam suggested.

"It won't hurt." Nick shrugged.

Pam disappeared into the room and returned a few minutes later with her phone to her ear. Damon paced as they waited to see if someone would answer.

"It went to voicemail." Pam sighed.

"It was a long shot." Nick turned to leave.

"Nick, something just hit me." Pam tilted her head.

"What's that?" Nick glanced back at them.

"If Greta died in the hospital, wouldn't someone have to claim her body?" Pam asked.

"Yeah." Nick looked confused.

"Wouldn't the person need to give their information to the hospital or the funeral home where the body was brought?" Pam glanced between Damon and Nick.

"Yeah, but it could be a fake address," Nick replied.

"The funeral would have to be paid for. How many people would pay for a funeral with cash?" Pam raised an eyebrow.

"Cuz, you're a fucking mastermind." Nick pulled out his phone, probably to call Sandy.

"My little genius." Damon picked her up and spun her around.

An hour later, Nick, John, Damon, and Trunk stood outside the address listed on the bill for Greta's funeral. It didn't look like much, but it was obviously lived in since there were cigarette butts overflowing a bucket next to the door.

Nick knocked on the door and stepped back. Damon scanned the front of the house and checked out all the windows. Some of the windows were open, and music floated out from the one on the main floor.

John knocked the second time a little louder. Trunk casually walked around to the side of the house and then back to the bottom of the steps. As the door opened, the man who appeared was in the middle of coughing, obviously from years of smoking.

"What?" the man snapped.

"Are you Lester Cox?" John asked.

"Waz it to ya?" the man grumbled.

"I'm Chief O'Connor with the Newfoundland Police Department. I'm looking for Lester Cox," John told the older man.

"Is dat old bag complainin' 'bout me music again?" The man hung out through the door and yelled at the house next door.

"Are you Mr. Cox?" John asked again, but Damon was getting impatient.

"Yes, b'y. Wat ya want?" Lester looked all of them up and down.

"We're here about your late wife. Could we come in and ask you a few questions?" John asked.

"Me late wife? Dat crazy bitch better be dead. Cost me over five grand to bury that loon," he complained. "But come on in."

Lester motioned for them to follow. Damon didn't understand why Nick and John both gagged, until he stepped inside the house. The smell of stale smoke, urine, and body odor was overwhelming.

"I'll just wait out here." Trunk smirked as he stepped back outside.

"Bastard," Nick mumbled.

"I guess none of ya can take a drink on da job." Lester sat on a shaky-looking chair and filled a glass with rum.

"No, sir." Nick smiled.

"Jesus, don't call me sir. Now, what do ya want ta know about Greta?" Lester asked after he'd slammed back the glass of booze.

Damon had to distract himself from the bottle on the table and turned to look around the house. Lester didn't have much, and he hadn't cleaned in a very long time. It was quite evident he lived alone.

"Do you know where we could get in touch with Greta's brother?" Nick asked.

"Her brudder? Never met da guy. He called a lot but when she lost her shit, never heard from him after." Lester shrugged.

"How did you meet Greta?" Damon was curious about how the woman could go from married to Warrick Blackwood to someone like Lester.

"Ya know, it was the damnest ting. She hit on me at da old watering hole down on Water Street. I was so fuckin' drunk I don't even remember da weddin'." Lester chuckled.

"You got married the night you met?" Damon asked.

"Yep, she was quite da sex kitten, if ya get wat I mean." Lester wiggled his eyebrows.

"Yeah." Damon locked eyes with Nick.

"Would you happen to have any pictures of your wedding?" Nick asked.

"Now yer askin' sometin'. I haven't seen dem in years." Lester looked around the house as if he was trying to remember where the pictures were.

"If I leave a card, would you have a look for them and give me a call?" John held out his card.

"Waz dis all about? I mean Greta's been gone fer several months." Lester narrowed his eyes.

"We're investigating a couple of abductions, and her name happened to pop up in our files," John explained.

"Don't surprise me. Dat ex-husband a' hers was a bastard." Lester shook his head. "Den again, she turned out ta be pretty nuts herself. Tried to bury me alive, she did." Lester slapped his hand on his leg. "Ta make da best of it; she took off wit dis guy wit a fucked-up scar on his face."

"Do you know who he was?" Nick asked.

"Nah, I never heard nuttin' else from her until da hospital told me dey had her ashes." Lester shrugged. "She's buried up da road at the old cemetery."

"Well, thanks for your help, Lester. If you remember anything else, please call." John shook the older man's hand.

"Will do," Lester shouted as Damon followed John and Nick out of the house.

On the way back to Hopedale, Damon couldn't shake the gut feeling there was something off with Lester. Not to mention the hair on the back of his neck prickled as if someone was watching them while they were in the kitchen.

"Keep the fucking windows open." John blew out a breath. "I swear I still have the odor of that fucking place in my nose."

"It was pretty fucking bad." Trunk chuckled.

"You coward, you didn't even go inside." Nick scoffed.

"I was smart." Trunk slapped the back of Nick's head.

"Is it just me or did anyone else get the feeling Lester wasn't on the up and up?" Damon asked.

"What do you mean?" Nick turned to look at him.

"Maybe it's my training, or maybe I'm just losing my mind, but I got a feeling someone else was in the house." Damon glanced around the SUV at the men, fully expecting them to tell him he was nuts.

"No, you're not losing your mind. We didn't really have a reason to look around the house." John shrugged.

"I got a picture of him, though." Trunk held up his phone.

"How the hell did you get that?" Nick asked.

"I'm good." Trunk smirked.

Back at Keith's place, everyone was sat down to supper. Pam, Lily, and Evie had joined them, and Melody was chattering about the dance and how Pam helped her pick out the perfect dress. Marshall was grumbling about having to wear a tie.

"I think guys look good in a shirt and tie," Evie announced.

Marshall's cheeks turned bright red and he seemed to become really interested in the food on his plate. Damon smiled as he met Pam's amused eyes.

"To be fifteen again." Nick chuckled.

"How did it go?" Alastair looked at them hopefully.

"We'll fill you in after we get a bite to eat." John nodded toward the kids.

"That means we should take our supper to the living room and turn the television up really loud." Lily picked up her plate as well as Patrick's bowl. "Come on guys, we'll go watch the *Lion King*."

"Love the *Lion King*." Evie took Noah's plate along with her own and motioned for Marshall and Melody to follow.

"Those kids are way too smart." Keith shook his head.

"They've been around too much of this shit." Nick plopped down on the chair Lily vacated.

"There's lots of food, dig in." Emily returned from the kitchen with plates for John, Nick, Trunk, and Damon.

"I'm not saying no to Emily's home cooking." Trunk grinned as he started to load his plate with chicken and vegetables.

Damon had to adjust his hearing aid because the kids had turned the television up so loud it was interfering with the conversation around the table.

"The guy was weird, and apparently Greta ended up in the hospital because she tried to bury Lester alive, but Trunk got a picture of him, if that means anything." Nick shrugged.

"Can I see the picture?" Pam asked.

"I doubt if you ever met him, cuz." John put a forkful of potato into his mouth.

Trunk handed her his phone with the picture on the screen. The conversation around the table continued, but Damon blocked it out when he saw the expression on Pam's face.

"Trixie, what's wrong?" Damon asked, and the conversation stopped.

"This is Vladimir Yugov, or at least it's how he introduced himself at the shop. He's the guy I was doing the order for the night I was taken." Pam held up the phone and pointed at the man Damon knew as Lester.

"Pam, that's Lester Cox," Nick told her.

"I don't care what he called himself today, but he's the guy who came to my shop and bought a ton of clothes for his wife. He used a credit card for Vladimir Yugov. He had an attendant with him all the time," Pam insisted.

"You're sure?" John asked.

"Positive." Pam nodded.

"If this is Yugov, then who was the guy we talked to when Pam was missing?" John asked.

"I'm guessing it wasn't Vladimir Yugov." Emily replied.

"What the fuck is going on?" Damon shook his head.

"Guess we're going back to town." Nick jumped to his feet.

Ten minutes later, they were ready to get back on the highway and head to Lester's house or maybe it was Vladimir's house. Either way, they were about to find out who the guy really was.

Chapter 28

Pam was furious. John would not allow her to go with them to confront Vladimir. Then she'd looked to Damon for support, but he'd agreed with John, which further pissed her off.

She was tired of being treated like she was a delicate china doll who couldn't take care of herself. She'd knocked down a man three times her size and escaped her abductors. She could surely handle a meeting with a man confined to a wheelchair.

"What's he going to do, roll over my foot?" Pam snapped at her cousin.

"Pam, the man we met today wasn't in a wheelchair," Nick told her.

"It's not like I'm going to be there alone. I want to confront this asshole," Pam argued.

"Trixie, we don't know if he's there alone and just how dangerous he could be," Damon reasoned.

"He was in my shop every week for almost four months. If he was going to hurt me, he would have done it then or at least turn his attendant on me. That guy was huge," Pam returned.

"I don't see the harm in letting her go," Emily interjected.

"Princess, stay out of it," Keith spoke up, calling her by the pet name he had for her.

"No, it's her right to confront the guy, especially if he's the one responsible for all this." Emily stood next to Pam.

"Do any of the women in this family have even an inkling of how hard it is to deal with them?" John sighed.

"Probably as hard as it is to deal with the men," Pam shot back.

"You're not going." John pointed at Pam.

"Fine, if you won't let me go with you, I'll go there myself." Pam crossed her arms over her chest.

"Not a fucking chance, Trixie," Damon roared.

"Don't yell at me. I'm an adult, and I can go wherever I like." Pam narrowed her eyes and glared back at Damon.

"Do you have a death wish? Maybe you want to be locked up in a room again?" Damon threw his hands up in the air.

"For God's sake, if you'd let me go with all four of you, what are the chances he'd even get to look at me, let alone do something else?" Pam asked.

"We need to get back there sooner rather than later and if any of you think you're going to win an argument with an O'Connor woman, then we might as well sit down now." Trunk propped his shoulder against the wall. "If it helps, I'll stick to her like glue."

"Fine, but whatever Trunk says, goes. Got it?" John ordered.

"I got it. I swear." Pam pressed her hand against her chest.

"Are you fucking kidding me?" Damon was looking at John like he'd lost his mind.

"You're more than welcome to try and talk her out of this, but I want to get back there before I get my pension." Nick waved his hand as he headed out through the door.

Pam hung her purse over her shoulder and followed Trunk out of the house. Seconds later, Damon sat next to her in the back of the SUV. She knew he was fuming, but she didn't care.

"I'll get Lily and Evie home later," Emily shouted as they pulled out of the driveway.

The drive back to town was quiet except for the soft country music on the radio. Damon had taken her hand and held it as if she would vanish any minute.

"I'll be fine," Pam whispered and lifted his hand to kiss his finger.

"Trixie, I love that you got a mind of your own, but I really hate the stubbornness right now." Damon released her hand and wrapped his arm around her.

"All women are stubborn," Trunk grumbled.

"They are when you act like an ass." Pam glared at the large man next to her.

She could tell he knew exactly who she was referring to. He'd already lost his chance with Abbie, and he found that out at Jess' wedding when Abbie brought her new man as her date.

John pulled up in front of a small house. Pam glanced at Damon, and he nodded to John and Nick. Pam had to roll her eyes because she knew what the nod meant. Damon was staying in the vehicle with her and Trunk.

Trunk rolled down the window, and they watched Nick and John make their way up to the house. John knocked, and they waited. After a few minutes, John knocked again, but still, nobody came to the door.

John pulled open the storm door and identified himself. After another minute he called out to Lester. Pam watched John and Nick disappear into the house, and it seemed to take a very long time for them to come out. Trunk and Damon must have thought so too because they started to get out of the SUV.

"Stay with her," Trunk told Damon and closed the door.

Before Trunk got up to the steps, Nick and John came out. John had his phone up to his ear, and Nick headed toward the SUV. A cold chill ran up Pam's spine, and she got out of the vehicle.

"He's dead," Nick told her.

"Dead?" Pam gasped.

"How the hell is that possible we were here less than an hour ago?" Damon grumbled.

"It wasn't natural either. He's been shot right in the middle of the forehead." Nick blew out a breath.

"If he's dead, then who killed him?" Damon asked.

"I wish I knew," Nick murmured.

Pam climbed back into the SUV and waited as John and Nick tied up the crime scene, and the body was removed. They'd offered to let Trunk take her and Damon home, but she didn't want to go anywhere.

The house was searched from top to bottom, but according to Nick, there was nobody else in the house, and it didn't look like anyone else lived there. Pam watched as officers went in and out of the house with masks covering their mouths and noses.

"Why are they wearing masks?" Pam asked.

"Probably to kill the smell. The place stinks to high heaven." Damon shuddered.

"I could smell it the minute the door opened," Trunk told her.

"He seemed like such a meticulous person. Every time he came to the shop, he was dressed impeccably." Pam shook her head in confusion.

"The first guy we talked to was dressed nicely, and he was in a wheelchair." Damon told her.

By the time they were headed back to Hopedale, it was dark. They hadn't found anything inside the house to tell them the identity of the man. As far as they knew he was Lester Cox. John said they would check fingerprints, but unless Lester or Vladimir was in the system, they couldn't be sure who he was.

"What do we do now?" Pam asked mostly to break the silence on the way back home.

"You don't do anything. You let us deal with this." John caught her eye in the rearview mirror.

"I didn't mean I was going to do anything." Pam rolled her eyes.

Pam was tired, and she was ready to crawl into her own bed after they got back to Hopedale. The only problem was she'd promised Emily she would spend the night with her. Lily, Evie, Melody, and Jess' stepdaughter, Ocean, were spending the night with Emily.

Emily invited the girls to the salon she co-owned with Sandy's sister the next morning. Marshall had opted to spend the evening with Bethany's nephew, Cameron. He was also going to the dance.

Lily decided that since Melody and Marshall didn't have dates, it was her job to find them someone to go with. So, Ocean was going with Marshall, and Melody was Cameron's date.

Pam wouldn't go back on her promise to Emily. She walked into the house and was surprised to see the kitchen table covered with all sorts of makeup. Sandy's sister Kim was helping the girls decide the best colors for them.

"Hey, Aunt Pam." Lily grinned excitedly.

"You're really loving this, aren't you?" Pam laughed.

She knew Ian and Sandy didn't let the girls wear makeup unless it was a special occasion. So when Evie and Lily got the chance to play with it, they were overjoyed.

"Aunt Kim said she's going to do our makeup tomorrow," Evie explained as she looked through some of the lip glosses.

"Dad said he didn't want me to wear it, but mom vetoed him." Ocean smirked.

She'd recently started to call Jess mom, and it was a little unusual the hear. Jess loved it though and would light up anytime Ocean would call her mom.

"She's the best." Pam smiled.

It was a little after two in the morning by the time the girls settled down. Emily and Pam sat at the table with a cup of tea. Emily was excited about being able to sleep in the next morning because Kathleen had taken the boys, and Emily's mother had taken Scarlett.

"It's honestly the first time since Scarlett was born that I could let her go for a sleepover. Keith's been feeling a little neglected, I think." Emily snickered.

"So you get rid of your own kids and invite a bunch of teenagers?" Pam smirked.

"I don't need to breastfeed them in the morning." Emily grinned.

"I'm assuming Keith may need to be." Pam glanced up when her cousin appeared in the kitchen.

"I may need to what?" Keith asked.

"To be breastfed." Emily winked.

"I love your breasts." Keith wiggled his eyebrows.

"I think the girls are all knocked out in the living room. I'm going to head up to the guest room." Pam laughed. "I don't want to hear any more about her breasts." She pointed at Emily.

Pam walked into the bedroom to see Damon sat up watching something on television. She glanced over her shoulders to see news coverage on the death of the man in the house.

"John said he'd let us know in the morning if they can get a positive id on the guy." Damon turned off the television.

Pam nodded as she slipped out of her jeans and sweater. She crawled into the bed and tucked herself into Damon's side. She really wanted to go to the community center the next night to see the kids all dressed up, but she had a feeling Damon and John were not going to agree.

"Girls all settled?" Damon asked.

"Yeah, they are so excited." Pam tipped her head back and looked into his eyes.

"What?" Damon smiled.

"Nothing." She rested her head on his chest.

Damon put his finger under her chin and tipped her face up, so she had to look at him. He ran his knuckle down her cheek and looked into her eyes.

"What's on your mind?" Damon whispered.

"I wanted to go to the dance tomorrow to see the kids all dressed up." Pam shrugged.

"And?" Damon raised an eyebrow.

"I know you and John would have a meltdown if I told you I was going." Pam rested her chin on his chest.

"Oh, like you would listen if you were adamant on going." Damon scoffed.

"Would you go with me?" Pam smirked.

"You mean dress up and go to a teen dance?" Damon chuckled.

"Yeah." Pam smiled.

313

"I can't see why not. It's not like you'll be there alone. I'll be there, and from what I heard, Ian and Wade are going to be there too." Damon laughed.

"Why?" Pam chuckled.

"Keith said they signed up to be chaperones after the girls decided to go to the dance." Damon grinned.

"The poor kids. Dad, Uncle Kurt, and Uncle Sean did the same thing when I was fourteen. Jess and I were so embarrassed when Uncle Kurt kept putting a bat between us and the boys we were dancing with. Kept telling them not to go any closer." Pam rolled her eyes.

"Sounds like a good plan." Damon laughed.

"It was so humiliating, by the end of the night, none of the guys would dance with us and Uncle Kurt was going around with the bat on his shoulder." Pam shook her head. "Of course, Mom and Aunt Alice gave him shit for it the next day."

Damon looked into her eyes, and his face turned suddenly serious. It was as if something was on his mind and he didn't know how to say it.

"You're so damn beautiful," he whispered.

"Thank you." Pam smiled.

"Do you want kids?" Damon tilted his head.

"Of course." Pam did, but she was getting close to forty.

"Me too." He ran a finger down the side of her face.

"With me?" Pam gazed into his eyes.

"I wouldn't want them with anyone else. I imagine a baby with your cute nose, those blue eyes, and your beautiful face." He brushed his lips against hers.

"You know, genetics says if we had a baby, it would probably have your color eyes. Blue is a recessive gene." Pam smirked.

"Well, aren't you the smart one." Damon chuckled.

"It's all I remember about biology from high school." Pam laughed.

"You know what I remember about high school?" Damon rolled her over on her back and hovered over her.

"Sex education?" Pam giggled.

"My favorite subject," Damon growled and covered her mouth with his.

Chapter 29

Damon tugged on the tie for the hundredth time since they'd arrived at the community center. The only thing good about being dressed up was Pam in a fitted blue dress showing off all her sweet curves.

As sexy as she looked, he was on edge being in a public place. He did feel better when Keith and his brothers stepped in as extra security. The last thing they wanted was one of the kids getting caught in a crossfire.

"If that fucking kid looks at her ass once more, I'm going to take him outside and run over him with my truck," Wade grumbled.

"She doesn't seem to mind." Damon chuckled.

"Isn't your nephew her date?" Wade motioned to were Marshall stood talking to Evie.

"I don't think it matters at this age." Damon laughed.

"How's Alastair doing since Tabitha passed?" Wade asked.

"Not really sure, I haven't been around him a whole lot. He and Malcolm are moved into one of the bunkhouses." Damon shrugged.

"What about that girl? I think Jess said her name is Kelsey?" Wade handed Damon a cup of punch.

"She's still staying with Keith and Emily. She's not talking much, but she did agree to see a therapist," Damon explained.

The truth was, he wasn't sure how Kelsey was handling things. He was starting to think she'd been kept a lot longer than she'd admitted, and Keith had said she was rather jumpy.

"I swear with this family, the therapists are making a bundle." Wade laughed.

"True," Damon agreed.

The dance ended, and Damon found Pam with Sandy helping to clean up the refreshment table. Except for a couple of waltzes, he'd hardly seen her most of the night. He didn't mind because she seemed to enjoy dancing with the girls to all the hip-hop music.

"Hey, need any help?" Damon asked as he loosened his tie finally.

"Yeah, go drag my husband away from over there. He's cramping Lily's style." Sandy laughed.

Damon looked over his shoulder where Lily was talking to a boy on the other side of the room. Ian stood within a couple of feet and seemed ready to break the guy's neck.

"I'm sure he won't kill the kid in front of people." Damon laughed.

His laugh faded when he looked up to see John running toward him. It wasn't because he was sprinting toward them; it was the look on his face.

"What the hell is wrong now?" Pam stepped next to Damon.

"I just got a call from our forensics team," John said as he stopped in front of them.

"And?" Pam waved her hand in a circle to get him to continue.

"I asked them to get a K9 team to run through the house. You know, grasping at straws and all. The dogs sometimes find things we miss," John rambled.

"You've been married to Stephanie too long; you're starting to ramble like her. Get on with it," Sandy urged.

"The dog found a body buried in a shallow grave in the back yard. Preliminary said it's been there at least six months," John said.

"Who is it?" Damon asked.

"It's male, and I've got a feeling it's the real Lester Cox. The prints on the guy killed yesterday came back as Yugov. They were on file because he was an immigrant," John went on.

"So, who killed Lester and Vladimir?" Pam asked.

"That's the million-dollar question." John sighed.

Damon listened to John and Sandy as they discussed the next step to finding who killed both men. He was so engrossed in their conversation, that he didn't hear his name being called.

"Damon, someone called Keith's phone looking for you. Said he couldn't get hold of you on yours." Crash tapped him on the shoulder.

"Mine is back at Pam's apartment. I didn't think I would need it tonight." Damon shrugged.

"It's kind of late, isn't it?" Pam glanced at her watch.

"He said it's urgent." Crash handed Damon a phone.

"Hello." Damon held the phone to his ear.

"Damon, it's Drake." His old friend's voice sounded strange.

"Drake, what's up?" Damon asked.

"You asked me to pack up your personal things and ship it back to Newfoundland. I got around to going over to your apartment today," Drake said.

"Yeah, there wasn't a rush." Damon shrugged, wondering what was so urgent.

"Damon, someone was in there. It was as if they were looking for something. All your military stuff was all over your room. The place is destroyed." Drake sighed.

"The building doesn't have great security. Probably somebody realized I hadn't been there in a while." Damon didn't understand the panic.

"Your handgun safe was open and it's empty, Damon. I'm sending a photo," Drake said.

Damon glanced up at the group around him, waiting to find out what was so urgent. It was unsettling to know his gun was missing. Someone could easily use it to frame him for something, or worse, the thief could use it to kill someone. He waited for the photo to come through and when he felt the phone vibrate, he opened it.

The photo showed his living room and it looked as if a hurricane blew through it. In the corner, he saw the opened door of his gun safe, but the writing above it made his hair stand up on end. Written on the wall in what looked like blood was the word, *revenge*.

"Thanks, Drake. Look, I'm going to send the police to check things out. Don't touch anything, and thanks for letting me know," Damon said.

"You got it, buddy," Drake replied.

Damon sent a quick text to a police officer friend of his in Toronto. He explained the situation and attached the photo. Seconds later his friend texted him back with a confirmation he'd deal with it. Then Damon held up the picture to show the group. He tried not to show his concern because he realized he was the target for this person, not Alastair. What was Tabitha trying to spell out the night she died?

"They took my handgun," Damon told everyone.

"What the fuck?" John took the phone and studied the picture.

"Do you think it's connected to what's been happening here?" Pam asked.

"Has to be," Sandy responded.

"This puzzle isn't fitting together." Damon shook his head as he tried to piece together everything they'd discovered.

"We just need to find a few more pieces," John murmured.

Who would be out to seek revenge on him? Whoever it was had learned a lot about him and his life, which was a little worrisome. If someone could find out the family secrets Damon didn't even know, it made him think, maybe it was someone closer than he expected.

The next morning, Damon sat at the kitchen table in Pam's apartment. His friend assured Damon that his gun was reported stolen and not to worry. He was slightly relieved but not enough to give up on figuring out who was out to get him.

Damon started to write a list of the people he knew who could be involved. Then he went through each name to try and narrow it down.

"Adrian? No fucking way," Damon mumbled to himself.

He put a line through his friend's name and moved on to the next. Considering Alastair's name started with the two letters Tabitha had written, he'd leave him on the list.

"Drake?" Damon whispered the name.

It was doubtful the club owner would have been flying back and forth to Newfoundland to kidnap and kill people or cause havoc. Drake could have hired someone, but why would he want revenge? Sure, Damon left Drake short-handed when he left, but Damon left to find Pam. Then there was Kelsey, she was taken months ago. He drew a line through Drake's name.

"Malcolm?" Damon looked at his brother's name. "No, unless he's a great actor, there's no way he knew we were adopted."

"Talking to yourself?" Crunch asked.

"No, trying to solve a puzzle." Damon sat back in the chair and blew out a breath as Crunch looked through the list.

"In my opinion, the only one that jumps out is your sister-in-law." Crunch tossed the paper on the table.

"Gail?" Damon pondered the thought.

"Weren't you supposed to marry her first?" Crunch asked.

"Yeah, but why would she want to expose the secrets? She lost Malcolm, the kids, and Alastair by revealing everything." Damon shook his head slowly. "No, she loses in that deal."

"I guess." Crunch shrugged.

"You know what gets me?" Damon looked up at Crunch.

"What?" Crunch leaned against the table.

"That I hurt someone so bad he or she will go through all this to get revenge. I mean, people were murdered." Damon pulled his hands down over his face.

"Sometimes, a person's sense of payback can be way out there." Crunch shook his head. "I've seen it a lot over the last several years."

Later that evening, after he'd returned from an AA meeting, he made his way to the bunkhouse where his father and brother had been staying. Pam was spending the evening with Isabelle, Jess, and Kristy, going over plans for Isabelle's wedding. Since Trunk and Shadow were at the apartment, Damon didn't worry about anyone getting to her.

"Damon, what brings you here?" Alastair asked as he looked up from the book he was reading.

"I wanted to see how you both were doing." Damon sat on the couch next to Alastair.

"I'm hanging in there. I don't get much time to sink too much into grief. Pam's grandmother is here almost every day, dropping off food. Then she goes around making beds and tidying up." Alastair smiled.

"We tried to tell her it wasn't necessary, but we were told to sit down, don't get in her way, and to stop calling her Mrs. O'Connor." Malcolm chuckled.

"Sounds like her." Damon nodded.

Pam's grandmother was very independent, and when she had her mind set on something, there was no stopping her. Pam was a lot like her grandmother in that way.

Damon glanced around the small living room. He never thought he'd see the day where he would sit in the same room with his brother and the man he grew up believing to be his father. It was a great weight off his shoulders to have the burden of anger gone.

"I'm glad you dropped by, actually." Malcolm handed Damon a cup of coffee. "Dad and I have something to talk to you about."

"Dad?" Damon glanced at Alastair and then back to Malcolm

"I can't get used to calling him by his name. Besides, regardless of what happened, he adopted and raised us, so technically he is our father." Malcolm shrugged.

"I understand. It's weird for me too." Damon glanced at Alastair.

"You can call me what you want, as long as you keep talking to me." Alastair met Damon's eyes.

"Agreed." Damon shook Alastair's hand.

"Dad and I had a long chat last night. We want to sell the estate," Malcolm told him.

"Really?" Damon was shocked Alastair would want to sell the place his father owned.

"That house might have some good memories, but from the moment Father was killed and Tabitha's decline into her depression…" Alastair stopped and looked down at his hands. "I want a home that hasn't been tainted."

Damon swallowed hard as he watched Alastair try to hold back the tears. It was obvious he didn't want to go back to where all the secrets began. They would probably find it difficult there without Tabitha too.

"The kids love Hopedale." Malcolm smiled.

"It's an addictive town." Damon chuckled.

"Mike's wife, what is her name?" Alastair tilted his head back.

"Billie," Damon informed him.

"Yes, she's going to get her friend to help us find a house here in Hopedale. I told Malcolm we could get one with an in-law apartment. He'll live in the house with the kids, and I'll stay in the apartment." Alastair nodded.

"Sounds like a great idea." Damon was glad they were starting new.

"I don't want to go back there, but we need to go through the house and figure out what we're keeping and what can stay there." Malcolm sipped from his cup.

"That's a lot of work." Damon snorted.

The estate had more than six thousand square feet with ten bedrooms and ten bathrooms as well as a large living room. Then there was Alastair's office with antique furniture worth a fortune. Not to mention the other rooms.

"We're only taking what is sentimental, necessary, or things we want to keep personally," Malcolm told him.

"Your room hasn't been changed since you left, and I'm guessing you'd like to take some of your old things." Alastair stood up and walked to the window. "Tabitha wouldn't allow anything in your room to be touched."

"We want to go by there in the morning and go through each room. Make a list of what we want to keep and then donate the rest to charity," Malcolm went on.

"Sounds good to me. Tomorrow is Sunday, and I'm sure Pam would come help as well. Maybe we'll leave the kids tomorrow. We'll get the big stuff done first. It's going to take more than a day or two to finish everything." Damon estimated it would take months to clear the house.

They made an agreement to get started first thing in the morning. Damon was concerned about how Gail would react when she found out what Alastair and Malcolm were doing. According to Malcolm, she wanted the kids with her, but they didn't want to. Since they were over the age of fourteen, they couldn't be forced to go with her.

His father could run his businesses from anywhere. Malcolm had become his right-hand man and took over the finance part. Alastair said Malcolm had a better head for that type of work.

Later in the evening, Damon lay next to Pam watching her sleep. She'd probably tell him it was creepy, but he loved to watch her. He was terrified someone would hurt her to get back at him. Damon wasn't sure how he survived when she left him before. Pam was back in his life and he wasn't about to let anyone take her from him.

"I love you, Trixie. You're my whole heart," he whispered as he pulled her into his arms.

Pam sighed and rested her cheek on his chest. Damon closed his eyes and said a silent prayer asking God to help find the person responsible for everything. When that happened, Damon was going to make Pam his wife.

Chapter 30

Pam walked into what seemed like the hundredth room and watched Malcolm place green stickers on everything the family would be keeping. Each label had a four-digit number on it, and Pam's job was to write down the number, what it was, and which room it was in.

It was incredible how many things Damon's family owned. Pam wasn't a professional, but she could tell most of it was antique and expensive. She noticed they were keeping less than a third of the items in the house. They were really planning on downsizing.

Pam and Malcolm were headed down over the steps behind Damon and Adrian when they heard a voice at the bottom of the stairs. When she looked up and around Damon, she had a feeling things were about to get ugly.

"What the hell are you doing here?" Alastair snapped.

"I could ask you the same thing." Gail stood next to the open front door.

Pam shivered as a chill skittered down her spine, and when Damon pushed her behind him, she could see he felt uneasy as well.

Malcolm and Alastair started down the steps, but Damon stopped them.

"This is my house." Alastair glared at Gail.

"Actually, according to my lawyer, it's Malcolm's house, and since there wasn't a prenuptial agreement, half of this house is mine." Gail clasped her hands in front of her chin. "So, whatever you're doing here, stop. Until we have a settlement agreement, you can't touch anything."

"You think you're smart, don't you?" Malcolm snarled at his estranged wife.

"I'm just looking out for my future and the future of my children," Gail sneered.

"I think we should probably fill them in on everything." A man stepped through the open door with his arms behind his back.

"What the fuck?" Adrian seemed surprised to see the stranger.

When Pam took a better look at the man, she recognized him immediately. It was Al, Vladimir Yugov's attendant. She was surprised to see him with Gail, but it was Damon and Alastair's reaction to Al's arrival that worried her.

"Alvin?" Alastair sounded completely dumbfounded.

"How do you know him?" Damon asked Alastair.

"We've been talking about a small commercial building outside of the city he wanted to purchase," Alastair returned.

"Damon, he's Vladimir's attendant," Pam whispered.

"You seem to know everyone here, Pop." Damon took a step down and stopped.

"I do." Alvin smirked, but it looked evil since only one side if his scarred face quirked up.

"What are you doing here?" Damon glanced at Adrian, and Pam noticed both men put themselves in front of her, Malcolm, and Alastair.

"Look at the heroes. Always the protector, aren't you, Damon? What was it we called you? Oh, yeah. Bulletproof." Alvin's words came out like a snarl.

"Pop, what are you doing with her?" Damon motioned toward Gail.

"Oh, she's been instrumental in my plan. She gave me a pretty good story on your beloved family here." Alvin wrapped his arm around Gail's shoulders.

While Alvin talked, Pam noticed his other hand dropped to his side. He had a gun. Damon must have seen it too because his back tensed as he and Adrian shared a worried look.

"What plan are you talking about?" Alastair asked.

"Oh, don't worry, Alastair, it has nothing to do with our deal. I do want to buy the property, but I needed to tie up some loose ends first." He glared at Damon.

"What does Gail have to do with your plan?" Damon asked.

"Well, you see, this all came to pass about a year ago. I walked into a strip club because unless I pay them, women tend to get turned off by this huge scar." Alvin slapped his own face. "Imagine my surprise when I saw my old friend at the bar with a drink in his hand. One of the men who were with me when this happened." He slapped his face again.

"Why didn't you come to talk to me?" Damon asked.

"Couldn't get near you with all the hot little sluts who were constantly around you." Alvin practically growled the words.

"I see," was all Damon said.

"You see, Pam, he was pretty popular at his little club. Me? Not so much." He reached back and closed the door.

"Get to the point, Pop," Damon growled.

"Don't want your little girl here to know you didn't really miss her too much?" Alvin sneered.

"Get on with it," Adrian snapped.

"You never even called to see how I was. Neither of you, but I don't blame you, Rock. You weren't the one who missed the fucking militant come from out of nowhere and use a grenade launcher to kill most of our team. You weren't the reason I spent months in a room having my skin peeled off and screaming in pain. It was our sniper's fault." Alvin glared at Damon

When he finished his rant, Alvin lifted the weapon and pointed it in their direction.

"It wasn't his fault, Pop," Adrian snapped.

"It was, Rock. I should have seen the guy first." Damon didn't flinch as he used Adrian's nickname.

"No, if we'd left when we should have, we would have been out of there before the guy got close." Adrian sounded pissed.

"Pam, why don't you, Malcolm and Alastair head up to the room and let us discuss this?" Damon waved his hand behind him.

"No, Pam," Alvin roared. "Let them stay and hear about what a failure you were on our last mission. How you let six fellow soldiers die, six friends be murdered because you didn't do your job." Alvin's face turned red as he continued.

"Why not just come confront me. Why take Kelsey, Pam, or Tabitha?" Damon asked.

"Well, Kelsey was actually Gail's idea." Alvin glanced at Gail.

She didn't look as cocky as Alvin continued to rant. Gail almost appeared scared and had stepped away from the unstable man.

"You see, her plan was for Malcolm to break their marriage vows by having an affair with his old flame. I didn't realize who Gail was the first time I saw her in the diner, but I heard her talk about how she couldn't wait until Tabitha finally died so she could become Alastair's wife. She's a little sick?" Alvin scoffed.

"How did you know about Pam?" Damon snapped.

"Actually, it wasn't as hard as you would think. Her old room mate, Lola, was not happy about Pam's sudden departure. It only took a couple of hundred dollars and a lot of liquor to get her to spill everything she knew about my old Army buddy. Turns out Lola knew more about your girl here than you did." Alvin sneered.

Pam glanced at Damon and Malcolm. They looked ready to kill, and Alastair didn't appear any calmer. As a matter of fact, the more Pam looked around the room, the more she realized she was in the middle of a shit storm, and it might just be ready to hit the fan.

Chapter 31

Damon shook with rage as Alvin continued to tell them how he and Gail planned to get Kelsey to set up Malcolm. His brother probably wouldn't have been able to deny her because she was the love of his life.

Damon was sure Malcolm didn't live like a priest since he'd been married, but Damon also knew he hadn't been intimate with Gail. Knowing his brother, he'd probably kept any affairs very quiet.

"You know that ex of yours, she's stubborn. I kept her locked up for over two weeks, alone with nobody to talk with. When we first asked her to do it, she adamantly declined. Even after I beat her black and blue, she still wouldn't do it." Alvin paced back and forth in front of the door, but his eyes were glued to Damon.

"You, bastard," Malcolm shouted.

"Yeah, but my mother was a whore." Alvin sounded so cold.

He wasn't the same man who they went through basic training with. The same guy who would short sheet beds to play a gag on one of the other guys. This scarred man in front of Damon had utterly lost his mind.

"Why Pam?" Damon asked.

"I needed to get you back here to put my plan for revenge into motion." Alvin glared.

"Why Tabitha?" Damon spat.

"Just to fuck with you. You see Vladimir was a doctor back in Slovakia where he and Greta were born. He took care of her while she was with me. He probably should be an actor too because he did a great stupid Newfie accent. We did get her back before it was too late. She recognized me from my meetings with Alastair. That surprised me." Alvin glanced at him as if he was expecting a thank you.

"So why kill Vladimir if he was your friend?" Damon asked.

"He'd served his purpose. Plus, he thought I was helping him get to Alastair. I had him convinced Pam was Alastair's new lover. He was buying all your clothes to use on you when he took you from Alastair." Alvin scoffed as he nodded toward Pam.

"What about Lester Cox? What did he ever do to you?" Damon wanted to get as much information as he could before he made a move and took Pop down.

"He became useless after Greta died. I didn't really need him, anyway. I got all the information I needed from Greta. You know she kept very detailed journals. She really hated you, Alastair. Greta blamed you for Warrick's death. I think her exact words were, *you were the reason he went after her the night he died.*" Alvin nodded.

"Pop, let them go. This is between you and me, isn't it?" Damon wanted to get everyone out of the line of fire if he started to shoot.

"You'd like that, wouldn't you?" Alvin raised his weapon and slowly waved it back and forth in front of them.

"I'm leaving." Gail started to back to the door.

"You know, I really don't need you for anything else. You should go." Alvin spun around and raised his weapon. "Right to hell."

Gail cried out for a split second and the loud pop of the gun sounded. Gail fell to the floor with a slap as she hit the marble.

Pam gasped, and Damon pushed her further behind him. Malcolm's eyes were wide as he stared where Gail lay motionless on the floor.

"He's fucking lost it," Adrian whispered.

"I guess you're a widower now, Malcolm. You're welcome." Alvin turned his weapon back to Damon.

"You didn't have to kill her," Damon snapped.

"Like you care. She told me you hated her." Alvin laughed as he scratched his scarred cheek with the barrel of the gun.

Damon reached behind him slowly and took Pam's hand. He pressed the top of her hand against his rear pocket where his phone was. Since she was behind him, he hoped she could send a message for help without being noticed.

"I may not like her, but I certainly didn't want to see her dead," Damon shouted as he felt Pam slip his phone out of his pocket.

"Enough, it's time I make you feel as much pain as I had to go through." Alvin lifted his arm, but his eyes focused in on Pam.

"Come here to me," he shouted.

"Leave her out of this, Pop," Damon warned.

"You don't think I was just going to kill you, do you?" Alvin laughed. "No, I'm going to make you watch every person you care about die by your own gun. You won't be able to do a fucking thing. Then you'll know just how I felt that day."

"It's not going to make the pain go away, Pop," Adrian shouted.

"How would you know? Look at yourself. You don't have a fucking mark on you. You lost the sight in one eye. Big fucking deal. Nobody looks at you like your dog shit on the side of the road," Alvin screamed.

"If a woman bases your worth on your looks, then she's not worth your time," Pam said, and Damon clenched his teeth, wishing she'd not spoken.

Adrian had distracted him from Pam, and Damon was hoping to get her out of sight. Now, Alvin was focused back on Pam, and that wasn't good. He seemed to have figured out hurting Pam would kill Damon.

"Right because the first thing you noticed about him was what, his personality?" Alvin returned.

"No, I noticed how handsome he was, but it wasn't what made me fall in love with him. I fell in love with who he was," Pam continued.

"Pam, please stop," Damon whispered.

"Alvin, when you came into my shop, did I ever treat you like you were less than a person?" Pam asked.

"No, but you didn't talk to me either." Alvin smirked.

Damon couldn't help but feel horrible for the damage on his face. When he smiled, only one side of his mouth turned up, his left eye looked as if it was pulled down. His left ear was basically gone, but it was the white cloud over his eye that made him look sinister.

"You stood next to the door like a guard. I didn't even know you were Canadian until you spoke just now. Vladimir never spoke to you. All he did was wave his arm. I thought you didn't speak English." Pam tried to step between Damon and Adrian.

"Stay back there, Pam," Damon whispered.

"No, let her come over here. Maybe it's time she and I had a chat." Alvin motioned for her to come closer.

"Not happening." Damon pushed her back behind him.

"Come here now, Pam." Alvin raised his gun and pointed right at Damon's head.

"Please, don't shoot him." Pam squeezed between Damon and Adrian and made her way down the steps.

"Pam, no." Damon reached for her, but she shook her head.

"I'll be fine." She looked back at him, and he could see the determination in her eyes.

Alvin grabbed Pam's arm and tugged her toward him until her back was flush against the front of him. When he buried his nose into her hair, Damon started down the steps.

"Stay right there, Damon. You don't want to see her pretty little brains all over this floor." Alvin sneered as he ran the barrel of the gun down the side of her face.

Damon felt Adrian start to tremble next to him, and he knew Adrian was pissed too. The problem was neither of them had a gun and Pam was now in Alvin's clutches.

"She smells like heaven." Alvin moaned as he continued to run his nose down the side of her neck.

"Don't even think about it, Pop," Damon growled through his teeth.

"Think about what? Getting me a piece of this pretty little ass?" Alvin grabbed the front of Pam's blouse and ripped it open, exposing her bra.

"Stop." Damon didn't even recognize his own voice he screamed so loud.

"Look at her smooth, flawless skin." Alvin moved his free hand around Pam and ran his hand across her bare stomach.

Damon met Pam's eyes. He expected to see terror or disgust, but all he saw was pure rage. She tilted her head away from Alvin, and the more he touched her, the more his weapon lowered.

"I bet you taste sweeter than honey." Alvin groaned as he brushed his lips against Pam's neck.

Damon saw red, but before he could move, Pam grabbed Alvin's wrist and spun around until the gun flew out of his hand. Adrian ran for the gun and Damon sprinted for Alvin, but before Damon could get to him, Pam lifted her leg and kicked at Alvin's knee. He dropped to the ground and screeched out in pain.

"I didn't spend ten years in Karate class for nothing. Thanks Uncle Kurt." Pam yelled.

Damon grabbed Pam around the waist and lifted her as he spun around to put her behind him. When she was out of Alvin's reach, Damon flew across the foot of space between him and his old friend and knocked him to the ground.

341

"You fucking bastard. How could you turn into such an evil son of a bitch? We were friends, comrades, looked out for each other, and you go and do this shit because you got fucking scarred. You killed people, Pop," Damon shouted as he fisted the front of Alvin's shirt.

"You killed people too," Alvin spat.

"I killed terrorists. Not people who were pawns in a fucking revenge plot." Damon pulled his fist back, wanting more than anything to slam it into Alvin's face, but he couldn't.

"You should have let me die out there. You should have let me die with the rest of them," Alvin cried out.

"If I'd known you were going to turn into this, I would have," Damon shouted.

"Then do it now. Put me out of my misery." Alvin shook with rage.

"It won't be that easy for you, Pop. You're going to pay for what you did the legal way." Damon stood up, leaving Alvin on the ground.

Without thinking Damon spun around to check on Pam. Alastair had wrapped his suit coat around Pam to cover her. He started to walk toward them, but there was a loud pop and his shoulder burned. He touched his shoulder and when he pulled his hand away, it was covered with blood.

"Damon," Pam screamed.

342

There was another pop, and Damon spun around. Alvin lay on the floor, a bullet hole in the middle of his forehead and a small revolver in his hand.

"He pulled it out of his waistband. I had to shoot him," Adrian choked out as he kicked the gun away from Alvin's motionless hand.

Damon caught Pam as she ran into his arms. He knew he'd been shot in the shoulder, but since he could still breathe, he figured it was just a flesh wound.

"We've got to get you to the hospital." Pam looked at his shoulder.

"I'm fine. We need to call the police," Damon told her as he guided her away from where the two bodies lay.

"We're here." Damon turned as John and Nick came into the house weapons aimed.

As if everything he'd felt over the last several minutes hit him at once, Damon dropped to the step and pulled Pam into his arms. She sobbed into his neck, and Damon couldn't hold the tears back any longer.

All of this was because his old friend couldn't deal with life after such a horrific injury. He blamed Damon because he wouldn't leave him there to die. War was hard, but when the aftermath made good people do horrible things, it made it so much worse.

The knowledge that Alvin wanted to die in the field where so many of their brothers were lost, was heartbreaking. The cryptic messages that he sent to Damon had meaning to Alvin. He wanted to die, and he wanted Damon to be the one to kill him. He might have wanted revenge, but he wanted his pain to end more. Hopefully, Alvin was at peace, and no matter what he did; a war hero deserved a little peace in the afterlife.

Chapter 32

Pam inhaled deeply as she strolled across the beach, watching the waves crash against the rocks and roll out again. It had been over a month since she'd had the freedom to take a walk anywhere without security, and it was incredible.

Damon and Adrian flew back to Toronto to return Alvin's remains to his family. John managed to keep Alvin's name out of the paper at Damon and Adrian's request. The only thing the news reported was the crimes were committed by an individual whose name was secured.

None of them wanted his family to go through any more pain, and Pam fully understood why. Alvin was mentally unstable because of what he'd been through and it was far to common with not only people in the military but first responders as well. She couldn't even begin to imagine what all those people went through. Pam admired Damon so much for the respect he used with Alvin's memory.

The two goons who had taken Tabitha were found dead in the house where Pam had been held. One of them was they guy Nick and John had talked to when she was missing. The one they thought was Vladimir. It seemed as if Alvin made sure anyone who could connect him to all the crimes was eliminated.

Her only problem was Damon had been gone for almost a week, and she missed him terribly. She hadn't slept much since he left, but thanks to a friend of James, she had a surprise for Damon when he returned. Actually, she had a couple of surprises for him.

He'd told her he would be returning in two days and she knew it would seem like a month. She laughed as she looked at the sweet surprise bouncing toward the waves and then yelping as they came back in after her.

"What are you barking at, Maisie?" Pam crouched to scratch the puppy's head.

The dog barked and wagged her tail frantically as she tried to lick Pam's face. The Golden Labrador puppy really loved the beach, and it was the only place Pam could let her run. Eventually, she was going to get too big for the apartment.

"What do you think Damon is going to say about you and my other surprise?" Pam laughed as the dog yelped and jumped up, knocking Pam on her ass.

"I think he's going to ask what the other surprise is." Damon's voice startled her.

"Damon." Pam shot to her feet and jumped into his arms.

Pam pressed her lips against his as if she hadn't seen him in years. Their kiss was interrupted by a very upset puppy not getting any attention. Maisie continued to jump up on Damon's leg and bark.

"This could become an issue if you don't let me kiss my woman." Damon crouched and rubbed the dog's head.

"Well, she's your woman now too." Pam smiled nervously.

"I see." Damon picked the dog up and cradled her in his arms.

"Her name is Maisie, and we can train her to be a service dog." Pam scratched the puppy's ear.

"I see," Damon repeated.

"Is that all you're gonna say?" Pam sighed.

"No, what's my other surprise?" He smirked.

"That will have to wait until we get back to the apartment." She poked him in the chest.

"Well, I like this one, but honestly, can we just let her be a puppy?" He put Maisie on the ground and grabbed the leash from Pam. "We need to worry more about this."

Damon pulled something out of his pocket. He held it up and looked at her with a raised eyebrow and a huge grin. She sighed as she grabbed it out of his hand.

"I didn't hide it very well, did I?" She smiled.

"No, but is it what I think it is?" Damon asked.

"What do you think it is?" She turned around and backed up as they walked back up the beach.

"I think this is going to change our lives. For the better." Damon grabbed her around the waist and pulled her into his arms. "Are you?"

Pam gazed up into his eyes and wondered how she could ever walk away from him back then. He was a piece of her heart and her soul. Damon was her life, and they created a life together.

"Yes, I'm pregnant." Pam grinned.

Five months later…

Pam stood at the front of the church and wiped a tear as Isabelle and Roman kissed for the first time as husband and wife. Pam was an emotional mess the entire day, and it wasn't even her wedding, but from what everyone told her, hormones were hell.

Isabelle had given birth in November to a ten-pound baby boy, and they named him after both their fathers. Little Grayson Kurt slept quietly in his little tuxedo between Kurt and Alice while his parents had a beautiful January wedding.

At the reception, Pam danced with Roman's brother and laughed when Damon narrowed his eyes as Demetrios whispered something in her ear and then winked at Damon. Of course, he was just teasing Damon since Roman's brother was happily married.

"I think I better go over and get my wife to take those daggers out of my back." Demetrios winked as she thanked him for the dance and escorted her back to Damon.

"He's lucky I like him." Damon smirked.

"He's also married." Pam laughed.

"That too." Damon sat down and pulled her onto his lap.

He covered her swollen belly with his hand and kissed her cheek. He liked to see if he could feel the baby move, but so far, he hadn't had any luck. They'd also decided to wait until the baby was born to find out the gender, much to her mother's dismay.

Damon and Alastair had come to an agreement and Damon had returned to calling him, Dad. He told Pam he could never get used to calling him Alastair and like Malcolm had said, the adoption papers said Alastair was his father.

Much to Malcolm's dismay, Kelsey had left Newfoundland for the mainland. She said being around the family was too hard for her because it reminded her of what she'd been through. Malcolm couldn't blame her.

"Did I tell you how beautiful you are tonight?" Damon whispered in her ear as they danced.

"Yes, several times, but thank you again." She smiled up at him.

"Hey, do you think we could get out of here for about an hour? I have something I want to show you." He grinned.

"Damon, you can show me when we go back to the apartment." Pam giggled.

"Dirty mind. That's not what I meant. One hour, I swear." Damon tugged her toward the exit, telling a few people they'd be back shortly.

He helped her into his truck and drove out of the parking lot of Roman and Isabelle's club. They'd closed the place for their wedding reception.

"Where are we going?" Pam said ten minutes later when Damon turned on to a dirt road.

"You'll see." He grinned.

"All these bumps are going to put me in labor." Pam grunted as they hit another bump.

"Are you serious?" Damon stopped the truck.

"No, I'm kidding." Pam laughed.

"That's not funny." They started to move again.

About two minutes later, they came to a large clearing. Pam had grown up in Hopedale and had seen the area dozens of times over the years. When they were teenagers, they'd even go there sometimes to drink when the adults had forbidden them to go to Greeley's Peak.

"Why are we here?" Pam asked as Damon opened the door and helped her out of the truck.

"Isn't this a beautiful area?" Damon walked around and motioned to the lake.

"It is. We used to drink here as teenagers and swim in the pond." Pam lifted her dress as she walked toward Miller's Lake.

"Nice place to live." Damon stood behind her and slipped his arms around her waist.

"Hopedale is the best." Pam sighed.

"Yes, but I mean this spot." Damon turned her around.

"What?" Pam looked up at him.

"Don't get mad, but I bought this property. I want to build a house and raise our little peanut right here." Damon released her and ran to the middle of the clearing. "We could have our bedroom right here facing the lake, or if you want, we could put the living room there. Whatever you want."

"Damon." Pam called out to him.

"We could have the nursery right here." Damon ran to another part of the field.

"Damon," Pam smiled.

"I know you love to create your designs and we could build you a room here." Damon ran to another part of the field.

"Damon," Pam shouted.

"What?" He stopped and looked at her.

"It's perfect." Pam walked toward him.

"You like it?" Damon asked as she stood next to him.

"You're going to pave the road though, because I'm not doing the bumpy road every day." Pam wrapped her arms around his neck.

"Done." He picked her up and slammed his lips against hers.

"I love you." Pam hugged him.

"I have a surprise for you." He grinned as he placed her back on her feet.

"It's great, Damon, and I know it's not much snow around, but I'm definitely not doing anything outside." She smirked.

"Jesus, your mind is in the gutter tonight." Damon laughed.

"It's where yours usually is." Pam poked him in the chest.

"Not tonight. Well, not at the moment." Damon winked. "Close your eyes."

Pam closed her eyes and waited. She could hear him move around and keep shouting for her not to peek. There was no way she could love him more than she already did.

"Okay, open them." His voice was barely a whisper and Pam opened her eyes.

Damon was in front of her, down on one knee, holding up a purple velvet box. He slowly opened it, and inside was the most beautiful ring she'd ever seen in her life. One square diamond sat in the middle, and it was surrounded by smaller diamonds. They were set on top of a rose gold ring.

"Damon," Pam gasped as she covered her mouth and blinked back tears of happiness.

"Pamela Louise Nightingale, I fell in love with you long before I ever knew it. My heart has never belonged to anyone but you. No matter what we went through and no matter what comes in the future, I want you by my side for everything. You're my light in a dark room. You're my peace, and you're my reason for breathing. I love you more than I could ever tell you. Pam, will you marry me?" Damon gazed up at her as a lone tear ran down his cheek.

"Yes," Pam whispered the word because she was so overwhelmed with emotion she couldn't get anything else to come out.

Damon placed the ring on her finger and pulled her into his arms. As he lowered his lips to meet hers, he stopped and looked down at her stomach.

"Was that the baby?" Damon's eyes were wide with surprise.

"Yep." Pam grinned. "I think he or she said yes too."

Damon dropped down to his knees and kissed her belly. When he stood back up, he took her in his arms and kissed her right there where they'd start their future.

Epilogue

Betty smiled as she watched the last of her grandchildren show off her engagement ring. It was the start of a new branch of her family, and Betty O'Connor couldn't be happier. At eighty-five years old, she'd watched her three children and eleven grandchildren find love and start families.

It made her sad that the man who helped her create this beautiful family only got to see some of the joy. Jack loved his kids and his grandchildren, but he would be over the moon to see the large number of great-grandchildren who had come into their family.

Betty looked up to see another man who had come back into her life when she never expected it. He'd disappeared when she was a teenager and left her broken-hearted. Then she met Jack, and although she never forgot her first love, she fell for Jack O'Connor.

Tom Roberts was still as handsome as he was back then. Older, but he still made her heart flutter. She never thought they would have a second chance, but they did. Most people would think at their age, love was the last thing on their mind, but Tom made her feel alive again.

"Darling, would you like to dance?" Tom held out his hand, and she gladly took it.

As they danced around the floor to an Irish Waltz, she glanced around. Of course, it was only the older folks dancing around the floor, but to Betty, it was as if it was just her and Tom. Jack was one half of her heart, but Tom was the other.

"Betty, I think it's time you made an honest man out of me." Tom smiled down at her.

The music stopped, and they were surrounded by her family as Tom reached into his pocket and pulled out a gold ring with two diamonds in the center.

"I'd love to get down on my knee, but I'm afraid at my age I may not get up again." Tom grinned.

"Tom, wat are ya doin'?" Betty stared up at him.

"Elizabeth, I've loved you since I was eighteen years old and my heart could never let go. It may have taken us nearly seventy years to get here, but I think we need to take a lesson from the youngsters."

"Stop callin' me Elizabeth." Betty pointed her finger at him as she tried to keep the tears from falling.

"Betty, I've asked every member of your family for their blessing, and it took a little while because they're multiplying like rabbits." Tom grinned as everyone around them laughed.

"Tom." Betty sniffed.

"Betty, would you do me the honor of becoming my wife?" Tom held out the ring.

The room around her was silent as they all seemed to hold their breath, waiting for her answer. As she glanced around the room and saw the huge smiles on their faces, she turned back to Tom.

"Yes, I'll marry ya." Betty smiled as she went to remove the rings Jack had given her.

Tom stopped her and shook his head as he slipped the ring on her finger, right next to the ring given to her by Jack.

"Don't remove the other rings. Jack is part of the reason we're all here tonight. He's part of you and to marry you; I want to marry every part." Tom wrapped his arms around her, and for the first time, they kissed in front of her family

The cheers and congratulations echoed in her ears as she got lost in the kiss with the man she would spend the rest of her life with. It didn't matter if it was a year or twenty, Tom was her first love and her last.

About the Author

What does someone say to describe themselves? You could start with giving what others say about you. Scratch that. It doesn't really matter what others think about you. It matters what you think of yourself. So here we go.

First of all, I'm a wife and mother. I'm also a grandmother. That alone would fulfill any woman's life and to be honest, it does. But.....

I'm also a writer. Someone who loves to tell stories of love, suspense, heartache, and of course happily ever after. For most of my life, I've written those stories for myself. A type of therapy, I suppose. I love the characters I create. They become part of who I am because there's part of me in them.

So... Now that you know this about me. I hope when you read my books and fall in love with them.

You should also know that I'm a Newfoundlander. What is that you ask? We're a proud people who live on an island, off the east coast of Canada. Some people believe Canada ends with Nova Scotia. It doesn't. If you keep going east, there is a beautiful island full of amazing people and magnificent scenery. That is where my stories are set because let's face it. The best stories always come from the places you know and love.

If there is anything else, you would like to know about me. Ask me!

O'Connor Brothers Series

Available on

Amazon and
Kindle Unlimited.

Dangerous Therapy

Book 1

Officer John O'Connor is giving up on life after a terrible accident. His family are at their wit's end when he refuses any kind of therapy. The only thing keeping him sane is his dreams of a beautiful woman he pulled in for a traffic violation months before.

Physical Therapist Stephanie Kelly is healing from a broken heart. When she is hired by Nightingale's personal care and physical therapy, she's ecstatic, but she's shocked when her boss asks her to take on a new patient. Shocked because the patient is her boss's nephew and he's not exactly keen on therapy. He's also the cop who's been heating up her dreams.

As Stephanie helps John get back on his feet, they grow closer, but someone is out to hurt Stephanie, or worse. After multiple attempts on her life, John's family tries to figure out who's after the woman he loves and stop them before it's too late.

Dangerous Abduction

Book 2

Widower James O'Connor has been fighting his growing attraction to his brother's sister-in-law for four long years, but when someone breaks into her home, destroying everything she owns, James takes her and her young son into his home. The break-in wasn't random. Marina and her son are in danger, and James swears to protect them, but can he keep them safe?

Marina Kelly dedicates her life to caring for her sweet little boy, Danny. Since she broke free from her abusive husband, she's sworn off men, but when James O'Connor keeps entering her thoughts and her dreams, it takes everything she has to keep her feelings hidden. Now, her sister and parents are out of the province, and she's in danger, Marina has no choice but to accept James's help and try to hide her attraction and growing feelings.

The attraction between them impossible to resist. Only her ex's family secret may tear it all apart. Can Marina and James unravel the family's hidden mystery without losing each other?

Dangerous Secrets

Book 3

Ian O'Connor has everything going for him. He's got the O'Connor drop-dead good looks, an incredible body and to top it off he's a doctor. Why wouldn't anyone want the man but none of that was the reason Sandy Churchill was head over heels in love with the man. After he had stood her up for their first official date, she was wary of taking another chance. When she ends up in the hospital because she turned her back on a criminal determined to get away from her, Ian admits that he loves her and wants another chance. A secret from his past throws Sandy into a tailspin, but she has a secret that she's hiding from everyone.

Ian's on cloud nine when he finally takes a leap of faith and tells the woman he's loved for four years how he feels and wants a chance to make up for his screw up. They have two weeks of bliss, but a murder and secrets come back to haunt him. Sandy's reaction tells him there's another reason why she's avoiding him. She's hiding something, but he has no idea what and to make matters worse there's danger coming from her past that could hurt the people he loves the most.

Dangerous Beauty

Book 4

When you come from a privileged family, you're expected to follow a particular path in life. Unless you're Emily Bradshaw. Defying her father, Emily turned down a full scholarship to Dalhousie University. Instead, she followed her dream and opened her own salon in the small town of Hopedale with her friend. She's happy. Then her mother vanishes. Her father receives threatening messages and hires Newfoundland Security Services to protect his children. Emily doesn't like the idea, especially when the man that walks into her salon dressed in a black leather jacket makes her weak in the knees. Emily knows she's in danger but not the kind her father is worried about.

Keith O'Connor isn't expecting his newest security job to be anything out of the ordinary. Then he walks into Snippy Gals, a beauty salon in Hopedale. Keith gets the shock of his life when an auburn-haired beauty turns to face him. Emily is defiant, sassy, and her sexy curves have him in a complete spin. Fighting his feelings for her becomes almost impossible, but when Emily's mother is found, a family secret is revealed turning Emily's life upside down. Can Keith help her cope and keep her out of the clutches of a vengeful stranger?

Dangerous Silence

Book 5

Mike O'Connor's reputation earned him the name Mr. Homerun, but after two hours with Billie, he's ready to change all that. There's one problem. She disappears before he can find out her last name.

Billie Carter had little choice but to leave when she received a desperate text from her friend. Peggy and her daughter have no family, both are deaf, and Billie wants to protect them from an abusive man.

When Peggy is brutally murdered, Billie is determined to protect Chloe. Like a dream come true, Mike walks through her door to help. They soon learn that the little girl is not the only one in danger, and it may take more than Mike to keep them safe.

Dangerous Delusion

Book 6

Lora Norris quit a great job and moved to Hopedale to escape an unknown stalker. Little did she know that finding employment at Jack's Place would lead her to some of the best friends she would ever have. Of course, there is also one man she wanted to be a lot more than a friend, but can't take a chance and put him in danger.

Nick O'Connor never thought the pretty waitress working at his Aunt's diner would give him a second glance. Especially with his playboy reputation. She's friendly toward him but doesn't seem the least bit interested.

When women show up dead and bearing a striking resemblance to Lora, Nick and his family do everything to protect her and her little girl. As they admit their feelings for each other, the danger moves closer than they even realize.

Dangerous Witness

Book 7

Aaron (A.J.) O'Connor is the youngest of seven brothers. His reputation for being a love 'em and leave 'em kind of guy is only a mask to cover the heartbreak he suffered at the hands of his high school sweetheart at the tender age of eighteen. Thirteen years later, she's still the one he dreams of.

Bethany Donnelly left Hopedale on the last day of high school and hasn't looked back since. Finding out the love of her life played her for a fool and only used her to win a bet broke her heart. Now her boss wants her to return to Newfoundland to investigate an employee he suspected of illegal activity. That means facing the one man who can destroy her. The one she's never been able to forget.

Now Bethany's back, and Aaron's determined to find out why she left. First, he's got to keep her safe from a killer intent on taking her away from him forever.

O'Connor Girls

Available on

Amazon and
Kindle Unlimited

Hidden Betrayal

Book 1

Kristy O'Connor never hid the fact that she wanted Dean 'Bull' Nash. He's kept her at arm's length since they met but he's pushed her away for the last time.

Dean loves Kristy more than he could ever tell her. He wants her desperately, but his family secrets could destroy them both.

When he can't stay away from her any longer, murder and a shocking betrayal shake them to their core. Can their new relationship survive?

Hidden Enemy

Book 2

Jess O'Connor has watched her seven cousins and younger sister find love and start families. She's happy for them, but she's ready to find her own happily ever after. She sees that with the sexy mechanic that makes her heart thump and her body ache.

Wade Rivers not only owns one of the best repair shops in the city but he's also a single father. When he decides to expand his business, someone doesn't want him to succeed. Even with concerns someone is out to hurt him, he loses his heart to the first woman to turn his head in years. Jess makes him feel whole again.

Will strange incidents at the garage bring them closer together or will things blow up around them??

Hidden Menace

Book 3

Isabelle O'Connor works hard to make her restaurant one of the best in the province. After she hires Roman Young, she struggles to keep her growing attraction for him in check. She fails miserably when, after a particularly crazy night, she breaks her own rule and sleeps with the sexy chef.

Roman Young falls fast and hard for his beautiful boss. He's thrilled when she finally surrenders to the chemistry between them. One night is enough to convince him they could be so much more but breaking down Isabelle's walls is going to take more than just great sex.

The least of Isabelle's worries is anyone finding out she and Roman have crossed that line. After a series of mysterious events, Roman believes it's more than bad luck. When a body turns up in Isabelle's kitchen, he's convinced. Someone wants to destroy Isabelle, but why? Is it greed, or is there another sinister reason?

Rhonda Brewer

Keep up to date on all things new.

Follow me on

Facebook

Twitter

Instagram

MeWe

All Author

Bookbub

Sign up for my newsletter and never miss another release!

http://www.rhondabrewerauthor.com/talk-to-me

www.ingramcontent.com/pod-product-compliance
Lightning Source LLC
Chambersburg PA
CBHW071156250626
47159CB00001B/110